PERIL ON PERN

Someday he would be the Masterharper, key figure in the history of a wondrous world of dragons and Weyrs. But now, Robinton is a young journeyman on his first posting, making the long, perilous trek from Harper Hall to Benden Weyr.

He must face the open dangers of storms at sea, beasts in the wilds, fire lizards, brigands . . . and more subtle—but no less real—battles of wit, riddles, confrontation and high diplomacy. If he succeeds, Robinton will begin a destiny among the Dragonriders. If he fails, Robinton won't die—but he'll be disgraced. Humiliated. Defeated . . .

And for a young man with dreams, humiliation can be far worse than death.

CROSSROADS™ ADVENTURES are authorized interactive novels compatible for Advanced Dungeons and Dragons™ level play. Constructed by the masters of modern gaming, CROSSROADS™ feature complete rules; *full use* of gaming values—strength, intelligence, wisdom/luck, constitution, dexterity, charisma and hit points; and multiple pathways for each option; for the most complete experience in gaming books, as fully realized, motivated heroes quest through the most famous worlds of fantasy!

All-new. With introduction and prologue by ANNE MCCAFFREY

ENTER THE ADVENTURE!

TOR'S CROSSROADS ADVENTURE SERIES

Dragonharper, based on Anne McCaffrey's Pern
Storm of Dust, based on David Drake's The Dragon Lord
Revolt on Majipoor, based on Robert Silverberg's Majipoor

COMING SOON

The Witchfires of Leeth, based on C. J. Cherryh's Morgaine
Prospero's Isle, based on L. Sprague de Camp and Fletcher Pratt's The Incomplete Enchanter
Dzurlord, based on Steven Brust's Jhereg
A Warlock's Blade, based on Christopher Stasheff's Gramarye
Encyclopedia of Xanth, based on Piers Anthony's Xanth
Warhorn, based on Lynn Abbey's Rifkind

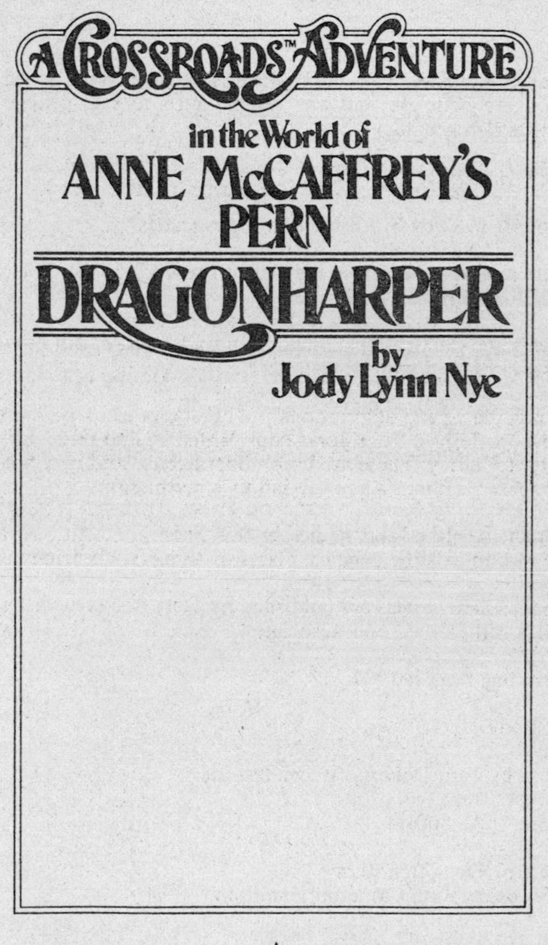

A TOM DOHERTY ASSOCIATES BOOK

This is a work of fiction. All the characters and events portrayed in this book are fictional, and any resemblance to real people or incidents is purely coincidental.

DRAGONHARPER

All characters, places and names in this book are fictitious, any resemblence to existing persons, places or things is coincidental.

Crossroads Game/novels are published by TOR Books by arrangement with Bill Fawcett and Associates.

First printing: August 1987

A TOR Book

Published by Tom Doherty Associates, Inc.
49 West 24 Street
New York, N.Y. 10010

Cover art by Doug Beekman
Illustrations by Todd Cameron Hamilton

ISBN: 0-812-56404-9
CAN. ED.: 0-812-56405-7

Printed in the United States of America

0 9 8 7 6 5 4 3 2 1

Dedication—

To my mother, Carole
to Diane
and to Anne,
thank you for
letting me play in your backyard

Special Dedication—

In Memory of
Judy-Lynn Del Rey

PREFACE
by Anne McCaffrey

AS EVERYONE KNOWS who knows me and my passionate possession of anything to do with *The Dragonriders of Pern* or *The Harper Hall Series,* it may come as a distinct shock to see Masterharper Robinton, in the days of his youth, in a Do Your Own Adventure book.

Actually, I had been approached on several previous occasions to allow Pern to be included, but I was most dubious.

However, when Bill Fawcett of Mayfair Games queried me about his projected series, I was considerably less dubious about the treatment my Favorite Characters would have at the hands of other beings without the Law. There may be rules, but there are also exceptions to rules. Also, I had come to realize how very popular and insidious these Adventure novels are: forcing young people who don't generally read a book to read books—a cunning ploy to catch the conscience!

So, I considered what a superb job Mayfair Games had done on their board game presentation of *The Dragonriders of Pern* and I knew that my Pernese friends would be in understanding and perceptive hands. I graciously announced that I would consider the project. But that I must, *must* have approval of any finished script and *who* would it be about?

When Bill, and Jody Lynn Nye, proposed following

the young Harper, Robinton, on his first assignment, Envy nearly consumed me. But, I had to face it; I didn't have the time, nor that particular turn of mind that can construct these special novelistic forms, *and* they promised faithfully and on their honor as Gentlepersons and Senior Evaluation and Exploration Scouts that nothing serious would happen to my budding young Harper.

I *am* pleased with the result, and I do feel that readers will be, too. Especially those that I am hoping will get so charmed by Jody's delightful, witty, inventive adventure for Robinton that they'll want to buy *all* the other Pern books, too.

Now, I'll get back to *Dragonsdawn,* the next breathtaking adventure set on this mysterious planet in the Sagittarian Sector of *Sppppppaaaaaacccccceeeee!*

ANNE MCCAFFREY'S PERN

RUKBAT, IN THE SAGITTARIAN SECTOR, was a golden G-type star. It had five planets, two asteroid belts, and a stray planet that it had attracted and held in recent millennia. When men first settled on Rukbat's third world and called it Pern, they had taken little notice of the strange planet swinging around its adopted primary in a wildly erratic orbit. For two generations, the colonists gave the bright Red Star little thought, until the path of the wanderer brought it close to its stepsister at perihelion.

When the aspects were harmonious and not distorted by conjunctions with other planets in the system, the indigenous life form of the wandering planet sought to bridge the space gap between its home and the more temperate and hospitable planet of Pern. At these times silver Threads dropped through Pern's skies, destroying anything they touched.

The initial losses the colonists suffered were staggering. As a result, during the subsequent struggle to survive and combat this menace, Pern's tenuous contact with the mother planet was broken.

To control the incursions of the dreadful Threads, for the Pernese cannibalized their transport ships early on and abandoned such technological sophistication as was irrelevant to this pastoral planet, the more resourceful men embarked on a long-term plan.

The first phase involved breeding a highly specialized variety of the fire lizards, a life form indigenous to their new world. Men and women with high empathy ratings and some innate telepathic ability were trained to use and preserve these unusual animals. These dragons, named for the mythical Terran beast they resembled, had two valuable characteristics: they could get from one place to another instantaneously, and after chewing a phosphine-bearing rock, they could emit a flaming gas. Because the dragons could fly, they were able to char the Thread in midair, and then escape from the ravages themselves.

It took generations to develop to the fullest the potential of these dragons. The second phase of the proposed defense against the deadly incursions would take even longer. Thread, a space-traveling mycorrhizoid spore, devoured all organic matter with mindless voracity and, once grounded, burrowed and proliferated with terrifying speed.

So a symbiote of the same strain was developed to counter this parasite, and the resulting grub was introduced into the soil of the southern continent. The original plan was that the dragons would be a visible protection, charring Thread while it was still skyborne and protecting the dwellings and the livestock of the colonists. The grub-symbiote would protect vegetation by devouring any Thread that managed to evade the dragons' fire.

The originators of the two-stage defense did not allow for change or for hard geological fact. The southern continent, overtly more attractive than the harsher northern land, proved unstable. The entire colony was eventually forced to move north to seek refuge from the Threads, on the continental shield rock of the north.

The original Fort, constructed on the eastern face of the Great West Mountain Range, soon grew too small to hold the colonists. Another settlement was started slightly to the north, alongside a great lake conveniently near a cave-filled cliff. But Ruatha Hold, as the settlement was called, became overcrowded within a few generations.

Since the Red Star rose in the east, the people of Pern decided to establish a holding in the eastern mountains, provided a suitable cavesite could be found. Only solid rock and metal, both of which were in short supply on Pern, were impervious to the burning score of Thread.

The winged, fire-breathing dragons had by then been bred to a size that required more spacious accommodations than the cliffside holds could provide. Two ancient cave-pocked cones of extinct volcanoes, one high above the first fort, the other in the Benden mountains, proved to be adequate and required only a few improvements to be made habitable. Such projects, however, took the last of the fuel for the great stone-cutters, which had been programmed only for regular mining operations, not for wholesale cliff excavations. Subsequent holds and Weyrs had to be hand-hewn.

The dragons and their riders in their high places and the people in their cave holds went about their separate tasks. Each developed habits that became custom, and which solidified into tradition as incontrovertible as law.

Then came an interval of two hundred Turns of the planet Pern around its primary—the Red Star was at the other end of its erratic orbit, a frozen, lonely captive. No Thread fell on Pern. The inhabitants erased the depredations of Thread, grew crops and planted orchards from precious seeds brought with them. They thought of reforestry for the slopes denuded by Thread. They even managed to forget that they had once been in great danger of extinction. Then the Threads fell again when the wandering planet returned for another orbit around Pern, bringing fifty years of attack from the skies. The Pernese once again thanked their ancestors, now many generations removed, for providing the dragons who seared the dropping Thread midair with their fiery breath.

Dragonkind, too, had prospered during that interval

and had settled in four other locations, following the master plan of interim defense.

Recollections of Earth receded further from Pernese history with each successive generation until memory of their origins degenerated into a myth muddled by the memory of the movement from the Southern Continent. People argued over whether there had been one Crossing or two.

By the seventh Pass of the Red Star, a complicated sociopolitical-economic structure had been developed to deal with this recurrent evil. The six Weyrs, as the old volcanic habitations of the dragonfolk were called, pledged themselves to protect Pern, each Weyr having a geographical section of the northern continent literally under its wing. The rest of the population agreed to tithe support to the Weyrs since these fighters, these dragonmen, did not have arable land in their volcanic homes. They could not afford to take time away from nurturing their dragons to learn other trades during peacetime, nor could they take time away from protecting the planet during Passes.

Settlements, called Holds, developed wherever natural caves were found. Some were, of course, more extensive or strategically placed than others. It took a strong man to hold frantic, terrified people in control during Thread attacks. It took wise administration to conserve victuals when nothing could be safely grown. And it took extraordinary measures to control the population and keep it productive and healthy until such time as the menace passed.

Men with special skills in metalworking, weaving, animal husbandry, farming, fishing, and mining formed Crafthalls in each large Hold and looked to one Mastercrafthall where the precepts of their craft were taught and craft skills were preserved and guarded from one generation to another. One Lord Holder could not deny the products of the Crafthall situated in his Hold to others, since the Crafts were deemed independent of a Hold affiliation. Each Craftmaster of a hall owed allegiance to the Master of that particular craft—an elected office based on the proficiency in that craft and administrative ability. The Mastercraftsman was responsible for the output of his halls and the distribution, fair and unprejudiced, of all craft products on a planetary, rather than parochial basis.

Certain rights and privileges accrued to different leaders of Holds and Masters of Crafts and, naturally, to the dragonriders to whom all Pern looked for protection during the Threadfalls.

Mankind has a history of forgetting the unpleasant, the undesirable. The Red Star did not pass close enough to Pern to drop its Threads. The people prospered and multiplied, spreading out across the rich land, carving more holds out of solid rock, and so busy with their pursuits, that they did not realize that there were only a few dragons in the skies and only one Weyr of the dragonriders left on Pern. The Red Star wasn't due back for a long, long while. Why worry about such distant possibilities? In five generations or so, the descendants of the heroic dragonmen fell into disfavor. The legends of past braveries and the very reason for their existence fell into disrepute.

INTRODUCTION AND RULES TO CROSSROADS™ ADVENTURES

by Bill Fawcett

FOR THE MANY of us who have enjoyed the stories upon which this adventure is based, it may seem a bit strange to find an introduction this long at the start of a book. What you are holding is both a game and an adventure. Have you ever read a book and then told yourself you would have been able to think more clearly or seen a way out of the hero's dilemma? In a Crossroads™ adventure you have the opportunity to do just that. *You* make the key decisions. By means of a few easily followed steps you are able to see the results of your choices.

A Crossroads™ adventure is as much fun to read as it is to play. It is more than just a game or a book. It is a chance to enjoy once more a familiar and treasured story. The excitement of adventuring in a beloved universe is neatly blended into a story which stands well on its own merit, a story in which you will encounter many familiar characters and places and discover more than a few new ones as well. Each adventure is a thrilling tale, with the extra suspense and satisfaction of knowing that you will succeed or fail by your own endeavors.

THE ADVENTURE

Throughout the story you will have the opportunity to make decisions. Each of these decisions will affect whether the hero succeeds in the quest, or even survives. In some cases you will actually be fighting battles; other times you will use your knowledge and instincts to choose the best path to follow. In many cases there will be clues in the story or illustrations.

A Crossroads™ adventure is divided into sections. The length of a section may be a few lines or many pages. The section numbers are shown at the top of a page to make it easier for you to follow. Each section ends when you must make a decision, or fight. The next section you turn to will show the results of your decision. At least one six-sided die and a pencil are needed to "play" this book.

The words "six-sided dice" are often abbreviated as "D6." If more than one is needed a number will precede the term. "Roll three six-sided dice" will be written as "Roll 3 D6." Virtually all the die rolls in these rules do involve rolling three six-sided dice (or rolling one six-sided die three times) and totaling what is rolled.

If you are an experienced role play gamer, you may also wish to convert the values given in this novel to those you can use with TSR's Advanced Dungeons and Dragons™ or any other role playing game. All of the adventures have been constructed so that they also can be easily adapted in this manner. The values for the hero will transfer directly. While AD & D™ games are much more complicated, doing this will allow you to be the Game Master for other players. Important values for the hero's opponents will be given to aid you in this conversion and to give those playing by the Crossroads™ rules a better idea of what they are facing.

THE HERO

Seven values are used to describe the hero in gaming terms. These are strength, intelligence, wisdom/luck, constitution, dexterity, charisma, and hit points. These values measure all of a character's abilities. At the end of these rules is a Record Sheet. On it are given all of the values for the hero of this adventure and any equipment or supplies they begin the adventure with. While you adventure, this record can be used to keep track of damage received and any new equipment or magical items acquired. You may find it advisable to make a photocopy of that page. Permission to do so, for your own use only, is given by the publisher of this game/novel. You may wish to consult this record sheet as we discuss what each of the values represents.

STRENGTH

This is the measure of how physically powerful your hero is. It compares the hero to others in how much the character can lift, how hard he can punch, and just how brawny he is. The strongest a normal human can be is to have a strength value of 18. The weakest a child would have is a 3. Here is a table giving comparable strengths:

Strength	Example
3	A five year old child
6	An elderly man

8	Out of shape and over 40
10	An average 20 year old man
13	In good shape and works out
15	A top athlete or football running back
17	Changes auto tires without a jack
18	Arm wrestles Arnold Schwarzenegger and wins

A Tolkien-style troll, being magical, might have a strength of 19 or 20. A full-grown elephant has a strength of 23. A fifty-foot dragon would have a strength of 30.

INTELLIGENCE

Being intelligent is not just a measure of native brain power. It is also an indication of the ability to use that intelligence. The value for intelligence also measures how aware the character is, and so how likely they are to notice a subtle clue. Intelligence can be used to measure how resistant a mind is to hypnosis or mental attack. A really sharp baboon would have an intelligence of 3. Most humans (we all know exceptions) begin at about 5. The highest value possible is an 18. Here is a table of relative intelligence:

Intelligence	**Example**
3	My dog
5	Lassie
6	Curly (the third Stooge)
8	Somewhat slow
10	Average person
13	College professor/good quarterback
15	Indiana Jones/Carl Sagan
17	Doc Savage/Mr. Spock
18	Leonardo dá Vinci (Isaac Asimov?)

Brainiac of comicbook fame would have a value of 21.

WISDOM/LUCK

Wisdom is the ability to make correct judgments, often with less than complete facts. Wisdom is knowing what to do and when to do it. Attacking, when running will earn you a spear in the back, is the best part of wisdom. Being in the right place at the right time can be called luck or wisdom. Not being discovered when hiding can be luck, if it is because you knew enough to not hide in the poison oak, wisdom is also a factor. Activities which are based more on instinct, the intuitive leap, than analysis are decided by wisdom.

In many ways both wisdom and luck are further connected, especially as wisdom also measures how friendly the ruling powers of the universe (not the author, the fates) are to the hero. A hero may be favored by fate or luck because he is reverent or for no discernible reason at all. This will give them a high wisdom value. Everyone knows those "lucky" individuals who can fall in the mud and find a gold coin. Here is a table measuring relative wisdom/luck:

Wisdom	**Example**
Under 3	Cursed or totally unthinking
5	Never plans, just reacts
7	Some cunning, "street smarts"
9	Average thinking person
11	Skillful planner, good gambler
13	Successful businessman/Lee Iacocca
15	Captain Kirk (wisdom)/Conan (luck)
17	Sherlock Holmes (wisdom)/Luke Skywalker (luck)
18	Lazarus Long

CONSTITUTION

The more you can endure, the higher your constitution. If you have a high constitution you are better able to survive physical damage, emotional stress, and poisons. The higher your value for constitution, the longer you are able to continue functioning in a difficult situation. A character with a high constitution can run farther (though not necessarily faster) or hang by one hand longer than the average person. A high constitution means you also have more stamina, and recover more quickly from injuries. A comparison of values for constitution:

Constitution	**Example**
3	A terminal invalid
6	A ten year old child
8	Your stereotyped "98 pound weakling"
10	Average person
14	Olympic athlete/Sam Spade
16	Marathon runner/Rocky
18	Rasputin/Batman

A whale would have a constitution of 20. Superman's must be about 50.

DEXTERITY

The value for dexterity measures not only how fast a character can move, but how well-coordinated those movements are. A surgeon, a pianist, and a juggler all need a high value for dexterity. If you have a high value for dexterity you can react quickly (though not necessarily correctly), duck well, and perform sleight of hand magic (if you are bright enough to learn how). Conversely, a low dexterity means you react slowly and drop things frequently. All other things being equal, the character with the highest dexterity will have the advantage of the first attack in a combat. Here are some comparative examples of dexterity:

Dexterity	Example
3 or less	Complete klutz
5	Inspector Clousseau
6	Can walk and chew gum, most of the time
8	Barney Fife
10	Average person
13	Good fencer/Walter Peyton
15	Brain surgeon/Houdini
16	Flying Karamazov Brothers
17	Movie ninja/Cyrano de Bergerac
18	Bruce Lee

Batman, Robin, Daredevil and The Shadow all have a dexterity of 19. At a dexterity of 20 you don't even see the man move before he has taken your wallet and underwear and has left the room (the Waco Kid).

CHARISMA

Charisma is more than just good looks, though they certainly don't hurt. It is a measure of how persuasive a hero is and how willing others are to do what he wants. You can have average looks yet be very persuasive, and have a high charisma. If your value for charisma is high, you are better able to talk yourself out of trouble or obtain information from a stranger. If your charisma is low, you may be ignored or even mocked, even when you are right. A high charisma value is vital to entertainers of any sort, and leaders. A different type of charisma is just as important to spies. In the final measure a high value for charisma means people will react to you in the way you desire. Here are some comparative values for charisma:

Charisma	Example
3	Hunchback of Notre Dame
5	An ugly used car salesman
7	Richard Nixon today
10	Average person
12	Team coach
14	Magnum, P.I.
16	Henry Kissinger/Jim DiGriz
18	Dr. Who/Prof. Harold Hill (Centauri)

HIT POINTS

Hit points represent the total amount of damage a hero can take before he is killed or knocked out. You can receive damage from being wounded in a battle, through starvation, or even through a mental attack. Hit points measure more than just how many times the hero can be battered over the head before he is knocked out. They also represent the ability to keep striving toward a goal. A poorly paid mercenary may have only a few hit points, even though he is a hulking brute of a man, because the first time he receives even a slight wound he will withdraw from the fight. A blacksmith's apprentice who won't accept defeat will have a higher number of hit points.

A character's hit points can be lost through a wound to a specific part of the body or through general damage to the body itself. This general damage can be caused by a poison, a bad fall, or even exhaustion and starvation.

Pushing your body too far beyond its limits may result in a successful action at the price of the loss of a few hit points. All these losses are treated in the same manner.

Hit points lost are subtracted from the total on the hero's record sheet. When a hero has lost all of his hit points, then that character has failed. When this happens you will be told to which section to turn. Here you will often find a description of the failure and its consequences for the hero.

The hit points for the opponents the hero meets in combat are given in the adventure. You should keep track of these hit points on a piece of scrap paper. When a monster or opponent has lost all of their hit points, they have lost the fight. If a character is fighting more than one opponent, then you should keep track of each of their hit points. Each will continue to fight until it has 0 hit points. When everyone on one side of the battle has no hit points left, the combat is over.

Even the best played character can lose all of his hit points when you roll too many bad dice during a combat. If the hero loses all of his hit points, the adventure may have ended in failure. You will be told so in the next section you are instructed to turn to. In this case you can turn back to the first section and begin again. This time you will have the advantage of having learned some of the hazards the hero will face.

TAKING CHANCES

There will be occasions where you will have to decide whether the hero should attempt to perform some action which involves risk. This might be to climb a steep cliff, jump a pit, or juggle three daggers. There will be other cases where it might benefit the hero to notice something subtle or remember an ancient ballad perfectly. In all of these cases you will be asked to roll three six-sided dice (3 D6) and compare the total of all three dice to the hero's value for the appropriate ability.

For example, if the hero is attempting to juggle three balls, then for him to do so successfully you would have to roll a total equal to or less than the hero's value for dexterity. If your total was less than this dexterity value, then you would be directed to a section describing how the balls looked as they were skillfully juggled. If you rolled a higher value than that for dexterity, then you would be told to read a section which describes the embarrassment of dropping the balls, and being laughed at by the audience.

Where the decision is a judgment call, such as whether to take the left or right staircase, it is left entirely to you. It will be likely that somewhere in the adventure or in the original novels there will be some piece of information which would indicate that the left staircase leads to a trap and the right to your goal. No die roll will be needed for a judgment decision.

In all cases you will be guided at the end of each section as to exactly what you need do. If you have any questions you should refer back to these rules.

MAGICAL ITEMS AND SPECIAL EQUIPMENT

There are many unusual items which appear in the pages of this adventure. When it is possible for them to be taken by the hero, you will be given the option of doing so. One or more of these items may be necessary to the successful completion of the adventure. You will be given the option of taking these at the end of a section. If you choose to pick up an item and succeed in getting it, you should list that item on the hero's record sheet. There is no guarantee that deciding to take an item means you will actually obtain it. If someone owns it already they are quite likely to resent your efforts to take it. In some cases things may not even be all they appear to be or the item may be trapped or cursed. Having it may prove a detriment rather than a benefit.

All magical items give the hero a bonus (or penalty) on certain die rolls. You will be told when this applies, and often given the option of whether or not to use the item. You will be instructed at the end of the section on how many points to add to or subtract from your die roll. If you choose to use an item which can function only once, such as a magic potion or hand grenade, then you will also be instructed to remove the item from your record sheet. Certain items, such as a magic sword, can be used many times. In this case you will be told when you obtain the item when you can apply the bonus. The bonus for a magic sword could be added every time a character is in hand to hand combat.

Other special items may allow a character to fly, walk through fire, summon magical warriors, or many other things. How and when they affect play will again be told to you in the paragraphs at the end of the sections where you have the choice of using them.

Those things which restore lost hit points are a special case. You may choose to use these at any time during the adventure. If you have a magical healing potion which returns 1 D6 of lost hit points, you may add these points when you think it is best to. This can even be during a combat in the place of a round of attack. No matter how many healing items you use, a character can never have more hit points than they begin the adventure with.

There is a limit to the number of special items any character may carry. In any Crossroads™ adventure the limit is four items. If you already have four special items listed on your record sheet, then one of these must be discarded in order to take the new item. Any time you erase an item off the record sheet, whether because it was used or because you wish to add a new item, whatever is erased is permanently lost. It can never be "found" again, even if you return to the same location later in the adventure.

Except for items which restore hit points, the hero can only use an item in combat or when given the option to do so. The opportunity will be listed in the instructions.

In the case of an item which can be used in every combat, the bonus can be added or subtracted as the description of the item indicates. A +2 sword would add two points to any total rolled in combat. This bonus would be used each and every time the hero attacks. Only one attack bonus can be used at a time. Just because a hero has both a +1 and a +2 sword doesn't mean he knows how to fight with both at once. Only the better bonus would apply.

If a total of 12 is needed to hit an attacking monster and the hero has a +2 sword, then you will only need to roll a total of 10 on the three dice to successfully strike the creature.

You could also find an item, perhaps enchanted armor, which could be worn in all combat and would have the effect of subtracting its bonus from the total of any opponents' attack on its wearer. (Bad guys can wear magic armor, too.) If a monster normally would need a 13 to hit a character who has obtained a set of +2 armor, then the monster would now need a total of 15 to score a hit. An enchanted shield would operate in the same way, but could never be used when the character was using a weapon which needed both hands, such as a pike, longbow or two-handed sword.

COMBAT

There will be many situations where the hero will be

forced, or you may choose, to meet an opponent in combat. The opponents can vary from a wild beast, to a human thief, or an unearthly monster. In all cases the same steps are followed.

The hero will attack first in most combats unless you are told otherwise. This may happen when there is an ambush, other special situations, or because the opponent simply has a much higher dexterity.

At the beginning of a combat section you will be given the name or type of opponent involved. For each combat five values are given. The first of these is the total on three six-sided dice needed for the attacker to hit the hero. Next to this value is the value the hero needs to hit these opponents. After these two values is listed the hit points of the opponent. If there is more than one opponent, each one will have the same number. (See the Hit Points section included earlier if you are unclear as to what these do.) Under the value needed to hit by the opponent is the hit points of damage that it will do to the hero when it attacks successfully. Finally, under the total needed for the hero to successfully hit an opponent is the damage he will do with the different weapons he might have. Unlike a check for completing a daring action (where you wish to roll under a value), in a combat you have to roll the value given or higher on three six-sided dice to successfully hit an opponent.

For example:

Here is how a combat between the hero armed with a sword and three brigands armed only with daggers is written:

BRIGANDS

To hit the hero: 14	*To be hit: 12*	*Hit points: 4*
Damage with daggers: 1 D6 (used by the brigands)	*Damage with sword: 2 D6 (used by the hero)*	

There are three brigands. If two are killed (taken to 0 hit points) the third will flee in panic.

If the hero wins, turn to section 85.

If he is defeated, turn to section 67.

RUNNING AWAY

Running rather than fighting, while often desirable, is not always possible. The option to run away is available only when listed in the choices. Even when this option is given, there is no guaranty the hero can get away safely.

THE COMBAT SEQUENCE

Any combat is divided into alternating rounds. In most cases the hero will attack first. Next, surviving opponents will have the chance to fight back. When both have attacked, one round will have been completed. A combat can have any number of rounds and continues until the hero or his opponents are defeated. Each round is the equivalent of six seconds. During this time all the parties in the combat may actually take more than one swing at each other.

The steps in resolving a combat in which the hero attacks first are as follows:

1. Roll three six-sided dice. Total the numbers showing on all three and add any bonuses from weapons or special circumstances. If this total is the same or greater than the second value given, "to hit the opponent," then the hero has successfully attacked.

2. If the hero attacks successfully, the next step is to determine how many hit points of damage he did to

the opponent. The die roll for this will be given below the "to hit opponent" information.

3. Subtract any hit points of damage done from the opponent's total.

4. If any of the enemy have one or more hit points left, then the remaining opponent or opponents now can attack. Roll three six-sided dice for each attacker. Add up each of these sets of three dice. If the total is the same or greater than the value listed after "to hit the hero" in the section describing the combat, the attack was successful.

5. For each hit, roll the number of dice listed for damage. Subtract the total from the number of hit points the hero has at that time. Enter the new, lower total on the hero's record sheet.

If both the hero and one or more opponents have hit points left, the combat continues. Start again at step one. The battle ends only when the hero is killed, all the opponents are killed or all of one side has run away. A hero cannot, except through a healing potion or spells or when specifically told to during the adventure, regain lost hit points. A number of small wounds from several opponents will kill a character as thoroughly as one titanic, unsuccessful combat with a hill giant.

DAMAGE

The combat continues, following the sequence given below, until either the hero or his opponents have no hit points. In the case of multiple opponents, subtract hit points from one opponent until the total reaches 0 or less. Extra hit points of damage done on the round when each opponent is defeated are lost. They do not carry over to the next enemy in the group. To win the combat, you must eliminate all of an opponent's hit points.

The damage done by a weapon will vary depending on who is using it. A club in the hands of a child will do far less damage than the same club wielded by a hill giant. The maximum damage is given as a number of six-sided dice. In some cases the maximum will be less than a whole die. This is abbreviated by a minus sign followed by a number. For example D6−2, meaning one roll of a six-sided die, minus two. The total damage can never be less than zero, meaning no damage done. 2 D6−1 means that you should roll two six-sided dice and then subtract one from the total of them both.

A combat may, because of the opponent involved, have one or more special circumstances. It may be that the enemy will surrender or flee when its hit point total falls below a certain level, or even that reinforcements will arrive to help the bad guys after so many rounds. You will be told of these special situations in the lines directly under the combat values.

Now you may turn to section one.

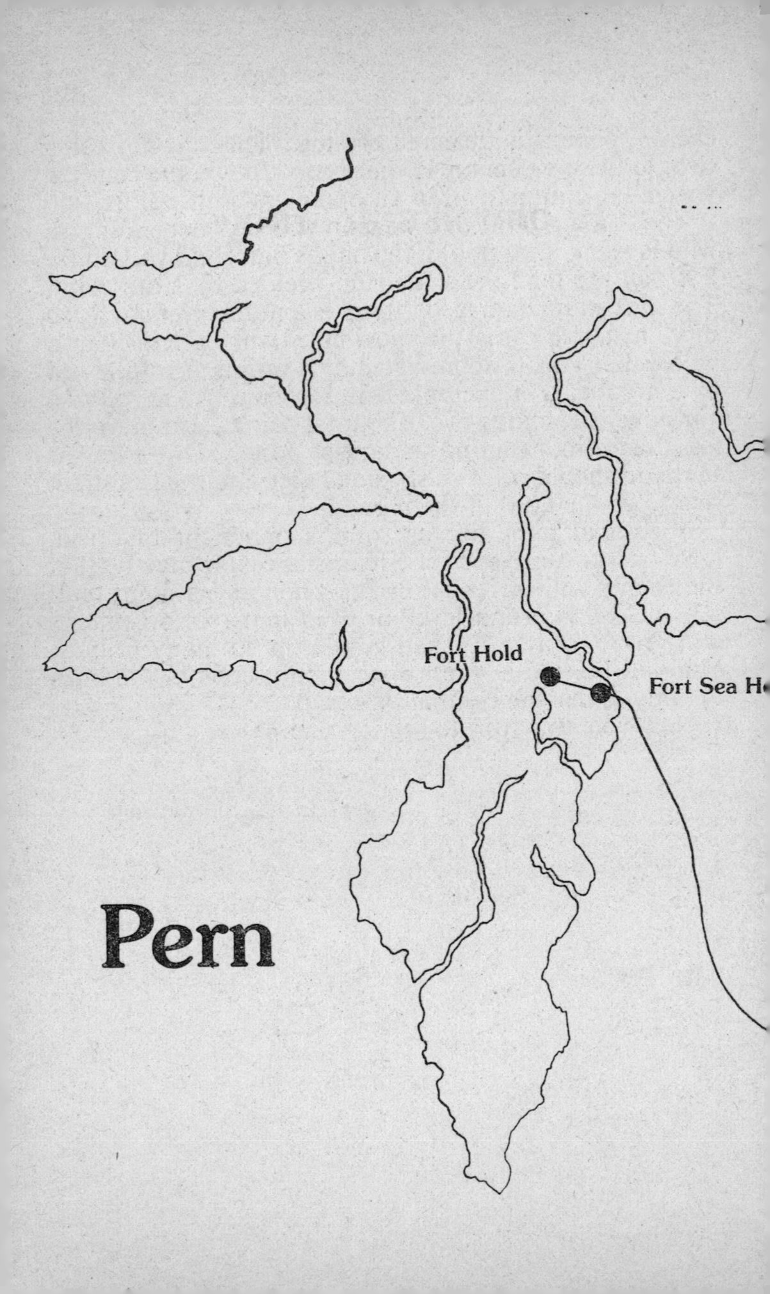
Fort Hold
Pern

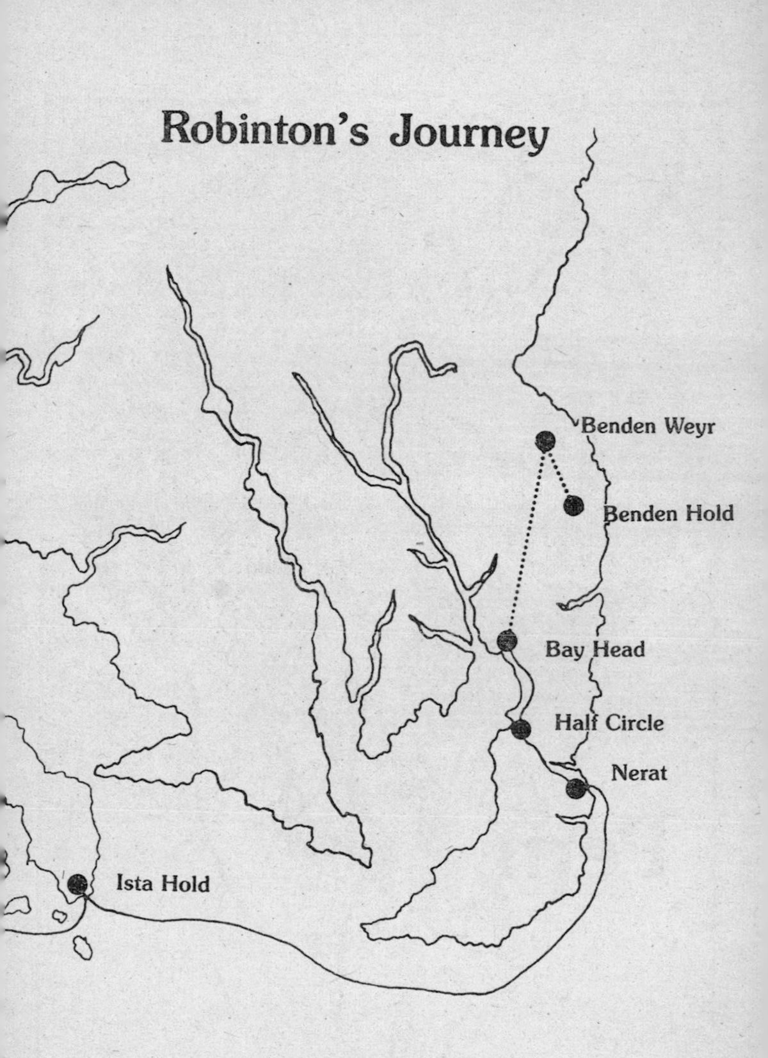
Robinton's Journey
Benden Weyr
Benden Hold
Bay Head
Half Circle
Nerat
Ista Hold

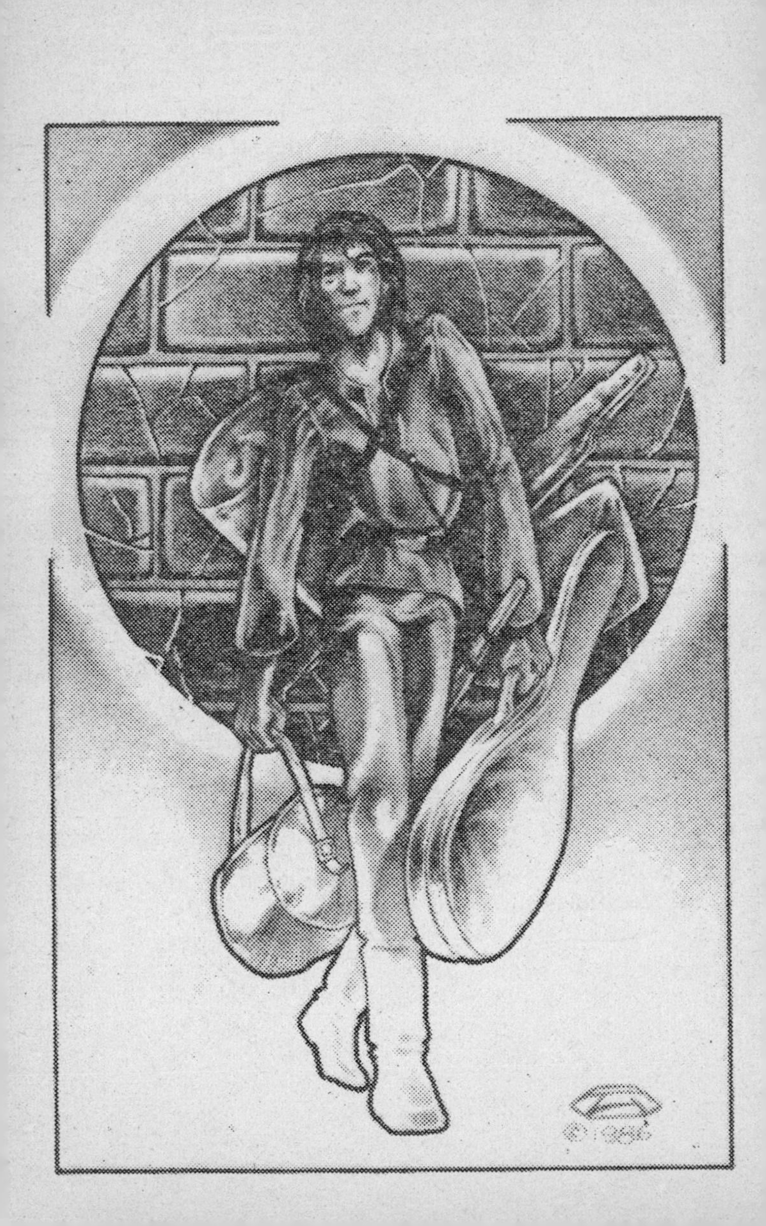

RECORD SHEET

Robinton, Journeyman Harper

Strength: 13
Intelligence: 16
Wisdom: 13
Constitution: 15
Dexterity: 14
Charisma: 15

Hit Points: 21

Marks: 15

Items Carried: Dagger; Gitar and Case; Drum, Tambourine and Case; Brass Horn and Case; Tenor Pipe and Case; Teaching Scores in a hide bag; Instrument Tools and Case; Cloak; Clothes

---

* 1 *

Robinton strode as quickly as he could toward the dining hall, flanked on every side with cases and bags which banged against him with every step. He tried to keep them in check, tugging irritatedly on the long, stiff straps, but not one of the heavy cases had the same balance. They tended to move out of rhythm with his walk, perversely pulling and pushing him across the floor like a distracted metronome. He'd been told, as were all the other journeymen, to report to the dining hall with all his belongings, in case he was to be given an assignment after the midday meal. The trouble was, a harper needed rather a lot of baggage. Carrying it all made his long arms and legs feel every bit as awkward as they did four Turns ago when he grew to his present height. He was a quick-witted young man, scarcely eighteen, but his masters let him know in their own ways that he showed great promise.

Harpering was by way of being a family occupation to him; his own father, Petiron, had once been Composition Master in the Harper Hall, though now he lived in Fort Hold as one of its Harpers. Petiron's own apprentice, Domick, a stocky, strong-looking lad whose blood family lived near Smithcrafthall, panted up next to him, carrying his own bundles.

"Hurry," Domick urged him. "Dinner gong will go any moment."

"I am hurrying," Robinton said, with irritation. "Why don't they give us more than an hour's time to get ready to go? And what if we don't have everything we need?" He shifted the instrument cases around, counting silently. He scowled, pulling his mobile face into a grimace.

Domick made a sound very much like a snort. "When you're Master Harper, you can organize journeymen-assignment your way."

"But I haven't got a harp ready to take with me. I gave the old one away. The joining on the new one I was making isn't dry yet. If I'd known a sevenday earlier, I wouldn't have begun. A sevenday later, and it would be ready."

"Then you'll make do without. I'll look after it. It isn't as if a journeyman goes into permanent exile, is it?"

"Well, no . . . but a harper without a harp!"

"Then send back for it, or make another! Oh, no, there goes the gong. We're late." Domick scuttled into the Hall just in front of Robinton, and slid his bundles to the floor. He took advantage of the cover provided by tables full of apprentices to move unobserved to his place at the oval journeymen's table. Masterharper Aldrem was engaged in deep conversation with Master Liesult, the Instrument Craftmaster, and didn't notice his entrance. The strap of one of his heavy wherhide cases caught on Robinton's tunic sleeve. When he finally managed to work it loose, the case slithered out of his grasp and banged to the floor. All the heads at the round Masters table shot up at the sound, and Robinton found himself the object of surprised and irritated scrutiny by not only the Masters and teachers of Harper Hall, but also his own father, Petiron. Robinton straightened up, swallowed a lump in his throat, bowed nervously to the head table, and made his way to his place, where his fellows were smothering laughter. He seized the serving platter of meat and began to heap slices onto his plate, wanting to build a meal high enough to hide behind.

"Hmph!" said Samel, teasingly. "They might send you out now just to get peace and quiet in the Hall."

"Isn't that your father, Robinton?" Domick asked out of one side of his mouth. "Did you know he'd be here this evening?"

"No," Robinton confessed, gloomily. "I wonder what's wrong."

"Cheer up," Garinael said. "If he's here it probably means you're getting a really good assignment. Boll, or someplace else warm."

"Not too warm, please," Robinton intoned dramatically, touching the back of one wrist to his forehead. "I couldn't bear it if I didn't have winters with breast-high snowdrifts. . . ." He fanned away imaginary heat. The others laughed.

"I could," Cyric muttered, refilling his cup with hot klah. "I'm from Igen Hold. I'll probably get sent to Telgar or Bitra."

"Oh, don't you worry," said Robinton. "To keep me from getting above myself, as Master Morshal has stated so emphatically, I'm probably bound for the northwestern end of Nowhere. And if he had anything to say about it, I would have to carry my bundles on my back all the way. No runner beast."

"You irritate him, Robinton. You always have," Domick said, reaching for the basket of bread. "No matter where you go, it won't be far enough away for him."

"That reminds me: Are there enough runners for all of us?" Samel asked, sounding worried. He was as thin as Robinton was, but nearly a head shorter. He didn't look capable of carrying heavy burdens for long.

"Of course not," Cyric snapped unsympathetically. "We're not all going."

A tapping from the head table brought their attention back to the front of the room. Masterharper Aldrem had risen, list in hand, and was facing them.

"Journeymen, I'm sure you have been guessing all the way through dinner which of you are going forth from the Harper Hall, and where. This is an exciting time for a young man, your first assignment in your craft. Will it please you? Will it suit? I can only hope so. I and the other masters have attempted to pick the job for the man, not just the man for the job. I'm sure that you will all make Harper Hall proud of you.

"This is the largest group we have assigned in a long time. But if you are ready to take on the responsibilities of a Harper, we must not hold you back. Journeyman Cyric, I can almost hear you shivering from here. But you will be assisting Harper Scotilar in Southern Boll."

Cyric smiled in relief and made a little bow to the Masterharper. The others at the table pounded him on the back in congratulation.

"Journeyman Garinael, there is need for you at Tillek Hold. Harper Dyadd died a month ago, but the message has just reached us. You're very strong in the teaching ballads and in instrumentation, and that's what is needed there. Journeyman Samel, you'll be returning to Ruatha to relieve Journeyman Coliman, who will be coming back here for further instruction; his composition skills are maturing, and we want him to get the maximum benefits from his talent.

"Journeyman Dollin, you'll be joining Masterweaver Diric at the Weavercrafthall in Southern Boll. He appreciates music, and there are those historical tapestries for you to examine with an eye toward new ballads. That's all. The rest of you can take your belongings back to your rooms and unpack. Your turns will come."

Master Liesult shook the Masterharper's sleeve, and handed up to him the second page of his notes, which had been hidden under a napkin on the table.

"One moment, please. There is one more assignment." The Masterharper smiled benevolently upon the young Harpers. "Journeyman Robinton, Harper Evarel wants you to join him in Benden Hold. Someone of your, ah, organizing talents and personality is wanted to help keep the importance of the Weyr in the minds of the people of Pern. You'll have plenty of opportunity to observe the dragons and their riders at Benden Weyr, and Weyrharper C'gan has offered to talk to you whenever you're free from your Hold duties. If the departing journeymen will join me in my quarters for a cup of wine?" The Masterharper rose and left the room.

Robinton sat in his place, feeling somewhat stunned. Benden! Why, that was a plum assignment. But it was also halfway across Pern. He wondered just how the Masterharper expected him to get there. Robinton only half-heard the others congratulating him, as he looked over to the Masters table and caught his father's eye. Petiron was beaming with pride. He motioned to his son to join him.

"The northeastern end of Nowhere," Domick said, cheerfully, thumping him on the back. "What did I tell you?"

"That's all, gentlemen," the Masterharper said, pouring himself another cup of wine. "Please remember that you have the dignity of this Crafthall to uphold. Though it seldom happens, your Lord Holder or Craftmaster has the right to send you back here if you prove to be a nuisance. I would be greatly disappointed, as I would be surprised, I might add, to have any of you returned to me in disgrace." He looked intently around at the six young men. "I would also expect you to keep in mind that anything you hear that would be of interest or of use appropriate to the Harper Hall, you will let me know. Send message slates or speak to a Hold Drummer. I won't insist on being the first to hear, but I should not be the last.

"I trust you all have sufficient funds to carry you until you reach your final destinations. You will be given a stipend there, as well as room, board and clothing, so you need only supply yourself for the journey itself. Anyone who doesn't have the marks to travel with can see me just before he sets out. The kitchens have made up supply bundles for you, too. Those of you with a long way to go and much to carry may report to the stables.

Farewell, Journeymen, and I hope not to see you too soon."

"Come on, my boy," Petiron said, capturing his son's arm and leading him outside. "You'll have to be on your way before long. The Masterharper asked me to arrange sea passage for you as far as Nerat. It'll take you the best part of a sevenday, maybe more. After that . . ."

"After that I'll make my way up the coast to Benden," Robinton interrupted eagerly. His eyes shone in his thin face. "It'll be a great opportunity to see Pern before I settle in at the Hold."

Petiron laughed. "You'll see plenty more of Pern before you die, boy. This is only your first journey. Come. Your mother wants to say goodby to you before you go." He shouldered some of Robinton's baggage, and they walked away toward Fort Hold.

Robinton's mother smoothed his crisp waves of hair and touched his cheek gently. She had slender, beautiful hands which her children had inherited, hands which looked natural doing fine work or on the strings of any instrument. She was a talented musician and singer herself, and had also lived in Harper Hall. "I hate to see you go," Merelan said, "but I can't put the dragonet back into the egg, nor should I try." She stood on her toes to kiss him on the cheek. "Look, listen, think, and remember there is a lot out there for you to learn. Beware arrogance. You're clever but you're young, and most people know more than you do." Belying her harsh admonition, her expression was soft and caring. She hugged him hard, and stood at the side of the road waving as husband and son set off eastward to Fort Sea-Hold.

It was a three hour ride by runner beast to the Sea-hold, and Robinton kept looking around anxiously at the scenery, wondering if he'd see an omen which would be a proper goodby to him. But the little cots along the cliff foot and the fields of crops just beginning to peep through the soil went on looking ordinary, everyday, until he realized that it would be a long time until he saw them all again. The very commonplace sights which he had found all but boring suddenly seemed very secure and solid. He chuckled to himself, knowing that he was being melodramatic. He glanced at his father, who was watching him closely, nodding, with a little smile at the corners of his mouth.

Robinton's throat was hoarse from calling farewells as he boarded the trading ship and waved to his father and the few friends from Harper Hall who had ridden down to Fort Sea Hold to see him off. He had dragged his many bundles off the runner beast and across the plank onto the *Sea Dragon,* a three-masted trading ship out of Ista. In a moment, the master and his men would slip anchor. The boat thumped against the stone wharf twice before they guided it out into the open water. The brightly colored sail was turned toward the wind, canvas snapping smartly above him. By the time the harbor was out of sight, Robinton's good spirits had returned. He might not see this harbor for a while, but this was not a sorrowful event. This was the beginning of his own first great adventure.

Lines of lazy trees brushed the tips of budding branches in the water by the shore, swaying slightly as the *Sea Dragon* glided by. Robinton tried cadences in his head as he leaned against the ship's rail. The captain, Elaus, had admonished him to stay out of the way, so he'd positioned himself at a point of vantage to see everything he could. Once they were well underway, the seamen paid more attention to the young Harper. The crew were all burly men, broad chested with sun-seamed brown faces. They watched with undisguised amusement as the youth explored as much of the ship as he could, all the time with hands held behind his back, so as not to touch something he shouldn't. The *Sea Dragon* had been recently painted white, with decks and trim a cheery red. Every pin and spar was neat, and all was clean and well kept. It smelled sea-fresh to Robinton. Wooden structures of any kind were rare enough on Pern, so Robinton admired the way the joining had been done, like a big musical instrument with pegs and dovetailing and caulk, wondering in amazement where all the wood had come from to build it. He resolved to learn more about ships and their construction.

His baggage had been stowed under a net amidships, and he stroked the smooth wherhide through the rope strands. He set himself in the bow to watch where the *Sea Dragon* was going, inhaling a deep breath of air flavored with salt. Up until now, this day, he'd lived landbound, with farm smells and hold smells around him. He was enjoying the novelty. There was more to being on a ship, he thought humorously, than met the eyes.

The ship chopped through a wave, jouncing him backward half a pace. His boxes under their net jumped up and slammed down. Concerned, he bent to examine them. No, they were in no danger of damage, though the edges of the cases would be well scuffed by the time they docked in Nerat.

"Shells, lad," the mate, Numa, said, coming over to peer up at him. Robinton had the advantage of half a span's worth of height over the sailor. "That all yours? You've got more bundles than a Holder's lady."

"The Harper's trade," Robinton replied, merrily. "That's my gitar. That's a drum with a small tambourine tucked in the bottom. Those two are a pipe and a brass horn. In that case are my tools for scribing or repairing instruments. The bag there contains written copies of teaching ballads and other music. This one here," he pointed to a very small bag indeed, "contains all of my clothes and things."

Numa laughed, slapping him on the back. "More your trade than you here."

"It inspires confidence in the craft," Robinton grinned. "I'd not think a lot of a seaman who could carry his boat on his back. Would you?"

"Oh, I once heard of a man who was so strong he *could* carry his boat around with him. Only that was in a song," said Numa, thoughtfully.

"It was? You must sing it for me," Robinton insisted. "Part of my duty is to collect new tunes. People at Gathers and feasts love to hear something new."

"So I shall. And so I would," the mate said. "I'd like to hear some new songs from you, too. I think I know by heart all the old ones there are."

"I wouldn't bet on that." Robinton laughed. "There are hundreds and hundreds a Harper has to learn that you've probably never heard—nor would care to."

"You're on, boy. After my watch is over we'll sit down together. We'll take turns at it." He nodded to Robinton and strode aft.

When night fell, the seamen filled lanterns and hung them around the ship's rigging. They made the homely old trading ship look like a net full of stars. Robinton made a note of the image for future use as he settled himself against a pyramid of barrels. The night was warm and pleasant. There seemed to be only a smooth light breeze blowing, though the sails were full. He supposed that it was because they were traveling with the wind that he didn't feel it. He tuned his gitar, strumming soft chords to the rhythm of the water rushing by the hull.

Numa loomed up through the darkness with a lantern swinging from one hand. Under one massive arm was a keg, and under the other a small tabor and stick. The lantern was hooked onto a metal ring on the wall of the cabin, where it hung flickering softly to the movement of the ship. Numa set down the cask, and moved one of the barrels against the mast and sat on it.

"Wine," said Numa, pointing at the cask. "When we have an evening sing, we drink. I don't think you could handle our grog, my lad, so I broke out some of the best. Benden wine, it is."

"Benden," Robinton echoed, eyeing it with pleasure. "That's a good wine. I've tasted it before. I'm going to Benden, you know."

"Ah, no, I didn't. We've only orders to take you as far as Nerat. We'll be making one stop in Ista Hold, to deliver these barrels. Ship's pitch." Numa pried the seal off the cork in the wine keg and poured some into two clay cups. "Here, try some of this. It's from the pressing of eight Turns back, and there's not a milder vintage to be had. Won't hurt a landbounder like you a bit."

Robinton took a cautious sip from the cup. He could probably count the times he'd had good wine. In the Harper Hall, wine was for special occasions and Gathers, and winesman stalls rarely had anything as fine as a Benden wine. The pressing was as smooth as Numa had promised. He held out the cup for a refill.

"Just one before a song," Numa warned him. "Our custom is, you sing a song and drain your glass. To earn a refill, you have to sing."

"All right," said Robinton. "The custom's the same at home." He picked up his gitar. "Here's one I know about a man who went fishing, and accidentally hooked the Great Sea Serpent." He struck the opening chords, and went into a lively strum.

When he finished the song there was applause and laughter, but not just from Numa. He'd been so intent in his singing that he didn't notice the other sailors joining them. Now that he peered around in the dusk, he could see six or seven others just out of the range of the glows. Numa scowled at them.

"Well, what are you hiding out there for? Sit down! It's a contest. We'll do all the better for more judges. But bring your own liquor. This is my best wine." He poured a cup out for Robinton. "Well sung, Robinton. Well sung. I've never heard those two verses before, where the poor fellow grabs Nerat by the tail, and spins Ista like a top. That'd explain some fuddleheads in Rocky Hold I know, it would."

"Those are new verses," Robinton told him. "That song's nearly as old as Pern itself and everyone knows it, so I sent him through a few extra perils. It still ends the same way, but it's like a new song because you don't know when his fishing line will break."

"The worm gave a heave and the line snapped free/With the hook in its mouth swam away/And the poor fisherman had a fish story/That no one believes to this day!" Numa sang, and cackled. "You have the talent, my lad, so you do. My turn." He picked up his tabor, and tapped out a rhythm to accompany himself.

The contest went on for several hours. Robinton hadn't had this much to drink in a long time, and was congratulating himself on how well he was managing to hold his liquor. Numa didn't seem at all affected, but Robinton knew that wine, especially one that tasted this delicious, was insidious, and they were both actually far drunker than they felt. Their audience came and went as the night watches changed, but all the seamen seemed to be having a good time listening. They were nearly out of wine around false dawn, when the lookout called down to the mate.

"Numa! Storm to the southeast!"

Numa was instantly alert. "How long have we got, Gurner?"

"It's about half an hour away, I'd say, sir."

"Batten her down, men! Storm approaching!" Numa shouted, springing to his feet. He handed the tabor to Robinton. "Look after that, would you? And get you below. I don't want you swept overboard." He ran forward, signaling to the men to reef the sails.

Robinton put his gitar back into its case and strapped it closed. He seized the tabor and headed around the cabin, feeling for the door. The sea was beginning to roughen under the ship, and the deck lurched out from beneath his feet. The gitar in its wherhide case was well enough padded to survive sliding down the ladder belowdeck. That left him with one hand free to guide himself along the handrail.

As he was moving down the steps, a voice behind him called out, "You! Help me! Catch that line!"

If Robinton should decide to go below, turn to section 2.

If he should decide to stay on deck, turn to section 3.

* 2 *

He turned around and squinted through the gloom at the speaker, a sailor gesturing frantically at him. The wind was already rough enough that the boat leapt along the waves, creaking angrily at having its rest interrupted. The wind which whipped at the sails was beginning to scatter tiny sharp raindrops over the ship. A line's tail, just over Robinton's head, smacked against the cabin wall. Its length disappeared into the darkness above. Most of the lanterns in the rigging had already been turned around to prevent the glows from scattering all over the deck. A muscular arm reached for the end of the tether at the same time that he did.

"Give me that, boy," said the sailor, sharply. "Get you below."

Realizing that he was out of his realm of experience here, and in everyone's way, Robinton clutched Numa's tabor tightly, and went down into the bowels of the rocking ship. On the wall there was a cagelike glowbasket with the gleaming fungi in it slopping back and forth, tossing the light now here, now there. He found his gitar in the corner of the bunk-room. Six low pallets were bolted to the floor and six more swayed in mid-air like long flat fish struggling in the net.

He bent low to keep from hitting his head as he scurried in, and tied himself and his gitar into one of the bunks. He intended to wait out the storm lying down. They'd sailed fully into it by now. Only a few hoarse shouts from the men were audible over the booms and growls and hisses of a sou'wester. The sea had become unfriendly to them.

Robinton found that he was frightened. This angry wind, which would have spent most of its fury before he would ever have seen it over Fort Hold, had its full potency out here on the ocean. This fragile wooden box couldn't last through a gale like this. It would be hammered to pieces on the rock-hard waves.

The *Sea Dragon* leaped sharply. He fancied it was trying to get away from its aggressor, that it was as terrified as he. Running away from a big, cruel, terrible beast with lightning bolts for teeth and wave-shaped claws that ate three-masters and seamen and young Harpers. Robinton shook himself. He didn't mind storms, but he hated being trapped anywhere, and it was playing tricks with his imagination. His fingers tapped out a nervous rhythm on the gitar case.

He tried to picture himself in a more familiar situation, say, riding a lively runner beast, bouncing up and down to the animal's gait. On his beast, he left Harper Hall, heading south along the forest road to Hold Gar to see his friend Sarle. On his left were ranged the little stone cots of the fisherfolk, and on his right, the fragrant needle-leafed trees that stood on the edge of the marshlands. The path was new-raked, and fresh white gravel crunched underfoot. Robinton smiled at the lovely spring day in his mind. But his runner had sped up, and was trotting a little too fast for his liking. He pulled back on the reins. Not a trot now, but a canter, a quick cut-time run that made his stomach turn over. And over. And over. Didn't the stupid beast understand that he wanted to stop? He grabbed the ropes and pulled hard. His runner bucked him off and galloped away.

Robinton sat up on the bunk-room floor, rubbing a sore spot on the back of his head. On his imaginary ride, he'd been using the pallet ropes for reins and had managed to untie himself. The ship, still tossing rhythmically back and forth, shot him across the deck to show how easily he'd been lifted off the bed. His instrument case spun away from him. It smacked against the wall, and Robinton cringed for his gitar. He had to retrieve it.

Roll 3 D6.

If the total is equal to or less than Robinton's value for Dexterity, turn to section 7.

If greater, turn to section 18.

* 3 *

He turned around and squinted through the gloom at the speaker, a sailor, gesturing frantically at him. The wind was already rough enough that the boat leapt along the waves, creaking angrily at having its rest interrupted. The wind which whipped at the sails was beginning to scatter tiny sharp raindrops over the ship. A line's tail, just over Robinton's head, smacked against the cabin wall. Its length disappeared into the darkness above. Most of the baskets in the rigging had already been turned around to prevent the glows from scattering all over the deck. A muscular arm reached for the end of the tether at the same time that he did.

"Give me that, boy," said the seaman, sharply. "Get you below."

"I can help," Robinton said quickly. "What can I do?"

The man hissed through his teeth. He snatched the line out of the young Harper's hands and made it fast to a metal cleat. "Help them take the sail down. But mind your head! And go below if the captain tells you, understand? Don't get in the way!"

"I understand," said Robinton. He put the tabor's strap through his belt, and joined the group of men gathering the broad sails into their arms and bundling them around the boom. The cloth was unbelievably heavy and rough, and he felt for the first time in his life as if his arms weren't long enough to be of use. The seamen worked quickly and silently. Robinton could understand why they were eager to waste no time. The storm was gathering itself close by. Thunderclouds the size of mountains assembled in a sky tinged a bruised and sickly violet.

He was soon wet clean through to his skin. The sails slid out of his arms, pouring buckets of water onto him. Palming his hair back out of his face, he bent to heave the rolls of wet cloth back up toward the boom. His companions accepted his burden, lashed it down. It was hard work, and he guessed that he might be of more assistance tying the sail up rather than trying to lift it. He signaled to Arloc, the seaman binding the mainsails from a coil of rope on his arm, to change places with him.

Nimbly, Robinton sprang up on top of the cabin. He kept the line taut as Arloc passed it up to him, and continued to do as he'd seen the other man do: draw a length of rope to the next bundle, pass the coil over and around, and catch the loop of the previous length. That way a separate length of rope was not required every time, an impossibility to manage in a storm. It looked exactly like sewing a giant hem.

In a very short time the job was done. All three sails were in place and their sheets secured tightly to the blocks. The five seamen who had been working on them went on to fastening down anything else on deck they could. Robinton hung on to a metal staple that had been driven into the cabin roof.

"You going below?" a seaman named Ritolon shouted up to him over the wind. "Last chance!" Robinton shook his head. "All right! Help me with the barrels!"

Rain pelted him so harshly that it felt like a whipping. Robinton's hands were becoming numb in the increasing cold. Ritolon threw the ends of two coils of line up to him. He passed them through the staple and back down. Ritolon looped the lines through the hawsers already holding the stacked barrels in place.

"Watch your fingers, boy! I'm going to haul on the lines!" the seaman called, throwing his weight against them. Robinton jumped back nervously, crossing his arms and folding his hands close against his sides. A Harper's hands are half his livelihood, and he was chary about damaging them. Moments later, the ends of the lines slapped the edge of the roof again.

"Once more and we've got it!" Ritolon shouted.

The ship was bucking fiercely under him, but Robinton managed to thread the lines and toss them back down again. Once the barrels were secured, he clambered down.

"Good lad!" Ritolon gave him a cheery grin and ran to aid his mates who were battening a hatchway which had come loose.

Robinton grappled his way toward the cabin, meaning to go below at last. He was cold and wet. The crack and boom of thunder shook the skies. The rain was falling harder now. Huddled under the eaves of the cabin,

Section 3

Robinton watched water pooling on the deck and pouring down the ladder into the hold. He'd have little chance of getting dry whether he was above or below decks. Lightning flashed, tearing great gashes in the storm clouds. For a split second, he saw the *Sea Dragon* and its crew painted in black and silver on the heaving sea, and then all was dark again.

"Arloc!" shouted Captain Elaus. "Rain cloaks!"

Arloc detached himself from the group forward and dashed past Robinton, heading for the ladder. The lightning flared again, illuminating the bow of the ship. Robinton caught a glimpse before the light went of his netful of luggage flinging itself back and forth against its restraints. Another good heave or so, and it would all go over the side!

He ran forward, sliding on the slick boards. Another thunderclap shook him to his knees. The jarring was punishing his insides and the wild sway of the boat made him dizzy. The boxes surged forward, there was a loud snap and the lines broke free.

Robinton dove for the net. The only thought in his mind was to keep it from being lost over the side. He seized handfuls of net and threw himself backward, straining against its weight. It felt twice as heavy waterlogged as it did dry.

Roll 3 D6.

If the total is less than or equal to Robinton's value for Strength, turn to section 9.

If greater, turn to section 10.

* 4 *

Robinton patted his tunic pockets, but it was in his pouch that he found the small ripe redfruit left over from his breakfast. With a flash of regret for his afternoon snack, he dropped it carefully amongst the gutting crew.

It landed with a splash of pulp and juice, surprising Arloc into jumping to his feet. Robinton heard the low growl of a curse and laughter from the others, as Arloc looked up to see where the missile had come from. As soon as he caught the cook's eye, Robinton signaled frantically, indicating Vanris's plight. He clung to the rope ladder, trying to keep his own movements to a minimum.

Never taking his eyes from the spectacle in the rigging, Arloc called for line and a net. Numa and Elaus came running. Vanris's face was suffused with blood under his deep tan and even his hands had swollen. There was no way to tell from Arloc's viewpoint if the crewman was awake or unconscious. It would depend very much on the young Harper whether they could get the man down safely or not. He squinted against sunlight at Robinton, estimating his mettle. Thin as wire that boy was. But the scrawny ones fooled you sometimes. It was often a surprise how strong that sort could be.

Kurram wound the coil of light rope over one arm, and began to shin up the mast. The others took up edges of a fishing net folded over and over again so that it would support the weight of a man. Arloc directed them to position themselves under Vanris. He thought of loosening or tightening the other sheets on the foremast, but decided not to try. Loosening the ropes might put slack into the rigging, which would be disastrous, and tightening them might well amputate the unfortunate crewman's feet.

The winds driving the *Sea Dragon* had slackened off somewhat, smoothing out the vibrations in the sails. Robinton reminded himself he had feeling in his fingers, and rubbed his whitened, ridged palms together. His eyes stayed on the unlikely twists of rope around the seaman's feet. The man was breathing in belabored pants, the pace increasing with fear.

"Listen to me, Vanris," he said, softly. "Kurram is climbing up the mast with a rope. The others have a net below in case you fall. It's all right. Stay relaxed." He felt rather than heard Vanris's breathing slow. Concentrating, willing him to keep calm, he began to sing, a slow ballad with a placid but definite rhythm. It was often used as a lullaby in Fort Hold, and it was the only thing at this moment to which he could remember all the words.

> "The dragons sleep within their Weyr
> No Thread dance dark against the sky
> The Holders know they've nought to fear
> When all is well, no dragons fly . . ."

"Robinton!" a voice hissed. He glanced up to see Kurram next to him. "Take this end of the rope. I've made it fast above, see?"

Robinton nodded, accepting the looped cord. "Vanris, did you hear?"

"I heard, lad."

"Good. I'll move very slowly. Bring your arms up—Yes, that's right. I'll lower this loop to you. Will your hands be able to grip?"

"I'm not sure," Vanris said grimly. "Be prepared to catch me if I can't."

Kurram braced himself on his perch and nodded to

Robinton. "All right," the Harper said. "We're ready."
"All right," Vanris said. "Here I go." Sliding the slip knot over one wrist, the seaman pulled gently down until the loop closed about his arm. He kicked his legs free.

Roll 3 D6.

If the total is less than or equal to Robinton's Strength, turn to section 20.

If greater, turn to section 15.

* 5 *

He lay down flat on the rigging, steadying the ladder by tilting his body first one way and then the other, to keep it from moving too precipitously until he was in place. At last, he was stretched full length, head down at a really uncomfortable angle. The ropes creaked where he pressed his hands, and sharp pitch-smelling strands poked him in the ribs.

He realized with a thrill of terror that he was going to have to lift both of his feet at once to hook them into the rungs if he wasn't to topple himself and Vanris off their perches. Concentrating on staying balanced, he gently shifted his weight to his midsection. He kept his arms flat, trying to use only the muscles in his stomach and back to lift his heels. The tendons in his neck stood out as he strained to move smoothly. Slowly. *Slowly.* A stray breeze danced by and blew down one pant leg, making him start violently. The ladder vibrated under him.

"I'm going to fall," Vanris gasped.

"No, you won't," Robinton said, forcing himself to

©1986

sound confident. He got his feet secured just as another gust sprang up. They swayed crazily and he gulped. There wasn't room for him to make a mistake. He could easily kill them both. "You're going to get down safely. Just stay calm. It's all right."

With his legs woven firmly if uncomfortably into the ladder, he wound his arms around Vanris's knees. "Can you draw yourself up? If I hold on to your legs, they won't come loose, and you can't fall."

"I think I can, yes. All right, steady." Vanris began to bend slowly in the middle. The swollen arms curved forward, the back bent a fraction at a time. Robinton shifted impatiently as the rope ladder pulled, sticking more fibrous bristles through his tunic and into his skin. Panting and red-faced, Vanris let himself drop limp, hanging loose in his bonds. With a sharp intake of breath, he heaved himself up and seized the rung just below Robinton's face. "There!" He began to kick at the knots around his feet.

The left came loose suddenly, and Robinton nearly caught it in the face. "Sorry, boy, did I hurt you?"

"Surprised me, that's all," Robinton said. Vanris laughed breathlessly.

More vigorous movement released the other foot, and Vanris was able to hoist himself up over the edge and onto the rope ladder. It swayed furiously, nearly throwing Robinton off. The young Harper nervously watched the deck twist to and fro under him. He was glad to let go of Vanris and see to his own safety. Holding on tightly to the rungs under his chest, he unhooked his own feet and turned himself right side up.

Vanris was already on his way down, shouting to the other seamen. They clustered about him, talking and asking questions. He sat heavily against a mast, displayed the contusions on his legs to Arloc, who sent a man running for bandages and numbweed. In the telling of his mishap, he must have mentioned Robinton's name, for all at once, every eye was on him. He felt gratified and a little embarrassed.

Turn to section 17.

* 6 *

"Yes," Arloc said. "It's mostly bruises. He's lucky not to have been killed, the young fool. I expect that he and Vanris were playing at some kind of game. Dangerous. A Harper wouldn't know, but a seafarer of experience should have known better. Have they found him yet?" Arloc called to Numa, who had taken charge of the rescue.

"Aye," Numa said, tersely. "He's been lucky. I can see him kicking. Yes, Dolgi's got a hold of him now. Stand ready to haul on the line." The men wound their hands into coils of rope and braced their feet. At Numa's signal, they strained back, drawing up their burden hand over hand. Panting, Dolgi appeared over the side, and dragged his dripping burden onto the deck.

Vanris just lay still for a time, gasping and holding his side. A quick examination by Arloc showed a couple of ribs had been broken, and a huge bruise was spreading quickly along his arm.

"It's intact," Arloc told him, feeling around the joint. "What happened to your legs? A tentacle fish?"

"Arloc, the boy's coming around." Junos held on to Robinton's wrists, keeping him from sitting up. The boy flexed and unflexed his hands, grimacing in pain. Color was beginning to come back into his face, and he moaned as consciousness returned.

"Robinton, can you hear me? Don't try to move. You've had a bad fall, but nothing is broken. Here, open your eyes. Good." Arloc clicked his tongue. The pupils were mere pinpoints of black in the wide gray irises.

Behind Arloc, Vanris was telling his story to Numa and Dolgi. ". . . and the lad tried to save my life. It's not his fault I wasn't careful enough. . . ." He broke off, coughing up seawater.

"That's enough," Arloc said, over his shoulder. "Put him to bed. I'll see to those ribs after he's had some fellis juice. And as for you, young Harper, it's bed rest for you. Drink this." He put his arm around Robinton and helped him to sit up. Robinton sniffed suspiciously at the bottle and batted it weakly away.

"None of that. It's fellis juice and wine. Drink it. Numa donated the last drops of the Benden you and he had last night. But you can't expect to get a good one like that every time. We don't want to encourage heroics just so you can get a drink."

"You can earn your drinks in a song contest, my lad," Numa added, leaning over him. "Before we land at Ista I want a rematch."

Robinton spent the next two days in a berth watching the ceiling and listening to Vanris regale his fellows with his mishap and Robinton's heroic attempt at rescue. He was much embarrassed, since he had failed, but it was the effort that interested the seamen rather than its result. One or two at a time, they sat with him, cheering him up and telling him stories. Arloc brought his meals to him and sat with him while he ate. He came down frequently during the day, ostensibly to make sure Robinton wasn't getting out of bed "before I say you can, my boy," but out of honest concern.

On the evening of the second day, he had Robinton carefully move one limb at a time and searched the youth's back with his fingers for sprained sinews. At last, he pronounced that Robinton would be able to get up the next morning. The young Harper was considerably cheered up by the news. He ate his dinner with improved appetite. His bruises were healing fast.

Roll 1 D6 per day for hit points regained by resting. *Turn to section 19.*

* 7 *

Robinton clutched a bunk leg and tried to reach the gitar with one foot. Just out of reach! Try again. Not wanting to let go of his anchor, he stretched out to his full length, attempting to hook the strap of the case. Bump! went the ship under his belly. He would have been shaken loose if his Harper's training hadn't strengthened the muscles and tendons in his arms to iron.

A big wave swashed loudly against the hull of the *Sea Dragon,* tipping the ship to starboard. Robinton took advantage of the rolling motion, and managed to capture his errant gitar as it skittered past his feet. He drew his leg up to where he could take hold of the strap with one hand. Draping it across his shoulders, he handed himself up onto the nearest bunk and resolved not to move again until morning.

His stomach reminded him that it had been subject to recent ill use and was on the verge of protesting rather more strongly. The sawing cry of the sea shouted in his ears and made him feel dizzy and sick.

"Too much wine," he said to himself, wryly. "But how was I to know there'd be a storm?"

His insides jumped again. He started to look around frantically for a bucket.

Water flowed along the deck down into the bunk-room. It must be raining harder now. Suddenly, one of the seamen, Arloc, dashed into the room. He passed

Robinton without acknowledgment, and threw open a huge press that was bolted down like the beds. From it he drew big oiled hides with ties and hoods attached, heavy-weather rain gear. He shouted over his shoulder.

"Come on, boy, help me!"

"Me?" Robinton asked, hearing his voice weaker than he remembered it.

Arloc turned to look at him, saw how white the young man's face was, and made a quick diagnosis. "Your belly griping you, lad?" he asked. Getting a nod, he tossed a few of the oilskins to Robinton. "Then by the shell, you'd best get up on deck! If you're sick down here, the men'll have your gizzards!"

He tucked the gitar under the blanket and stood up. Somehow, he managed to follow Arloc up the stairs with the heavy cloaks. Hands took them away from him, and guided him roughly but kindly to the rail. The rain plastered his hair and clothing against him, but the winds were dying down. He let his stomach heave away, seeing the edge of daylight close approaching from the east. Sunrise.

"Landbounder," said Numa behind him, with amusement in his voice.

Turn to section 8.

* 8 *

The sun was balancing on the horizon now, like a ball in a juggler's trick. The darkness sped away from it, shading the sky in ever lightening blues. Under their feet, the ship's rhythm had died to a calm rocking, and the sea, purring, rubbed itself affectionately against the hull.

Already, a man stood by each mast, ready to unfurl the

bound sails on the merchant captain's orders. Others seized the mainsheets. Elaus squinted at the sun, took a sniff at the air, and nodded his head. In a moment, the sails were aloft, and filling with the breeze.

"Last watch, to bed!" Elaus called. "Fine weather today, I'll warrant. Get you to bed, too, young Harper lad. It takes three storms to make a seaman. You've two to go."

Robinton acquiesced gratefully, following the others back toward the bunk-room. His back and shoulder muscles ached, and he felt tired right through to his bones. He handed the rain cloak back to Arloc, slipped off his wet clothes, and climbed into the nearest empty bunk. In a very short time he was asleep, soothed by the lullaby of the gentle sea.

When he awoke, it was dark in the cabin, but very warm. Around him in the many bunks huddled forms wheezed and snored companionably. He put out a hand to find his clothes and discovered they were not where he'd left them. In their place lay a long soft tunic and a belt.

He tried the shirt on. It had been made for a much larger man than he, falling as it did just to his knees, but it was roomy and comfortable. He belted the tunic at the waist, discarded the thought of wet shoes, and made his way up the stairs, taking care not to wake anyone else.

Brilliant sunshine greeted him as he emerged from the dim stairwell. Protectively shading his eyes with a forearm, he took a quick look around. The merchant's men had been busy while he was asleep. The deck was clean and dry again, the ropes freshly coiled, and the netted cargo back where it belonged. Robinton heard voices humming up over his head. He squinted up to see two seamen, Vanris and Junos, clambering through the rigging, singing as they worked. The tune was a simple, rollicking one, and Robinton resolved to hear it in full before he went ashore. There were brightly colored pennants fluttering from the lines. Robinton laughed out loud when he realized that the "pennants" were clothes, his and the crew's.

"This trip will make a grand song, if I live through it," he said to Arloc, who also served as ship's cook. "I'd like to learn more of your craft." Arloc dished him a bowl of cereal, and motioned to where he could find a cup of klah and slices of a thick salt bread. Small sweet-smelling redfruits gleamed from a heavy wooden bowl next to the klah pots.

"It's just our business, same as Harpering's yours," Arloc said. "There's some who'd say that you should keep to your own tasks, but I think it's grand that you're so minded. You'd make a fair sailor, you would, but you've got to learn to hold your wine better than that."

Robinton threw back his head and laughed. "I will, I promise you. Do you have many storms like the one we had last night?"

"Oh, a few, a few," Arloc said, grinning at the young Harper. "We might be able to treat you to another before you go ashore."

"I beg you, don't go to the trouble!"

"Ah, here you are, my lad." Numa poked his head under the flap of the cooking tent. "Your things are about dry. If you want to give Junos a hand with them and the others? After you finish your breakfast, of course. I never saw a youngling so eager to go to work." He raised a hand to stay Robinton from rushing out immediately.

"Thank you, Numa." The seaman grunted and disappeared.

"There you are," Arloc said. "You're accepted. He usually ignores passengers. They can't be bothered to stir during a storm, they barely speak to us except when they want something, so they're nothing to us but cargo. Land folk don't understand sea folk."

"That isn't right," Robinton insisted. "We're all Pernese."

"You're one of the few who thinks that way, then." Giving him a searching look, he collected Robinton's empty bowl and cup and turned away.

The day was fine and clear, as Elaus had foretold. Once he had his clothes back, Robinton enjoyed himself climbing around in the rigging with the other two crewmen. With three pairs of hands, the work went quickly. The men's clothing was taken down, folded and stowed away before midafternoon. When they were through, they sat swinging their bare feet in the breeze, laughing and exchanging yarns. One of the other seamen, Tarosi, passed underneath carrying a small keg under his arm.

"Hey!" Junos yelled down to him. Surprised to be addressed from above, the man raised his head. Junos held out his hands. Tarosi grinned in comprehension, and tossed the keg lightly up to him. The seaman took a swallow, wiped his mouth on the back of his hand, and passed the barrel to Robinton.

It was quite a trick to drink out of the heavy cask while sitting on swaying ropes high over the deck. He had rivulets of ale running down his neck by the time he got any into his mouth. With a jaunty grin, he handed the keg on to Vanris.

"So, what is it like living landbound?" Junos wanted to know.

"We don't exactly think of it as being bound. It is different, though, not just because a Hold isn't always moving, as a ship is. In the Harper Hall, we get to know each other very well, because there aren't many people living in it. We don't have to rely upon one another in life and death situations, as often as you do on shipboard. On the other hand, we can go off farther when we don't get along." Robinton gestured to take in the whole ship. "The folk on land, Hold and Hall, do interact and cooperate in important ways. Everyone has their special tasks. There's a song we play mostly for children of Teaching age, called the Song of the Holdless Holder." He squinted off into the sky, humming to himself for a moment to get the tune, then began to sing aloud.

Each of the verses of the song described the hapless farmer's attempts to find something he liked doing better than farming. So humorously inept was he at everything he tried that the two seamen were helpless with laughter by the time Robinton finished the song. He signaled for the keg, and took a long swallow.

"A good lesson, Harper," Vanris said. "Children would learn from that well. You know your landsmen, to be sure."

"I'd wager you've learned about all there is to know about your mates without a song like that."

"That's so," Vanris nodded.

"No, 'tisn't," Junos corrected him. "There's some you never get to know well. Like Gurner."

"Well, yes, Gurner's different."

"Who's Gurner?" Robinton asked. "A former mate of yours?"

"Shell and scale, no, boy! But it's small wonder you don't know him. He's forever up in the lookout." Vanris pointed upward. There was a tiny basket woven of strips of hide atop the main mast. "He's up there in any weather but storm, sometimes sleeps up there. He loves the sea, but can't abide anyone else at all, though he'll listen well to Numa and the captain. If he wasn't such a good worker, Elaus would put him ashore."

"I didn't see him last night."

"Oh, belike enough he was down here helping. He's the one spotted the storm coming."

"He was taken on three seasons back. And I'll tell you now that I know less about him than I did then. Never gets matey with the rest, never drinks with us. Never seems to notice what cargo we're carrying. Almost as if he hides up there in his little basket. As if he has something *to* hide."

Robinton craned his head back, trying to see if there was any movement in the lookout. The little basket was deep enough that he wouldn't be able to tell who was in it unless he climbed all the way up to it. It didn't strike him as a perch he'd like to sit on for very long. Each snap of the sails in the breeze caused the mast to thrum throughout its length, shaking the lookout like the top of a child's rattle. His brains would be properly addled after a sevenday up there, let alone three whole seasons of trading. Gurner must treasure his privacy above physical comfort.

A netful of fish was dragged up on deck by Arloc and two other seamen, Dolgi and Kurram. They hauled the catch to the foredeck, so the stench of gutting would be blown forward with the wind. Robinton, with a hopeful glance for the safety of his wherhide cases just steps from piles of fish entrails, fled farther up the rigging with his two friends away from the smell.

From his seat high up over the sea, Robinton felt like a gossamer-spinner in its nest. But the crawler, hunting as it was for food, never had so grand a view as he. With one arm around the mast for support, he could swing his body in any direction. A single day's voyage out of Fort Sea Hold, and there was not a speck of land in sight. Robinton searched the horizons, but all he beheld was length after length of glass-green water. A cone of white ripples followed the *Sea Dragon* in her path, and curling, foaming waves ran before her.

On the foredeck, under the shelter of the jibsail, the three tiny seamen toiled at their minuscule task, looking like worker insects gathering grains. Every so often, an insect would pick up a piece of shining silver and throw it over the side of the ship. Robinton noted that larger gray flecks, bigger fish, followed the morsels of fish guts along the ship's sides, and devoured them greedily. There was, in fact, a whole school of large deepwater fish in the *Sea Dragon*'s wake, far enough under the surface that they seemed insubstantial. The gleaming shadows appeared to take turns feeding on the offerings cast to them.

Arloc seemed to sense scrutiny from above and raised his voice. "You lot can come down here and help. If you want to eat, that is!"

Laughing, the seamen started down to the deck. Robinton took a final sniff of the clean sea air and prepared to follow.

Junos paused when he was still at quite a height over the others. He leaped, springing off the cracklingly tight rigging, threw his arms and legs about the smooth mast-tree, and slid spiraling down its length. At the bottom, Kurram and Arloc cheered his daring, and Dolgi congratulated him by presenting him with an especially big and slippery fish to gut. Junos accepted the fish with a grimace, but drew his knife and set to work with alacrity.

Robinton grinned in admiration at Junos, then set about finding a safer way down for himself. He wound both hands tightly into the stiff, pitch-smelling rope ladder, and began gingerly to feel for his first toehold. It was much easier to climb up than down. He felt envy for the crew who had been scaling the riggings so long they did it without effort or thought. Especially thoughts of falling, or breaking bones, or drowning. Robinton grinned at himself. What a terrible sailor he'd be, always imagining disasters.

"Well, come on, Robinton. There's no supper for lazy lieabouts, is there?" Vanris chided, pointing down. "Plenty of gutting left to do." Then, shrewdly guessing the young Harper's misgivings, "Want me to go first?" Robinton nodded. "This way, then!"

The sea man leaned away from the rigging for a taut line stretched along the angle of the sail, reaching from mast-head to boom. "You climb the ladder. I'll just swing down and stay below you all the way."

Robinton felt a little foolish being protected like a child taking its first steps, but grateful, too, that Vanris wasn't making fun of his nervousness.

"Here we go," Vanris called. He hung on the rope, moving out of Robinton's way.

There was a sudden loud snap, and Vanris's line broke free of its mooring, robbing him of his support. With a strangled cry, he fell. Robinton flailed at the air in panic, grabbing for the seaman's arm. Before Robinton could catch him, Vanris was hanging upside down in mid-air, casting about wildly for a handhold. His ankles held his whole weight in a pair of accidental slip knots which could undo themselves at any moment. The deck was very far below. If Vanris fell, he would surely be killed.

Robinton started forward to draw him back up. The ladder swayed in the wind and he nearly fell off. They were both in danger.

If Robinton should attempt to rescue Vanris, turn to section 13.

If he should decide to wait for help, turn to section 4.

* 9 *

The ship leaped again, jarring all his bones, but he hung on to the precious bundle. Panic twisted in his guts. He couldn't let his beloved instruments be lost overboard. The wet strands cut into his palms, but he ignored the pain.

Section 9

"Help me!" he cried, trying to outshout the storm. He could feel his feet slipping. Gathering all his strength, he drew a deep breath and pulled.

For a moment, he thought his shoulders would pop out of their sockets. His fingers were growing numb from lack of circulation. In the roar of the wind he fancied he could hear the storm laughing at him, trying to reclaim his toys from its grasp. It yanked once more at the net, but as the *Sea Dragon* tacked against the gale, there was a lull just long enough that Robinton could haul the bundle in.

He sat down on the deck with a thump, the wherhide boxes suddenly in his lap. He laughed for pure joy then, his battle won. Scooting closer to the cabin with the net in tow, he secured the broken ends of the rope to a ring at the foot of the mast.

The winds were dying down. He sat on the deck with his back to the cabin wall, panting. His hands hurt. So did his back. The stitch he felt in his chest made him remember early singing lessons. He decided not to move.

Someone walking by dropped a raincloak on him, and he put it on. The other men appeared to be relaxing as the storm spat out its last burst of fury and abated. Robinton breathed in and out, his body following the rhythm of the ship. Abruptly, his wine-laden stomach took umbrage. It reminded him that it had suffered recent ill use, since he had mistaken it for a wineskin that wanted filling. His exertions had stirred up his digestive processes to the point at which he felt very hungry, but he was sick all the same. He felt his way over to the rail and let his stomach heave away, seeing the edge of daylight close approaching from the east. Sunrise. Behind him the men cheered.

"Landbounder," said Numa, with amusement in his voice. "I'll wager you feel like you've just landed the

Great Sea Serpent all by yourself, don't you?" he asked. "Well, never mind. You're a brave one all the same."

Subtract one hit point for damage.

Turn to section 8.

* 10 *

The ship leaped again, jarring all his bones, but he hung on to the precious bundle. Panic twisted in his guts. He couldn't let his beloved instruments be lost overboard. The strands cut into his palms, but he ignored the pain.

"Help me!" he cried, trying to outshout the storm. He could feel his feet slipping. Gathering all his strength, he drew a deep breath and pulled.

For a moment, he thought his shoulders would pop out of their sockets. His fingers were growing numb for lack of circulation. In the roar of the wind he fancied he could hear the storm laughing at him trying to reclaim his toys from its grasp. The net was yanked once more, and as the *Sea Dragon* tacked into the gale, he felt himself lifted off his feet and over the side, still clutching his instruments.

"Help me!" he cried, trying to outshout the screaming winds. A chasm opened in the waves, and he fell into it. Dark, cold water rushed in on him, pushing him down, dragging him down. He gulped mouthfuls of bitter salt water, trying to free his fingers from the tether lines. The more he struggled, the more his hands became entangled. Kicking wildly, he struggled to the surface and sucked in gasping breaths of air. "Help!" he called. "Man overboard!"

There were already faces squinting down from the rail

far above. He tried again to cry out to them, but a wave slapped him in the face, filling his mouth and eyes. He gagged, vomiting sea water and wine.

Something large hit the water near him, sank under the surface and bobbed up again. In a moment, he could feel an arm grasp him around the waist. He thrashed against the restraint.

"Easy, Robinton," said Numa's voice in his ear. "You'll drown us both." The seaman took in his predicament in a glance and treaded water strongly enough to keep them both afloat. He signaled to someone above. A rope hit the water, and they were hauled aboard.

One of the seamen cut the ropes off his wrists and opened the net to examine the boxes for damage. Robinton watched him anxiously, rubbing his hands together to restore feeling.

"Nothing's ruined," the man said. "These cases are well built."

"Thank goodness," Robinton said, sighing with relief. "I'll never skip Master Liesult's classes again." He started to wring out his tunic.

Numa stood over him, dripping seawater. "Your baggage was nearly the death of you, lad. I'll wager you feel like you've just landed the Great Sea Serpent all by yourself, don't you? Well, never mind. You're all right for a landbounder. But for your skin's sake, don't try to help any more, eh?"

Subtract two hit points for damage.

Turn to section 8.

* 11 *

"Thank you, Numa," said Robinton, feeling honored by their regard. He prepared to set foot on Ista with all dignity in his craft. He strode proudly forward. The crossing looked simple enough, but from one or two steps along, the canvas seemed to stretch for dragon-lengths until it met at last the safety of the dock. He stole a quick look over his shoulder. The others were waiting patiently.

At the moment he was about halfway across, they all rushed as one to the port side of the ship. The *Sea Dragon* tilted sharply, and the sling dropped out from under his feet.

Turn to section 24.

* 12 *

Arloc peered at him bleakly. "Yes," he sighed. "He'll live. It's mostly bruises, but there might be a few bones broken as well. He's lucky not to have been killed, the young fool. I expect that he and Vanris were playing at some kind of game. Dangerous. A Harper wouldn't know, but a seafarer of experience should have known better. Have they found him yet?" Arloc called to Numa, who had taken charge of the rescue.

"Aye," Numa said, tersely. "He's been lucky. I can see him kicking. Yes, Dolgi's got a hold of him now. Stand ready to haul on the line." The men wound their hands into coils of rope and braced their feet. At Numa's signal, they strained back, drawing up their burden hand over hand. Panting, Dolgi appeared over the side, and dragged his dripping burden onto the deck.

Vanris just lay still for a time, gasping and holding his side. A quick examination by Arloc showed a couple of ribs had been broken, and a huge bruise was spreading quickly along his arm.

"It's intact," Arloc told him, feeling around the joint. "What happened to your legs? A tentacle fish?"

"Arloc, the boy's coming around." Junos held on to Robinton's wrists, keeping him from sitting up. The boy flexed and unflexed his hands, grimacing in pain. Color was beginning to come back into his face, and he moaned as consciousness returned.

"Robinton, can you hear me? Don't try to move. You've had a bad fall, and you may be badly injured. Here, open your eyes. Good." He examined the boy's pupils. They were mere specks of black in the wide gray irises. "Not in shock, I think. There's a good big bump on the back of his head."

Behind Arloc, Vanris was telling his story to Numa and Dolgi. ". . . and the lad tried to save my life. It's not his fault I wasn't careful enough. . . ." He broke off, coughing up seawater.

"That's enough," Arloc said, over his shoulder. "Put him to bed. I'll see to those ribs after he's had some fellis juice. And as for you, young harper, it's bed rest for you. Drink this." He put his arm around Robinton and helped him to sit up. Robinton sniffed suspiciously at the bottle and batted it weakly away.

"None of that. It's fellis juice and wine. Drink it. It tastes bad but it'll keep you from feeling the pain while I see to those poor bones of yours."

"How are the patients?" Numa asked in a low voice as Arloc came up the stairs from the bunk-room.

"I've bound up all the injuries. Vanris is not too badly off. After all, he did land in the water. He's been expecting a reprimand, but I think he's punished himself enough. Thinks it's his fault the lad got hurt. By what he's saying, I think they can share the blame."

"And Robinton?" Numa knit his brows in concern.

Arloc sighed. "In my opinion, he's not fit to finish his journey to Benden. I recommend we make provision for him in Ista, and see him on the next ship back to Fort Hold."

"Very well. 'Tis a shame, but we'll do what you suggest. I wish him a swift return home and a speedy recovery."

Turn to section 29.

* 13 *

"Hold on!"

Robinton scrambled as far down the rigging as he dared. To move too close too quickly would probably shake the seaman loose from his life-saving knots. Vanris, hanging head down and fully aware of the danger he was in, was twisting slowly, slowly around. He seemed to be gauging if there would be time to swing toward and capture one of the lines just out of his reach, before the rigging straightened out and dropped him. He tilted his head up just enough to see the frightened young man perched above him.

"What do I do?" Robinton called. His words were muffled by the crackle of canvas. He projected his voice to be heard over it. "I can't go down for help. You'd fall."

"Can you reach any loose lines?" Vanris panted. The

blood rushing to his head was beginning to darken his vision. "There might be . . . one close by. The end of a sail tie?" Vanris forced himself to relax and let his arms hang loose. He'd seen many a shipmate break bones by being rigidly tense in a fall. It was important to stay calm. But it was a long drop to the deck. "Hurry, lad!"

Robinton looked around. Every line he could see was tied tightly just out of reach, and he had no knife to cut one loose, even if he could guess which one would not bring the whole mainsail down on his head. If the crew below didn't look up, they'd never know Vanris was in trouble until he fell on them.

"Wait, I know what to do!" the young harper cried.

If Robinton now decides to call for help, turn to section 4.

If instead he decides to help Vanris up by catching hold of his legs, turn to section 5.

If instead he decides to help Vanris up by catching hold of his hands, turn to section 16.

* 14 *

"No, thank you for the honor," Robinton said, stepping back and making a slight bow. "I'll wait my turn."

Junos guffawed and slapped his knee. "He's on to you, Numa. Good for you, lad." He stepped off the side of the ship and leaped onto the slings. The ship curtsied slightly under his weight, rolling toward the dock. The other seamen followed, each following the rocking motion of the ship, and choosing a moment to cross when the ship was bowing toward the shore.

Robinton put a cautious foot on the sling. The *Sea Dragon*'s sway was much more noticeable on something less solid than her boards. He lifted himself cautiously onto it, and stepped lightly, arms held out for balance.

Roll 3 D6.

If the total is greater than Robinton's value for Dexterity, turn to section 24.

If less than or equal, turn to section 30.

* 15 *

There was a sharp jerk on the cord as Vanris entrusted his whole weight to it. Robinton on his perch in the rigging was bounced up and down like a parcel on runner back. The rope burned out of his grasp. He lunged for it, sacrificing his own balance to save his friend. The ladder wobbled under his knees.

Kurram cried out as Vanris's entire weight yanked at his arms. He managed to hold the line steady. The men holding the net ran to stand under the mast. Vanris smacked into it, hard. Hands shaking, he undid the loop around his wrist, wound his limbs around the mast, and slid to the bottom, where he lay, moaning in pain.

Robinton stared at his palms. Great blisters rose while he watched. He started down toward the deck, gripping with great care for his sore hands.

Turn to section 17.

* 16 *

He lay down flat on the rigging, steadying the ladder by tilting his body first one way and then the other, keeping it from moving too precipitously until he was in place. At last, he was stretched full length, head down in a really uncomfortable angle. The ropes creaked where he pressed his hands, and sharp pitch-smelling strands poked him in the ribs.

He realized with a thrill of terror that he was going to have to lift both of his feet at once to hook them into the rungs. If he wasn't to topple himself and Vanris off their perches, he had to stay perfectly balanced. Gently, he shifted his weight to his midsection. He kept his arms flat, trying to use only the muscles in his stomach and back to lift his heels. The tendons in his neck stood out as he strained to move smoothly. Slowly. *Slowly.* A stray breeze danced by and blew down one pant leg, making him start violently. The ladder vibrated under him.

"I'm going to fall," Vanris gasped.

"No, you won't," Robinton said, forcing himself to sound confident. He got his feet secured just as another gust sprang up. They swayed crazily and he gulped. There wasn't room for him to make a mistake. He could easily kill them both.

He thrust one long thin arm through the mesh toward Vanris. "Can you reach my hand? If you bend very slowly upward, I can catch your arm and pull you up.

"All right. Steady, now." Vanris began to draw himself up. The swollen arms curved forward, the back bent a fraction at a time. Robinton shifted impatiently, pushed his shoulder through and strained his fingers forward, extending to the very end of his reach.

Grunting and red-faced, Vanris let himself fall limp, hanging loose in his bonds. With a sharp intake of breath, he heaved himself up, arms out-thrust. "Catch me, boy!"

Robinton shoved his hand forward, scraping his cheek on the lines. He seized the man's wrist firmly. The other hand clamped about his own. "Now I can loose myself," Vanris said, kicking at the knots around his feet. "Hold tight!"

"I am!" Robinton assured him vehemently, winding his other arm fast into the rigging. His cheek stung from the pressure, but he concentrated on keeping his head positioned just as it was. He didn't want the rope to slide into his eyes. Vanris was no light weight, and Robinton's shoulder felt nearly wrenched apart holding him so.

The fierce grip on his wrist let go, and the rigging dipped just under his head, as Vanris caught hold of the side behind his right shoulder. "Just hang on to me another moment, Rob-me-lad, and I'll be free." More kicking, but at least the pressure on his arm was relieved. The side of his face felt raw with little pin pricks of irritation. He wished he could scratch.

"—There!" Vanris exclaimed. A hard kick in the belly announced to Robinton that one foot was free, the left. "Sorry, boy, did I hurt you?"

"Surprised, that's all," Robinton said. "Go on."

A deep chuckle. "You're a good sport. You can let go now. I'll need my hand back. I never tied so good a knot with my fingers, let me tell you."

Robinton let go gratefully. He could not have held on much longer in any case. His palm was slippery with sweat. He watched Vanris worrying at the loops around his trapped ankle, his free leg kicking at the air. At last the loops shot over the end of the man's bare foot, and he dropped to hang from the rigging by one hand.

The sudden movement overbalanced the ladder, and it flipped over. With a cry, Robinton lost his grip and fell off, plummeting to the deck. As it turned back, Vanris was flung off to the side. He flew in a broad arc that deposited him with a crash on the portside bulwark. Moaning, he dropped over the side into the sea.

In an instant, the other sailors swarmed into the foredeck, trying to see what had happened. There was a cacophony of shouting, as everyone demanded information or tried to take charge at once. Three men took the ends of ropes and dove into the sea with them, seeking after their companion. Arloc and Junos knelt next to Robinton, trying to assess the extent of his injuries.

"Numbweed!" Arloc shouted, and a seaman went running. He put a hand on the boy's throat, feeling for a pulse. It was there, though weak and shocky. They eased him onto his back, frowning with concern at the drawn white face.

"What happened? Will he live?" Junos demanded.

Roll 4 D6 for damage and subtract the total from Robinton's hit points.

If the total is greater than or equal to Robinton's hit points (whether it brings him down to 0 points), turn to section 6.

If less, turn to section 12.

* 17 *

Robinton made his way somewhat unsteadily down to the deck. His arms and legs were shaking from tension and excitement. Vanris beckoned him over.

"I owe you my life, young Harper, and it's been an interesting one so far. I'm glad to be able to hold on to it for a while longer."

The young man reddened. "Anyone would have done the same," he said.

"I'm grateful for the calming voice as well. I don't deny I was afeared. You're a fine Harper, and a fine fellow."

Arloc handed Vanris a small flask. "Drink this, mate." He eyed Robinton. "You look like you might need a little of this, too, my lad."

Robinton took the bottle and sniffed it suspiciously. "What's in it?"

"Fellis juice and wine. In your honor, it's some of the good Benden, though you can't expect that every time. We don't want to encourage heroics so you can get a drink."

Turn to section 19.

* 18 *

Robinton clutched a bunk leg and tried to reach the gitar with one foot. Just out of reach! Try again. Not wanting to let go of his anchor, he stretched out to his full length, attempting to hook the strap of the case. Bump! went the ship under his belly. His stomach reminded him that it had been subject to recent ill use and was on the edge of protesting rather more strongly.

A big wave swashed loudly against the hull of the *Sea Dragon,* tipping the ship to starboard. Robinton lost his grip on the post and was thrown under one of the other bunks. Water flowed along the deck down into the bunkroom, dampening his clothes with sea spray. It must be raining harder now. He saw the gitar skitter past his feet, and tried to recapture it. The ship lunged again, slamming Harper and instrument against the other bulkhead. Robinton was sure he'd be one big bruise by daylight. Handing himself carefully across the deck, he managed to get a hold of the gitar strap just before the rolling motion took it away again. He examined the case closely. There was a long shallow slice in the wherhide from some unseen nail. He looked down at his arm. Yes, he'd been caught by it, too. There was blood, and the sleeve was torn. A minor injury. Draping the gitar across his shoulders, he handed himself up onto the nearest bunk and resolved not to worry about it until morning.

The sawing cry of the sea shouted in his ears and made him feel dizzy and sick.

"Too much wine," he said to himself, wryly. "But how was I to know there'd be a storm?"

His insides jumped again. He started to look around

frantically for a bucket. Suddenly, one of the seamen, Arloc, dashed into the room. He passed Robinton without acknowledgment, and threw open a huge press that was bolted down like the beds. From it, he drew big oiled hides with ties and hoods attached, heavy-weather rain gear. He shouted over his shoulder.

"Come on, boy, help me!"

"Me?" Robinton asked, hearing his voice weaker than he remembered it.

Arloc turned to look at him, saw how white the young man's face was, and made a quick diagnosis. "Your belly griping you, lad?" he asked. Getting a nod, he tossed a few of the oilskins to Robinton. "Then by the shell, you'd best get up on deck! If you're sick down here, the men'll have your gizzards!"

He tucked the gitar under the blanket and stood up. Somehow, he managed to follow Arloc up the stairs with the heavy cloaks. Hands took them away from him, and guided him roughly but kindly to the rail. The rain plastered his hair and clothing against him, but the winds were dying down. He let his stomach heave away, seeing the edge of daylight close approaching from the east. Sunrise.

"Landbounder," said Numa behind him, with amusement in his voice.

Subtract one hit point for damage.

Turn to section 8.

* 19 *

Two peaceful days passed while the *Sea Dragon* glided over smooth green waves, heading toward Ista. Robinton was soon over his uneasiness about the rigging, and was enjoying the light breeze under the shadow of the center mainsail. The sun was hot, and the merchant's men wore only knee-length trousers while working on deck. Robinton had taken his pipe out of his baggage, and played a few sprightly tunes for the pleasure of the men, and the sheer joy of playing.

A new tune began to come into his head, a neat little air in a major key, but no words, no subjects, suggested themselves to go with it. He tried one phrase and then another, perfecting the song. A bridge joined the melody, and the chorus just wove itself under his fingers. Too bright and insubstantial for an instrumental piece, he mused. It needs words. A comic song, perhaps.

The mast creaked loudly behind him, disturbing his concentration. All his half-formed ideas were driven away, though he still had the tune. He felt a little frustrated. It was like crafting one shoe. It'd be no good until the other half of the pair was finished.

Vanris was back on duty this morning, too. The rope burns on his ankles made him walk stiffly, but he went at his tasks willingly. He was clearly happy to be freed from enforced idleness. His whistling echoed Robinton's tune, as he sat in the shade mending nets.

"We're more traders than we are fishermen," Vanris explained. "But a nice catch of fish means we don't have to load on as many supplies. More room for cargo. Since every man has a share of the profits, there's not many objections you'd hear when we load on a bale or two instead of a side of herdbeast."

"Does every man have a say in what you choose to take on?"

"Well, a suggestion or two don't go amiss, but it's the captain who has final approval. The size of a man's share depends on how long he's been on board, and his say has the same weight. Junos and me, we're best friends. We signed on together. Our shares are just exactly the same. We're saving to have a ship of our own one day." Vanris sighed wistfully. "We'll call her *Misty,* after our home Hold. Junos was my foster-brother. We wanted to call our ship after my blood mother, Alina, but she wouldn't have it."

"I was never fostered out," Robinton admitted. "When I was of fostering age, I began my apprenticeship at the Harper Hall. My parents live in Fort Hold."

"You've missed something, then. Have you other blood kin?"

"Oh, yes."

"Well, I haven't. My father died when I had just twelve Turns, so there's only Junos, my mother and me. Though I'm grateful for what I have. I could be all alone, as Gurner is, for example. And if I do say it, he's got less of a talent for making friends."

Gurner. Robinton craned his head back. Above him, the woven basket shifted, as whatever was within it moved. Robinton decided impulsively to greet this mysterious crewmember and get acquainted. Nimbly, he scaled up the rope ladder to the top of the mast. Seizing the rim of the basket, he hauled himself upward.

He got one elbow over the edge, then the other, keeping his feet hooked into the rigging. The man seated in the lookout stared at him in irritated astonishment. He swore a fierce oath.

"How do you do? My name's Robinton," the young Harper said, cheerfully, ignoring the seaman's evident hostility. "Are you Gurner?" No reply. "I'm sailing as a passenger on the *Sea Dragon* to Nerat Hold. How quiet it is up here. You could easily fall asleep on warm days, couldn't you? Fine weather today, Elaus said."

"Stow your babbling and get away. I've work to do," Gurner snarled. When Robinton showed no signs of moving away immediately, the seaman set one hand against the young man's chest and pushed him away.

Robinton squawked in surprise as he tried to keep from falling. More upset by Gurner's reaction than even from the memory of his experience of the day before, he ducked quickly out of sight. Before he was gone, the lookout had withdrawn to the padded furs on the far side of the tiny space, and was pointedly ignoring him. Robinton went down to his previous perch to think.

He sat on the boom, idly tapping out a drum beat with his fingers. A sharp tug on his foot brought his mind back to the present moment, nearly surprising him into toppling over and eliciting another squawk. Numa grinned up at him.

"My poor heart!" Robinton grinned back, clutching at his chest dramatically. "When it starts again . . ."

"What, you? If all Harpers were as fearless as you, we wouldn't need the dragonriders. Perhaps you should write a ballad about yourself. You can sing it this evening. We might have another song contest, if you're up to one," Numa offered.

"I'd enjoy that," Robinton agreed.

The sky was bright from end to end with the jewel points of stars. Neither moon was out, so the sparkling carpet was uninterrupted to the horizons. There were no clouds at all, and the night air had a sharp nip to it. Robinton moved his seat so there was a barrier between himself and the cool wind.

"Have no fear, lad," Numa assured him. "After a drink or two, you'll think it's an Igen summer. Shall you begin, or shall I?"

"If you would," Robinton said. "I need to get my gitar out of my baggage." He handed his flute to one of the others who were gathered to judge the contest, and walked out of the ring of glows.

As he peered through the darkness, feeling his way forward, he could see a silhouette against the stars just where the cargo net would be.

"Hello?" he called out. "Who's there?"

The figure straightened up, startled. It appeared to crane at the darkness, trying to see who was addressing it. Before Robinton could identify it, it moved into the shadows. He started after it. Silently eluding him in the dark, it vanished. Robinton barked his shins on an unseen obstacle and had to halt his pursuit.

"Hello?" he repeated, softly. No reply. Puzzled, he bent to examine his bags. Nothing had been moved or changed. Perhaps one of the seamen had fixed an undone knot for him. Perhaps the figure hadn't heard him call to it. The roars of laughter Numa was earning from the audience might easily have drowned him out. He retrieved his gitar and rejoined the others.

Just after he sat down, Tarosi sauntered into the circle of light and sat down, nodding calmly to everyone. He appeared to be somewhat preoccupied. Robinton felt concern for him. Tarosi was a kindly man, usually very cheerful. He resolved to find him later on and ask what his worry was.

The contest ended while it was still full dark. Robinton was judged the winner by unanimous acclaim. The crew agreed with him that his new song was a jolly one, but it needed to be sung, not just played. The party broke up into little groups of two and three men, some of them still humming snatches of tunes. Numa refreshed himself with a long draught of ale and went off to bed, saluting Robinton with his tabor stick. Not long afterward, Robinton too sought his bunk.

He caught up with Tarosi early the next morning and

drew him aside. "Is anything troubling you?" he asked. "I noticed that you didn't seem to be enjoying yourself during our contest."

"Oh, it's nothing, Robinton. I think I must be driving my poor wits Between. I had a handful of pretty shell and freshwater gem necklaces, to use as trading goods here and about, and I must have traded the last ones, for I can't seem to find them. And yet, I was sure I had at least four left after we set out from Fort Sea Hold. I mind that I put them aside in my press. We dock early tomorrow, and I wanted them handy."

"Can I help you look?" Robinton asked. "Perhaps you've walked by them a hundred times searching, and all you need's a pair of fresh eyes."

"I'd be grateful," Tarosi confessed. "I've done that many times with other things I've mislaid; just overlooked them though they were in plain sight. You're probably right."

But after a thorough and exhaustive search of the bunk-room, the deck and the galley, Robinton began to doubt his easy assurance. The necklaces were nowhere to be found. "Could someone have stowed them in the hold for you?" he asked, sitting down on a bunk and fanning his hot face. Tarosi repacked the press they'd just looked through.

"If someone did, I'll have his left ear! I would never find them in time for the early trading." He sighed, letting the lid fall with a boom. "Ah, never mind. They'll last until the next time." Then, noticing Robinton's long face, "Oh, don't look like that, boy! It's not my children's legacy I've lost. In fact, it's more the fun of barter than the marks. Come, we'll have breakfast and start the day."

Ista Sea Hold slowly crept up toward them, growing bigger and brighter as the sun rose behind them. At first, it was a dot on the horizon between the two southernmost of five volcanic islands which Elaus had shown him on his maps. Gradually, as they changed course it grew, from bead size, disappearing behind another island, to doll size when it reappeared, to a lively dock with a broad stone wharf behind it and a great stone hold above and beyond that. From a standard high up in the rocky cliffs flew a gather flag. The merchant's men dumped most of the air out of the sails so the ship would skim majestically and ever slower toward the dock.

The *Sea Dragon* settled smoothly into its place, between an intricately patterned red-and-yellow sail from Igen and a red-and-white-striped one from Boll. Two of the seamen leaped out onto the pier as soon as the ship was near enough, and made painters fast to bollards. The port side touched stone.

The young Harper stood in his favorite vantage point in the bows, watching as the other ten seamen prepared to unload the cargo. The crew looked festive in bright vests with crisp white shirts beneath. Robinton thought he looked rather well himself. He had on his second best, a handsome blue tunic, banded with journeyman light blue around the sleeves, shoulders and hem. Under strict instructions from Elaus, he was pledged to stay out of the way while the merchant's business was conducted.

The barrels of pitch, unlaced from their webbing, were rolled into a line near to where the gangplank was being laid down. Cloth-wrapped bales emerged from a hold back of the sleeping quarters, and were placed alongside seasoned tree trunks, Elaus's precious shipment of timber which would now travel northward to Igen.

Men of Ista Harbor were waiting patiently on the dock to greet Captain Elaus and take the cargo ashore. One of them, a tall man with a slate in one hand, exuded an air of authority. His badge, visible even from the ship, showed him to be Harbormaster.

Two lengths of canvas, sort of cloth slings, were secured between the ship and the landing, and the heavy gangplank was placed between them. The board had two thick felted pads that straddled the bulwark of the ship and one which cushioned its landward end. Elaus walked upon it, stamping first at one end, then the other, to make sure it was securely set. He strode off toward the Harbormaster, who greeted him as an old friend, clasping his hand and thumping him on the shoulder. The harbor fee changed hands, and Elaus signaled to the men to start unloading the cargo.

One by one, the barrels rolled off the ship. Two men stood in the slings, carefully steadying the barrels as they went by, ensuring that the heavy casks wouldn't topple off the narrow plank. When those were all safely across, the wrapped bales were tossed from man to man until they too stood in a heap on the dock. The Harper's gitar went the same way. Once all the cargo was accounted for, the plank was lifted off and stowed away. The men gathered amidships, waiting for their signal to come ashore.

Numa beckoned Robinton down from the bow and courteously took his gitar from him. "You're our guest, my lad. If you'd care to lead us, we can all go gather together." He gestured to the canvas slings.

Robinton eyed the cloth walkways warily.

Roll 3 D6.

If the total is less than or equal to Robinton's value for Wisdom, turn to section 14.

If the total is greater, turn to section 11.

* 20 *

There was a sharp jerk on the cord as Vanris entrusted his whole weight to it. Robinton was bounced up and down on his perch in the rigging like a parcel on runner back, but he never let go of the line. His knees and shins, bruised already from last night's storm, vibrated against the rung-knots, battering the same sore places.

Right side up once more, the seaman nimbly sawed his legs back and forth until he bumped into the mast. Wrapping his legs around it, he undid the loop from his wrist and slid down. He slumped at the base of the mast, rubbing his ankles. Robinton's cheer was drowned out by the joyful outcry of the men below.

Turn to section 17.

* 21 *

The look on Lord Dinesdan's face told Robinton he understood the joke, and though he wasn't sure he approved, had decided not to enlighten his friend. Robinton was deeply grateful. Neither of them was prepared for Raid's next statement.

"You must sing it at tonight's feast."

"Oh, no, Raid," Dinesdan protested.

"Well, why not? What's your name, Journeyman?"

"Robinton, sir."

"Robinton, eh? Why do I know . . . Oh, yes. You're Evarel's new assistant, aren't you? It will be a pleasure to have you in Benden. I'll look forward to hearing that song often, then."

Robinton groaned inwardly. If he had to sing it frequently, he would have only himself to blame. Raid continued on, not noticing the Harper's change of expression.

"You're on your way there? I won't be returning for a couple of sevendays. Would you deliver a message tube to my Warder for me?"

"I would be honored, my lord." Robinton recovered himself.

"Good, good. You can collect it at the feast tonight."

He bowed and escaped, followed closely by Caitlon.

"Why didn't you tell me you were going to sing something like that? If he had construed it as an insult, you would have been on your way home now," Caitlon said, sternly. "As it is," his expression changed to one of rueful amusement, "you'd better teach it to me. I can tell it's going to be popular."

Turn to section 23.

* 22 *

"Well, come on then, we've missed half the day already," Arloc said, pointing up the street. "It's this way."

The young man retrieved his gitar from his baggage and started to follow the *Sea Dragon* crew. His first few steps were awkward stumbles, and he landed painfully on one knee. Puzzled, he picked himself up and started walking again. It was almost as if he were back on the ship again. The land felt as if it was moving. Simultaneously, both knees gave, his long legs folded up, and he sat down hard on the ground.

"You'll need to get your land legs again, son," one of the seamen told him, helping him up. "Take it slow."

Robinton nodded, shouldering his gitar and struggling to his feet.

Ista Sea Hold was one of the smallest major Holds. The original Hold building was excavated from the stone heights beyond Ista Harbor, but when the settlement expanded, it did so by erecting rows of small stone cots with tiled roofs, rather than mining deeper into the mountain.

The people here were nearly all sun-browned and had mariners' squints in the corners of their eyes. The greatest difference between the Holders and any ship's crew he saw was that anyone fresh off the sea tended to have a more rolling gait. The sunlight was much brighter here than back home in Fort Hold, though the temperature was much the same at this time of day. A cool breeze was blowing in from the southwest and the sun was not yet at its height. It would be very hot indeed by midday. Robinton was glad for the light weight of his clothing.

The oldest stone cots stood closest to the seaside. They were built in a style similar to ones he knew in the western part of Pern, but they had more windows, though all with wide metal shutters thrown back to let the cool morning zephyrs flow through. One shutter had broken free of its fastening and was creaking noisily back and forth. The sound set the Harper's teeth on edge. He longed to pound on the cottage's door until someone opened it up and he could tell them to oil their hinges.

Here and there a paving stone had been pulled up near a cot and a little kitchen garden dug in the space. The newer cots had more garden space still, and wooden doors and shutters. Worried about these departures from tradition, Robinton found himself humming a teaching tune to himself and tapping the beat on his gitar case.

"Lord of the Hold, your charge is sure/In thick walls,

metal doors, and no verdure," Robinton sang, only half to himself. His mellow baritone voice carried, low pitched as it was, through the stone streets.

A cotholder, working in his garden, perked up his head at the sound. His brows lowered.

"Aye, that's the way that it is in High Reaches, where we come from," said Tarosi, nodding his head. "We remember our Teachings."

"You, Harper," said the cotholder, stopping work and coming over to them. "Are you criticizing Ista? You're a stranger here, aren't you?"

"My apologies. No offense is intended," Robinton said, amiably. "I'm from the Harper Hall in Fort Hold. I've never seen green things growing so close to cotholds before."

The Holder's eyes narrowed. He looked Robinton up and down, eyes coming to rest on the Journeyman's badge on his shoulder.

Roll 3 D6.

If the total is less than or equal to Robinton's value for Charisma, turn to section 25.

If greater, turn to section 31.

* 23 *

The six Harpers escaped from the eager crowd with some difficulty that evening. Only by promising to play the same songs next Gather were they able to dispel the assembled listeners and make their way up the steeply inclined path toward the Hold.

Around the main cliff, greenery was, to the Lord's

credit, not at all in evidence. It was all decent stonework, as was proper. The massive metal doors were ornamented with sea creatures done in the style Robinton recognized as a lost art: metals so finely wrought and crafted as to suggest that the beasts depicted had been magically frozen in place, then gilded.

These doors were thrown back against the walls to admit the cool evening breeze. Robinton found the temperature drop soothing after the oppressive heat of the afternoon.

On a dais in the dining hall, Lord Dinesdan and Lord Raid sat at the center of the long head table, flanked by master craftsmen and guildsmen, Elaus and the Harbormaster among them. A shorter table stood just below the one for the Harpers and their guests. A taller chair at its head was evidently meant for Caitlon. Bowing to their hosts and to the assembled, Robinton and the others seated themselves. Elaus nodded affably to the young Harper, and went back to his conversation with a guildsman seated next to him. The fireplace, laid but unlit, lay at the side of the room closest to Robinton and Noray.

The Harpers' meal was served by two drudges assigned especially to their table. One of them kept all mugs full, first with hot klah during the meal, and with wine afterward. The other drudge kept a steady pace of the many platters which arrived laden with delectable dishes and left empty. Robinton neglected to ask how many courses were intended, and was full by the time the third meat dish was served. He took tiny portions of all that followed, but he was sorry he hadn't followed the example set by the others of taking small servings to start with. One way or another, though, there was room for the dessert, a sweet pastry made with seabeachplums that had a sticky but delightfully flavored filling.

After the second course, Jelan excused himself, and began to play incidental music for the lords while the others ate. In a short while, Caitlon replaced him, followed by Noray, who was grateful to perform without having to sing. Blake played the last set while the dessert was served.

When the last dishes were removed, Robinton washed the sticky plum filling out of his throat with more wine, and joined the others tuning up their instruments. The music segued gracefully from a smooth dinner accompaniment to a lively instrumental number. By then everyone else had finished with their meals and joined clapping or stamping the beat with the music. When that ended, a snapping one-two-three-four stamp from Caitlon set the five Istan Harpers off into a dance number which Robinton recognized from that afternoon, and added his gitar's voice to the others at the first bridge. The arrangement, he knew, called for a harp, not a gitar; and he sighed for the frame sitting unfinished in a vise in Master Liesult's workshop.

The Holders helped the drudges push tables out of the way to clear a wide dancing floor. Ladies, shy at first, joined their men in the middle of the room. To Robinton's surprise, Numa appeared among the dancers, hand in hand with a girl who must have been the one who kept him waiting that morning. Numa caught his eye, and affirmed his suspicion with a broad wink. Faster and faster the dancers whirled, hands and heels following the complex rhythm of the song. Their dance seemed impossibly intricate to Robinton until he noticed that it was the same pattern of steps repeated over and over again with variations in the hand movements. The Harpers played until most of the dancing couples were out of breath and calling for more wine.

The air in the hall began to cool, and the fireplace was lit, to Noray's great relief. While they waited for the roar of the tinder catching to die into a quieter crackle, the Harpers refreshed themselves.

Caitlon and Blake repeated their duet of the afternoon, to the delight of their audience. As they finished,

Holder and crafter called out their requests. Caitlon let the Istan Harpers play several tunes until Lord Dinesdan signaled for attention.

"Perhaps our guest has a tune he would like to hear?" Dinesdan acceded gracefully to Lord Raid.

The Benden lord smiled. "I would like to hear a song about dragonriders, good Harpers. Let us not forget the Weyr which protects Pern." Murmurs of agreement whispered about the hall. And some low tones of dissent, Robinton noted.

The Istan Master Harper bowed and sighed so low that only the Harpers could hear him. Blake lowered his brows. It was evident that there was long-lived disaffection between this island and the dragonweyr. Robinton had heard the stories from journeymen who had returned to Aldrem, dismissed by their lords for singing too often of dragonriders and Weyr Ways. Giant parasites, one Holder had called them. Ungrateful fools.

Nevertheless, Caitlon smiled in the direction of the Lord Holder, and sketched the time to the others. They broke into a traditional Ballad about the Weyr's duty to Pern. Raid and Dinesdan listened, seeming pleased with the performance. There were sections of the ballad traditionally sung as solo, a dragonrider speaking to his dragon, and Caitlon pointed to Robinton to perform them. He did so, projecting his voice smoothly to the furthest corners of the room. The song ended to scattered applause, and Raid stood up, his wine glass raised to the Harpers.

"The new voice of Benden," he toasted Robinton, and sat down.

Robinton sat on his stool, cheeks burning. There was such an air of arrogant possession in the Lord Holder's voice that Robinton felt insulted. His ire of the afternoon returned, and he looked to Caitlon for permission to sing.

He strummed the chorus to give the others time to

pick up the beat, took a deep breath, and sang.

He felt a little guilty, because he knew it was a sharp parody of Raid, but he had to express his irritation somehow. The other Harpers gave him sidelong glances as he went through the verses, wondering how he had the nerve to make fun of a Lord Holder like that. Raid was tapping his fingertips on the table in time, a broad smile on his face. It was clear he had no idea as to the real subject of the song, and what's more, he seemed to like it. It annoyed Robinton no end that his victim hadn't an inkling at all that he was on the receiving end of a joke. In fact, that ignorance served to make Robinton feel even more guilty. Lord Dinesdan had a little wintry smile on his face, knowing precisely what the song concerned, but was unwilling to say anything about it.

The Holders had joined in the chorus by the fourth verse, and the laughs were louder, and mixed with tumultuous applause at the conclusion.

Robinton took a long draught of wine as he sat down.

"You had better give me all the words to that song before you go," Caitlon warned him. "It'll be requested at any event a Harper attends for many sevendays to come."

After a short break, the Harpers played more dance tunes, and after another wave of requests, the lords excused themselves and went to bed. A servant delivered the message tube Raid wanted Robinton to deliver. He made a courteous reply that he would convey it to Benden just as soon as he could. The servant bowed and withdrew.

Robinton received many a compliment from his listeners. Before the evening drew to an end, he was asked to sing his song and several others beside. Several pitchers were drained drinking to the Harper's health.

As he had promised, he sat down with Caitlon and Noray, who was a quick, accurate scribe, to set out the song.

"Would you like a copy for yourself?" the apprentice asked.

"No, thank you," Robinton said, "but if you'll send one off for me to the Harper Hall, I'd be grateful. Better send it to my father, Petiron, in Fort Hold," he added, after a moment's consideration. His father could review the composition structure, and analyze how this comic ditty could best be brought to the attention of the Master Harper without getting him, Robinton, in any trouble. Aldrem was chary of offending the Lord Holders, and quite rightly, too.

"Gladly. Will you send us copies of anything else you compose?" Noray asked.

"If you wish, I would be happy to do so. Though they probably won't be as popular as this one."

"Excuse me, Journeyman."

Robinton looked up from the score Noray was scribing to see the red-haired crafter girl from the baker's booth at the Gather. He scrambled to his feet. "How do you do?"

"My name is Natala. You're a wonderful musician."

"Um, thank you. Oh, my name is Robinton."

"I know."

Behind him, he could hear the apprentices snickering. He must sound fully as awkward as he felt.

"I have enjoyed your playing," the girl went on. "In fact, I stayed past the time my father went home. I wondered," she said, coyly, "if you might walk me home? I don't live far away, but the streets are very dark."

Caitlon stood up and put a hand on Robinton's shoulder. "Well, good night, lad. I must be getting back, or my wife will wonder what happened to me." He turned to his apprentices. "Are you through with that score? Well, then, off to your quarters. It's late. Robinton, it was a pleasure to meet you. I wish you good fortune in your endeavors. *And* at Benden." With a nod, he left the two of them alone.

Section 23

Robinton watched them leave, then looked back at Natala. "I'd be happy to walk you home," he said, extending an arm to her.

Later, he made his way back to the dock by the light of an occasional glowbasket and the single crescent moon. It wasn't quite as chilly as it had been the night before. He could see a few of the crewmen sleeping out on deck. The *Sea Dragon* creaked and groaned softly under his feet as he crossed the canvas walkway. It was very late.

"Who's there?" a voice called.

"Robinton," he answered, sounding hoarse even to himself.

The voice chuckled. "Must have been a good Gather for you, too. Get some sleep while you can. The cargo arrives soon, at first light. Good night."

"Good night," Robinton echoed.

The first bales thumped to the bottom of the stairs, waking Robinton out of his dreaming. Tarosi and Kurram jumped down and climbed over them, and began to haul them out of the way before others hit in exactly the same spot. Dolgi appeared a moment later, and the three men formed a line, tossing the bales hand to hand into the hold. Robinton seized his clothes and flattened himself against the wall, trying to struggle into his pants while avoiding being hit by one of the huge bundles. After a while, there was a lull in the procession.

"Hold it!" Numa called down to them. "There'll be more in a moment."

Kurram stood peering up the stairs, hands on hips, waiting. Dolgi ran into the hold to stack the cargo more neatly, and Robinton seized his opportunity to scramble up the stairs and out of the way.

He finished dressing in the bow of the ship, watching the crew and harbormen load more bales from a long burden beast-drawn cart. The lacing on his tunic turned out to be too long on one side and too short on the other.

Shaking a rueful head at the fascinating sights that could distract a poor Harper, he undid the lace all the way and started over. His gitar he had stowed the night before; staggering in happily exhausted and a little wine-flown he had still lavished a Harper's care on his instrument. He patted the case through the net holding it and his other property secure.

A little music might be just the thing for this early morning. He felt somewhat useless having to stand by while others worked, though it was work they did well and quickly. Perhaps they would enjoy a tune, too. His fingers felt rough from the long Gather day; perhaps horn or pipe? He hummed a song to himself that he felt like playing. It was well suited to either instrument. The pipe's case was closer to the tied edge, so he fished it out and opened it. It was empty.

Robinton pinched his lower lip and furrowed his brows in thought. Where had he last seen his pipe? Oh, yes, at the song contest two nights ago. He had put it in the care of one of the merchant's men. But who? Dolgi? Vanris?

"Arloc," he called, seeing that seaman temporarily unoccupied. "Have you seen my wooden pipe? I handed it to someone in the circle during our contest the other night, and I must have forgotten to reclaim it."

"Indeed I did, lad. It was on your bunk yesterday, put there by Ritolon. I know, for he asked me what he should do with it. I said, if he can't learn to use it, he should give it back to you! That's a joke, if you can see it. He can't tell one note from another. By the way, it was a fine performance you gave at yesterday's Gather. You've a truly fine voice, and a wicked way with words." A hard elbow, all but pickled from long Turns on the salt sea, jabbed Robinton in the ribs. "A fine joke. His Lordship's a good man, considerate to his folk and all, but it's true he can't see what's right under his nose." He laughed heartily on his way back to the galley.

Once the cargo was all on board, Elaus shouted orders, and the *Sea Dragon* was once again under way. Robinton waited until all the men had cleared the bales and packages into the hold to search for his pipe.

He shook the sleeping furs out, carefully, in case the pipe had slipped into a fold during the night. It hadn't. Next, he pulled the rush bag out of the narrow wooden frame and felt around next to the wall. Not there. Nor was it under the cot, nor anywhere else on the floor. By now, he was upset, wondering if someone had moved it for a joke.

He thought of going to Captain Elaus, and asking for help in finding the missing pipe, but he was reluctant to take up the time of such a busy man and even more to imply he was accusing someone on the *Sea Dragon* of theft. For a long time he pondered what he should do.

If he decides to go to Elaus, turn to section 34.

If he decides to wait and search some more, turn to section 33.

* 24 *

With a surprised cry, Robinton swung his arms in the air, frantically searching for balance. The folds of cloth skipped from under his feet like a stone in the mud, and he plummeted into the harbor.

He surfaced, sputtering. Above him, the men were leaning over the rail laughing and pointing. A hand was extended to him from dockside. He clutched it and was hauled bodily out of the water.

"You're one of us now," Elaus called, watching the fun from a safe distance. "There's your baptism."

Robinton looked around at the others. Every one of them was grinning mischievously at him. Numa slapped him on the back and handed the gitar back by its strap. "Welcome to Ista, Harper. Let's go see the Gather."

Robinton decided he didn't want to waste time returning to the ship. Shrugging his shoulder uncomfortably, he decided to let his clothes dry on the walk to the Hold.

Turn to section 22.

* 25 *

"Well, that's as may be, young Journeyman, but you've got to be more careful about things people might take amiss. My neighbor Gaford, for example, would take offense at your song, never taking into account that you're a stranger and all."

"My apologies, Holder," Robinton said again. "I'm afraid that Harpers tend to take the teaching ballads literally. After all, they meant a great deal to our ancestors, especially during Threadfall."

The man turned slightly pale at the mention of the ancient menace. "Well, there's been no Threadfall for hundreds of Turns. Probably it will never happen again. Times change. We do things differently here in Ista."

"And yet we keep instructing children in the Teachings," Robinton said, turning a palm up in supplication. "Our fathers meant us to be ever-vigilant. Even in what they called the Intervals."

The Holder gave a derisive snort. "You talk like a ballad yourself. You're here for the Gather, are you? Well, it's up that way." He pointed up the street. "Two rows up, and turn right. You'd best get a move on."

They thanked him and trudged on. Robinton looked

over his shoulder before the cot was entirely out of sight. The cotholder was standing deep in thought, staring at his garden.

Turn to section 39.

* 26 *

When his turn came, he strode boldly to the center of the stage, and began to strum out the chorus of his song. The other musicians picked up the beat. Jelan looked a question at him.

"A new song," Robinton told him, and began to sing.

He had to admit it was a very pointed parody. He heard more than one gasp from the audience during the first verse, but there were more appreciative noises made as he sang the chorus. In fact, the positive acclaim grew greater as the song progressed. But when he dared a glance at Raid, that lord had a strained expression on his face, his eyes narrowed at him, nodding in concentration. Robinton felt his heart sink. He was in trouble. But he was committed now, so he went on to finish the last verse.

Loud applause resounded about the dancing square, and hoots of laughter underlined it. Robinton bowed nervously, wrapping his fingers around his gitar neck to keep them from trembling noticeably. A loud guffaw startled him, and he straightened up to see where it was coming from. At the table in the wineseller's booth, Raid was beckoning to him, with tears running down his cheeks. Robinton exchanged glances with Caitlon, and the two of them went to wait on the lords.

"D'ja hear that, Dinesdan?" Raid chortled, pounding

Section 26

Robinton heartily on the back. "This fellow's got a new song about old Corman of Keroon! I've never heard it before, but it's him to the life. O'course you couldn't call him by name, could you, young man?"

Dinesdan looked from his guest to the Harpers and back again. It was clear *he* knew who the butt of the song was meant to be.

Roll 3 D6.

If the total is less than or equal to the value for Robinton's Charisma, turn to section 21.

If greater, turn to section 37.

* 27 *

When his glass was empty, he stood up, and felt in his belt pouch for a small mark piece which he set down on the table.

"What are you doing?" Numa demanded, picking up the mark and placing it back on his palm. "No one's asked you to pay, did they? This drink is on me. You can buy me one later today, if you wish."

"I'd be happy to," Robinton said.

"It'll be hot this afternoon. A cool glass of wine wouldn't go amiss then. Are you off to see the Gather?"

Robinton gestured toward the musicians. "I should introduce myself to the Istan Harpers. If they need an extra gitar or voice for their program today . . ."

"Supporting your craft, eh? Good! I'll look forward to hearing you sing." Numa looked around. "There's a lass I know who lives hereabouts. She promised me a dance or two when I should come back to Ista. It's my home Hold, you know. I'll be here for a time if I'm needed."

He poured out more wine for himself and settled back to wait, in no hurry.

Until the current song came to an end, Robinton stood aloof, mentally critiquing the performance. Two gitars and a pipe accompanied a tenor and a baritone. Three little girls seated to the side, all of whom bore a strong family resemblance to the baritone singer and to one another, nervously clutched a musical score. One of them was mouthing the words to herself. Evidently, they were next up.

When the Harpers finished, the little girls made their way timidly to the center stage, looked to their tutor for encouragement. They began to sing a song about planting and harvest. They weren't too bad, Robinton decided. But they had an advanced case of stage fright.

Once the little ones were well begun, the baritone turned away from them and approached Robinton. He was the eldest Harper there, showing two streaks of gray in the thick brown hair over his temples, and bore a Master's badge on his tunic. Extending a hand palm up, he looked Robinton over from head to toe, and cast an approving eye on his gitar.

"A visitor?" he asked, sounding pleased. "Where are you from, journeyman?"

"Sir, my name is Robinton. I've just come from the Harper Hall, on my way to Benden Hold."

"Well met, Robinton. I think I met you when you were no higher than my girls, there. I am Caitlon."

Robinton's brows climbed in recognition. "Yes, sir. My father has spoken of you."

"And how is Petiron? And your lovely mother?"

"Very well, thank you. Have you any use for an extra Harper today?"

"Certainly yes! And any new songs you know would be welcome." Caitlon gestured toward the others. "My apprentices, Jelan, Noray and Maur. The other is Blake, from Rocky Hold."

Section 27

Robinton nodded to them all, and covered the palm of the last named, who bore a journeyman's badge like his own. "I think we can fit you in early so you can get back to Gathering," Blake said. "We've got a dance turn next, and a group song. And you can always come back later for more, and a chat." He peered over Robinton's shoulder at the little trio. "I think I'd better find some fruit juice for those three. Marga looks like she's going to cry." Inviting the young Harper to take his seat, Blake rose and disappeared into the crowd.

"We are to be much honored today, Robinton," Caitlon said, leaning over to tap his knee. "Your future master Lord Raid is here, paying a visit to our Lord Holder Dinesdan."

The young man's eyes widened. "Here?"

"Yes, indeed. They are old friends and distantly related, too. Of course, most of the families of the Blood are distantly related. We will sing for him tonight as well. I had looked forward to speaking with his Harper, Evarel, but I'm told he couldn't attend because of his many duties. I expect he'll be more free after you've arrived to help him." Caitlon gave him a measuring look. "We have a program worked out, but you must perform with us, then. Give his Lordship a chance to meet you."

"It would be an honor, sir."

"Good. That's settled."

Robinton did his turn with the Ista Hold Harpers, and then performed a solo of the song written and sung for the Lord Holder of Ruatha on the birth of his first child only a few months before. None of the other Harpers there knew it, and Robinton could see Caitlon out of the corner of his eye tapping out the slow rhythm. He rose to much applause, and was dismissed until the afternoon to the Gather.

Turn to section 28.

* 28 *

After finding himself a meal at the baker's booth, served by the baker's pretty red-haired daughter, and enjoying some more of the sights around the Gather, Robinton went back to the dancing square. As he was not needed immediately by the Istan Harpers, he sought around for a lass who looked willing to dance. Several girls looked shyly at him through their lashes, liking what they saw of the tall Harper lad. He bowed to a girl with long bronze-colored plaits, and she giggled, but took his hand.

Deciding that it would not do for him to play favorites at a Gather, he thanked the girl for the dance, and picked another, a slim crafter lass with wavy brown hair. The Harpers struck up a fast whirling number. The crafter girl was a fine dancer, and they were both out of breath by the time the music stopped. Caitlon caught his eye, and gestured him over. He bowed over his partner's hand and excused himself.

Murmurs he picked up from the crowd informed him that Lords Dinesdan and Raid had at last decided to walk the Gather, and were now ensconced at a table in the wineseller's booth, watching the Harpers. He could see them from where he stood, and hear them, too. Lord Dinesdan of Ista was a tall, strong-looking man of forty or fifty Turns, with the healthy complexion enjoyed by most of his Holders. Lord Raid of Benden, approximately the same age, was of medium height, paler than his friend, very thin and wiry, but with a pursed mouth that turned down at the corners. He appeared to be pointing out to Lord Dinesdan only the parts of the performance in which he was displeased. But it could have been the heat of the day.

Section 28

Robinton's professional pride was stung. He felt that Caitlon's troupe was very good indeed; witness the acclaim from the audience, if he couldn't trust his own reactions. Stupid man. Only half consciously, he started to imitate Lord Raid's expressions, copying the sour-faced scowl on his own flexible features. Marga, Caitlon's little daughter, noticed that he was making faces. She pointed at him and laughed. He decided he'd better stop before he was drawn to the attention of someone who'd recognize the original of his mimicry. But he had to admit that it was funny, too. He made a couple of horrible faces at Marga, which caused her to squeal with glee.

When Marga was at last distracted away from him, Robinton found he had at least half a verse and most of the chorus in his head for the comic tune he'd made up the other day. But it wouldn't do to call the protagonist Lord Raid. He would need another suitable one-syllable name.

Caitlon noticed that Robinton had returned, and signaled to him that he would follow the next dance tune. Robinton nodded assent, and began to look for rhymes that would scan in his song, racking his brains for all that he had ever heard of the Lord Holder of Benden.

If Robinton should decide to sing his comic parody of Lord Raid now, turn to section 26.

If he should decide to sing it later in the evening, turn to section 32.

* 29 *

"It is very good of you to bring him home, C'gan," the Master Harper said, looking disapprovingly at a half-conscious Robinton. The lad slumped in his chair with his head down.

The dragonrider smiled. "Well, I never expected to find him there at all, but I waited so long for him to appear in Benden, that I just went looking. He's a nice young one. Tagath likes him, and he's never wrong."

"Well, he's a reckless one, nevertheless. I thought we'd seen the back of you, young Robinton, but I see we're stuck with you for a while yet. A journeyman should know enough of his world to be more careful in it. Well, you are dismissed to your quarters until we decide just what will be done about you." Aldrem waved him away.

Return to section 1 and start over.

* 30 *

Robinton could hear snickers from the men already gathered on the pier. He was determined not to make a fool of himself. The sling swayed and dipped under his feet, so he concentrated on each step as carefully as if he were walking on a narrow path on a cliff face. He hoped desperately that he wouldn't fall in. A fine way for a harper to show himself off in a new Hold!

One step, another, another, and finally, solid ground underneath his feet. The crew cheered him. Numa came over and slapped him on the back and handed the gitar back to him. "Welcome to Ista, Harper. Let's go see the Gather." The men prodded him and joked with him merrily, to show that he was one of them.

Turn to section 22.

* 31 *

"Well, that's as may be, young Journeyman, but you shouldn't go around casting slurs against your betters. Especially when you're an outsider, see?"

"My apologies, Holder," Robinton said again. "I'm afraid that Harpers tend to take the teaching ballads literally. After all, they meant a great deal to our ancestors, especially during Threadfall."

The man turned slightly pale at the mention of the ancient menace. "And you're suggesting that we don't learn our Teachings here? Eh?" He curled his hands into fists.

"No, not at all," the young man stammered, throwing his arms up for emphasis. "I mean that . . ."

Robinton is so intent on convincing the Holder of his innocence that he never sees the fist the enraged cotholder snaps into his jaw. Robinton staggers backward, his arms windmilling madly as he struggles to keep his balance. He's astonished by the man's reaction, and tries to pull his wits together. The cotholder stalks him, his face contorted with rage.

"Tell me what to do, will you?" the Holder snarls through clenched teeth. His jaw is thrust forward as he moves forward. Robinton, easing his gitar to the ground, scans the gathering crowd for some sign of help. The three sailors who came with him from the *Sea Dragon* have their hands full keeping four of the Holder's friends from joining in the fray. No one else seems to want to take on the burly seamen so they can intervene. Robinton is on his own.

Reluctantly the Harper raises his own hands, more concerned about possibly damaging them than about striking his opponent. He is adverse to causing trouble, but it seems that he is forced to defend himself. Speculatively Robinton wonders if that outthrust jaw is as solid as it looks. He is still considering striking out at it when his retreat is blocked by a most solid-feeling stone wall. And the angry man is glowering down at him.

The cotholder, his face purple, draws his arm back for another blow.

COTHOLDER
To be hit: 11 To hit Robinton: 13 Hit Points: 5
Damage with fists: both men do one hit point per hit.

This is not a killing combat. When either of the men reaches 0 hit points they will be unconscious and will take 3 hit points of real damage. The winner will receive no damage.

If Robinton knocks out the cotholder, turn to section 36.

If Robinton is knocked out, turn to section 40.

* 32 *

When his turn came, he strode to the center of the stage, and began to strum out the chorus of the "Catching of the Great Sea Serpent," so that the other musicians could pick up the beat. Jelan looked a question at him.

He caught the glance, and nodded back, modulating

his strum into the melody of the song. Jelan raised a brow in comprehension, and picked up the harmony.

When he got to the two verses he had added, he watched his audience carefully, deciding they didn't mind that he had tampered with a traditional song. The people around him, dressed in bright hues not commonly used back in Fort Hold, raised intent, sun-browned faces to him, all grinning broadly. His confidence returned. He emboldened the tempo, and the audience began to clap along.

Loud applause resounded about the dancing square, and peals of laugher underlined it. Robinton bowed, wrapping his fingers around his gitar neck to keep them from trembling. Though he had enjoyed it, he had played longer and harder than he would in a Turn of Gatherings in Fort Hold. A lone Harper had a tougher job to do working outside the Harper Hall. A loud guffaw startled him, and he straightened up to see where it was coming from. At the table in the wineseller's booth, Raid was beckoning to him, with tears running down his cheeks. Robinton exchanged glances with Caitlon, and the two of them went to wait on the lords.

"D'ja hear that, Dinesdan?" Raid chortled, pounding Robinton heartily on the back. "This fellow's clever! What's your name, Journeyman?"

"Robinton, sir."

"Robinton, eh? Why do I know . . . Oh, yes. You're Evarel's new assistant, aren't you? It will be a pleasure to have you in Benden. You're on your way there? I won't be returning for a couple of sevendays. Would you deliver a message tube to my Warder for me?"

"I would be honored, my lord."

"Good, good. You can collect it at the feast tonight."

Lord Dinesdan, who too had clearly enjoyed his song, smiled at him. "You must sing tonight for us then, too."

"It would be a privilege and a pleasure, my lord," Robinton said, bowing.

Behind him, some of the audience was chanting for him to come back. Bowing to the lords again for permission, Robinton returned to the center of the stage. He held up a hand for quiet, and began to strum a soft song about the dragonriders' love of Pern. At first there were some mutters of protest from listeners who wanted another comic song, but those dissenters were quickly quieted by their neighbors. Lord Raid nodded approvingly.

The applause at the end was even louder than it had been for the first song. Caitlon beamed at him as he left the stage. The other musicians assembled to lead another group song with the happy crowd.

Turn to section 23.

* 33 *

Arloc came upon him then, while he was sitting with his chin propped up on his hands.

"If you've nothing to do, I wouldn't mind some assistance in the galley. There's a quartered herdbeast hung up back there which I need to butcher into usable portions for the next several meals, and I've not enough hands to do that and pare roots at the same time."

"Of course," said Robinton, and followed him.

There was a huge amount of roots to be peeled and pared, and a quantity of other fresh vegetables beside. "They've an earlier growing season in Ista than back home," Arloc explained. "The men enjoy a change from preserved food when there's room. When we reach full trading season, there won't be a spare span on this ship to set a plate down, so we take advantage now."

Seeing no paring tool, Robinton took out his belt knife

and set to work. In a short time, the floor around his feet was littered with parings.

"What do I do with those?" he asked Arloc, pointing to the mess with the blade of his knife.

"Oh, throw them overboard. The fish think they're worms. The big hungry ones will wait for the trimmings from this meat."

Robinton set the knife down, and swept up the wet peelings. When he dropped them over the side, some of the long silver fish, who seemed always to be following the ship, now that he had noticed them, scooped up the bits of vegetable almost before they hit the surface of the water. He brushed the few clinging bits from his hands to the hovering fish.

"No waste on the ocean," Arloc said, with satisfaction. "By the way, why aren't you using my paring knife to do that? Don't care for the balance?"

Robinton looked around. "I don't see one here."

"No? It's a bit gaudy for the job, I confess. A short-bladed knife, made of hardened bronze, with a fancy knobbed hilt."

"Not here" Robinton shook his head.

"Well, if you don't mind using yours, go on. Like as not one of the others took it to carve wood with. It takes a fine edge, though it needs sharpening more frequently than good steel."

"When did you last see it?" Robinton asked, a suspicion growing in his mind. He pushed aside the piles of vegetables, but the knife wasn't beneath any of them. Arloc scratched his head with the handle of his cleaver.

"Oh, yesterday. I don't know. Don't think anything of it, lad. It's like there's no private property on a ship."

Forcing himself to sound casual, the young Harper went on with his peeling. "You must be right. Some of the others have complained about their possessions being moved to where they can't find them."

"Your pipe, do you mean?"

"No, there're others, too."
"Ah. Have you spoken to the captain about that?"
"No."
"Well, mind you don't. You're talking about theft, you know. A serious accusation, and you an outsider."
"But your knife . . . ?"
Arloc carved savagely at the side of herdbeast. "It'll be found. I have no doubt of that."
Robinton shook his head, but returned to his paring.

If he decides to go to Elaus, turn to section 34.

If he decides against going to Elaus, turn to section 35.

* 34 *

He waited nearby while Elaus saw to several problems that needed his attention. The captain, while still in the midst of lists of the new cargo taken on board, examined boxes and barrels of supplies, marked the heading the *Sea Dragon* now sailed, and heard out from Numa an item-by-item recitation of profits made on the merchandise traded in Ista. He seemed pleased by the last, and even more pleased at some of the things he found noted down as being in the hold.

"Nerat will welcome fine fabrics like these," Elaus mentioned in an aside to Robinton, showing him an entry on the manifest. "The Masterweaver here claims that they were woven underwater to keep the threads from breaking."

Or, "Fruit preserves. Now, that we can take back with us to Tillek. Their fruit harvest last Turn wasn't all they had hoped. Not a large shipment, to be sure, but I think it'll find a home."

When at last he was satisfied that all was in order, he turned his attention fully to Robinton. "Yes, lad. And what may I do for you?"

"I'm sorry to take up valuable time, Elaus . . ."

"I can always find things to take up my time, my boy. Right now I'm spending some of it on you. You're not 'taking it up.'"

"Yes, sir, I'm grateful. It's a small thing, but I am unable to find my tenor pipe."

"Ah," Elaus's brows went up. "The little instrument which sounds like marsh-dwellers singing. Yes? Well, without a doubt, it's underfoot in the men's quarters."

"It isn't there, sir. I've already looked."

"No?" The brows lowered and joined over the captain's thick nose. "And, d'you know that I've heard of other things going missing and not being found?"

"Yes, I do. Tarosi spoke to me."

"And to me, too." Elaus sighed. "A ship's a small place, Robinton. I've been afraid of this for a long time. It's a bad thing if you find there's someone aboard you can't trust. Well, no use putting it off. We'll start a search."

Elaus summoned Numa, and had him call the whole crew to the deck. Even the surly Gurner was signaled to light from his high perch. When they were all assembled, Elaus outlined the problem of Robinton's missing pipe, alluding only generally to the other things suspected to be missing. "And if any of you has placed it somewhere for safe-keeping, no reprimands will be given you. I'm sure you'd all do a favor like that for a shipmate—" he put a hand on Robinton's shoulder—"however new he may be."

The crew nodded and muttered among themselves. Vanris and Junos stood a pace apart from the others, defying anyone to accuse them. But not an eye was turned in that direction, nor toward anyone else as far as Robinton could judge.

"Very well, then I have no choice but to ask your help. We will search the *Sea Dragon* thoroughly to determine what has become of the little pipe."

Numa and Arloc were put in charge of two search parties, and the crew was divided between them. Arloc's group, grumbling about wasted effort, was set to clear out the hold and repack it, looking for the lost flute.

Numa's group, with Robinton among them, had the deck and galley to search. Tarosi carefully undid the baggage net and shook each empty case to see if the pipe had gone into the linings. Robinton, as the thinnest, had to crawl into the deep shelves where Arloc kept his pots and dishes, and emerged smudged and dirty, but still empty-handed. He brushed himself off, looking dejected.

Junos hoisted himself up to the galley roof and began to climb the mast to the lookout, with Vanris nervously watching him go. Gurner, who had just completed an inspection of a heavy press against the cabin wall, noticed Junos, and leaped toward the mast, intending to climb up after Junos. Vanris seized his arm.

"Where are you going?" he asked, mildly.

"He's no right to go through my things," Gurner growled, struggling to get free.

"He won't hurt your things," Vanris assured him, but didn't let go. "You didn't stow Robinton's toy for him, did you?"

"Of course not," Gurner snapped.

"Numa!" Junos shouted from high above. Everyone looked up at him. He waved a small cylindrical object. "Here it is! And look what else I've found!"

Vanris gave Gurner an angry shove. "So you didn't have it, eh?"

"That one's not his," Gurner said, quickly.

"We'll see."

Junos tossed the pipe to Robinton when he was still halfway up the mast. "There you go, laddie."

Section 34

"Well?" Numa asked.

"It's mine. Here is my initial 'R' carved opposite the G-stop hole."

"How did it get up there, Gurner?"

"Oh, well, I might have taken it up there to try. I learned how to play a pipe in my youth."

"Look at these," Junos said, jumping nimbly off the galley roof. He poured a handful of sparkling objects into Numa's hands. "And there's more, but I'd need a basket to get it all down."

"Tarosi's necklaces!" Robinton exclaimed, and then clapped a hand over his mouth. He was actually accusing Gurner of theft!

Numa smiled at his belated discretion. "Don't you worry, boy. I've heard about them, too. And seen one, come to that. I gave one to Lorra, my girl, the last time we were in port." His expression changed abruptly as he turned to confront Gurner. "What have you got to say?"

"It's that one's fault," Gurner said, pointing at Robinton. "He must have planted those things up there, knowing I'd be blamed." Suddenly shaking off Vanris's restraining hands, he leaped at Robinton.

GURNER
To be hit: 14 To hit Robinton: 10 Hit points: 7
Both men do one point of damage per hit.

There will be three rounds in this fight before the combatants are separated.

If Robinton wins (does more damage), turn to section 51.

If Gurner wins, turn to section 46.

* 35 *

After the midday meal, Robinton helped clear away the bowls and cups. Arloc, pleased to have so willing an assistant, made quick work of the tasks, and sent him "out of my way," in a very short time.

Robinton, running down into the bunk-room, came upon Kurram and Dolgi, usually the best of friends, having a violent argument.

"I tell you no one came past me yesterday!" Kurram shouted.

"And I tell you that someone must have! While you took an afternoon nap, belike."

"I did no such thing."

"Then you tell me what happened to my son's belt, eh? A commission which took half my earnings from the last trading run to pay for? Has it gone Between, and it'll be back when it feels like?"

Kurram rumpled his black curls in frustration. "I don't know what happened to it. It was here when you left it, and it was still here when I went off watch and left for the banquet. You can ask Terti where it is."

"He never saw it. So it must have been gone before you left!"

Robinton backed out of the room and tiptoed up the stairs. He had no wish to be caught in a personal argument. But it was clear there was something more widespread going on on this ship than just his missing flute.

If he decides to go to Elaus now, turn to section 34.

If he decides against going to Elaus, turn to section 44.

* 36 *

The angry man punches out, putting his weight behind his fist. Robinton notices, almost impersonally, that he is sighting at his midsection and whisks himself out of the way in time to avoid the blow. Overshooting his mark, the Holder strikes the wall with his fist. A scream of frustration and pain echoes between the stone walls as the man clutches his bruised hand near the wrist.

By now, Robinton has put his own fists up, and swings a right uppercut at the other man's jaw. He connects, but it is not a solid blow. The Holder shakes his head and works his jaw uncomfortably; obviously Robinton's punch has done some small damage.

Once again, the two men circle, each looking for the best opening. The onlookers are cheering on their favorites. Robinton can already feel the unfamiliar heat beginning to affect him. Sweat is running down his temples and into his eyes. He blinks it away, not daring to move one of his hands out of guard to wipe his face. The Holder strikes out at him, a quick one-two with his fists, feinting to the head with the first blow, and catching the younger man in the stomach with the second.

Breath explodes out of Robinton as he folds around the other man's punch. He cries out involuntarily. The world swims in his eyes. He straightens up, blocking the Holder until he can gather strength enough for a renewed attack of his own. His breaths come in short, agonized gasps. Behind his opponent, the crew of the *Sea Dragon* have their hands full trying to keep the other Holders in check.

"Can't you . . . do better than that?" Robinton says, trying to look as if it doesn't hurt him to utter every syllable.

The Holder sneers at him. "You can't last, sonny. Come on, try again. Come on, Harper boy." And sticks his chin out again, that irresistible chin.

It was Robinton's turn to feint, left hand darting down toward the Holder's midsection. The man collapses, drawing his belly away from the Harper's fist. His action leaves his chin out-thrust, hovering, available, waiting for just a split second. Robinton's right crashes into the side of the Holder's jaw, bone striking bone. The man looks startled. His eyes close over his astonishment, and he slumps to the ground, unconscious.

Robinton clutches his sore right hand in his left, hissing at the pain. Suddenly, he is aware of noise again. Onlookers crowd around him to congratulate him. A few eye him coldly and crouch by their mate, trying to coax him back to consciousness.

Drawing himself up with returning confidence, Robinton signals to his friends, and they walk away, leaving the Holders to argue details of the fight. From the sounds he can hear, the Gather isn't far away. Robinton nurses his sore hand, accepting the congratulations of his friends. He wipes the sweat off his face with evident relief.

Turn to section 39.

* 37 *

The look on Lord Dinesdan's face told Robinton he understood the joke, and he didn't approve of it at all.

"You must sing it at tonight's feast," Raid said, looking to his friend for agreement.

Section 37

"Oh, no, Raid." Dinesdan protested.

"Well, why not? What's your name, Journeyman?"

"Robinton, sir."

"Robinton, eh? Why do I know . . . Oh, yes. You're Evarel's new assistant, aren't you. It will be a pleasure to have you in Benden."

"He won't be going to Benden, will you, Journeyman?" Lord Dinesdan made a curse out of his rank.

"What? Why not?" Raid asked again.

"Because I don't think you would want a Harper under your roof who parodies you to your face."

Raid's expression changed to one of utter astonishment, and then resumed its former sourness. "Is this true?"

Robinton hung his head. "In a way, my lord. It was meant to be a humorous song."

The Lord Holder nodded. "I see. Well, Dinesdan, perhaps you have a small room to accommodate this disrespectful fellow until passage can be made for him back to the Harper Hall?"

"Yes, I do." He signaled to one of his servants to take Robinton's arm. "You're a disgrace to your craft, you know that, don't you? I shall send a full report of your action to the Master Harper. Take him away."

"Too bad," Raid's voice followed him as the guard escorted him toward the Hold. "I thought the song was quite funny."

Turn to section 29.

* 38 *

When his glass was empty, he stood up, and felt in his belt pouch for a small mark piece. He drew out a thirty-second bit and laid it on the table.

"What are you doing?" Numa demanded, picking up the mark and placing it back on his palm. "No one asked you to pay, did they? This drink is on me. You can buy me one later today, if you wish."

"I'd be happy to," Robinton said.

"It'll be hot this afternoon. A cool glass of wine wouldn't go amiss then. Are you off to see the Gather?"

"Yes, I am."

"Well, I'll be here a while yet." Numa looked around. "There's a lass I know who lives hereabouts. She promised me a dance or two when I should come back to Ista. This is my home Hold, you know. I'll be here for a time if I'm needed." He poured out more wine for himself and settled back to wait, in no hurry.

Robinton let himself be lost in the growing crowd of happy Holders and crafters now assembling in the meadow. Dozens of small children in brightly colored tunics sped by him laughing and calling to one another. The fine weather had so infected everyone's mood that instead of being annoyed at them, adults were smiling indulgently at the children's antics.

A performer in a faded green tunic coaxed two trained canines to stand up on their hind feet and perform a creditable parody of a popular dance. Craftsmen haggled about the price of new, gleaming knives. A very pretty girl with red hair smiled at him over the counter of a baker's stall. He smiled back, and she waved at him to come over.

Section 38

Another journeyman Harper dashed past him, bearing a long tube of fruit juice. He stopped and turned around to look at Robinton, brow furrowed as if trying to place him. "Excuse me," the Harper said. "Are you Lord Raid's Harper?"

Surprised, Robinton forgot about the girl and went over to him. "No, not yet. I'm on my way to Benden Hold to assist Harper Evarel. I left the Harpercrafthall only a few days ago. My name is Robinton."

"Pleased to meet you, Journeyman Robinton. I am Blake of Rocky Hold. Have you introduced yourself to Harper Caitlon yet?"

"Well, no. I was going to see a little of the Gather first," Robinton said, and then wished he hadn't. Blake showed his obvious disapproval.

"It is only courtesy, I admit," Blake said, with asperity, "but a Harper is supposed to make himself known to the Master Harper of any Hold he visits as soon as he can. You are very young; is Benden to be your first assignment?"

"Yes," Robinton answered, much abashed.

"Ah." Blake curtly turned away from him and started walking toward the dance square. "If you would please follow me."

"Well, well, Petiron's son," Harper Caitlon said, extending his hand, palm up, to the young Harper. He was the eldest Harper there, showing two streaks of gray in the thick brown hair over his temples, and bore a Master's badge on his tunic. Extending a hand palm up, he looked Robinton over from head to toe, and cast an approving eye on his gitar. "When I saw you last, you were only so high." He held his hand only a short distance above the ground. Robinton blushed uncomfortably. "I wish that you could have helped us earlier today. We could have used another voice in the group song."

"I meant to come and speak to you sooner, sir.

I . . . got distracted by everything else going on at the Gather." Robinton's discomfort only increased as he tried to explain himself.

Caitlon's expression was kindly. "Gathers are for the young, after all. Well, my son, would you like to redeem yourself? Will you take the place of my apprentice Noray for the rest of the afternoon? He says he feels his throat is getting sore, and I want to save him for our performance tonight. Lord Raid of Benden is visiting, and we had a program worked out."

"Robinton has been assigned to Benden Hold," Blake put in.

"Has he?" Caitlon said. "Well, good. You must perform with us, then. Give his Lordship a chance to meet you."

"It would be an honor, sir."

The afternoon crept by. He had time only for an occasional cup of wine between pieces. The Istan Harpers had planned it so the solos were followed by group songs and then dances, so that the dancers had time to rest between sets. The audience requested certain chanteys and popular songs again and again. Robinton performed one number which elicited much applause from the assembled Gatherers: the song written for the Lord Holder of Ruatha on the occasion of the birth of his first child, a daughter. None of those present except possibly a few traders had heard it. He was asked to sing it several times more during the day.

By the time he was dismissed to the Gather, his own throat was dry, and he was hungrier than before.

Turn to section 28.

* 39 *

The Gather meadow was already full of people, animals and carts. Those who had occupied their pitches early were in full swing of trade by now, cheerfully drawing attention away from latecomers by their cries.

"Hot pies! Hot pies! Meat rolls, fish rolls! Hot pies!"

"The fastest runners on Pern!"

"Fresh fish!"

"Smooth hides, cut and crafted to your specifications!"

"The best here!"

Robinton wandered after the seamen, drinking it all in. He enjoyed Gathers. They were frequent in Fort Hold and in the other nearby Holds to which Robinton, as an apprentice and journeyman of the Harper Hall, had gone to play with resident musicians and singers. During the day to come, there would be singing, solos and ensemble songs by the Harpers, and group sings led, not to mention dance music and requests from the audience. One young man in blue was in the dance square already, playing the lap harp for a group of children. Robinton squinted at him, trying to decide if he knew him. There was too much noise to recognize the music he was playing.

He was distracted at that moment by a craftsman who called out, "Your pardon, masters!" and dodged in front of them carrying a box full of wooden toys. Robinton followed him and watched him set them up in his stall. They were finely crafted and painted: little boats; animals; herdbeasts, canines, runners, wherries; and dragons, a few of each color.

"May I?" he asked the craftsman, stretching out a tentative hand.

"O' course!" the man assented, heartily. "If they won't take a little touching they'll not last a sevenday in a home with children, now will they?" He put a hand-sized bronze dragon into Robinton's palm. "Feel like satin, don't they? And yet they're made of hardwood. Do you care to buy?"

"Well, I have no children myself," he began, lamely, and then laughed. "I won't deny I might like one for myself. But I've only just arrived. It'll take a little while until I decide what to do with my marks."

"Take your time," the man said. "I hold in Ista, so I'll be here all day long."

Robinton stroked the little dragon once more, and then put it down. A fine little thing, beautifully proportioned. They reversed the usual image: a dragon you could put in your pocket, instead of the other way around. If dragons had pockets.

"Ah, there you are, lad." Ritolon stood before him, hands on hips. "We've found the wineseller's booth. We're all for a drink before we split up to see the Gather. Join us?"

"Yes, of course." Robinton hurried to follow him.

The wineseller's was positioned cleverly just to one side of the dancing square. His lads were already setting up seats so that tired dancers would be handily served when they sat down. More Harpers had joined the single musician in the square, and were tuning their instruments.

From one corner of the booth, Numa beckoned to him and Ritolon. They had pushed two small tables together, and a pitcher of wine was already making its rounds.

"You have but two instructions for today," Numa said, raising his glass. "First, be back at the *Sea Dragon* no later than dawn tomorrow, for loading on our new cargo, or you'll be left behind. You may sleep aboard if you wish, but that's up to you. Second, stay out of trouble. Anyone who's taken up by the Warders will find his belongings on the dock."

The men around the table muttered assent. Robinton nodded along with them. Numa looked around at them all, trying to look stern, and then broke into a wide grin. "D'you mean I have to tell you to have fun, too? It's a Gather Day, you louts!"

They cheered him, raising their glasses high. A wine-man's boy came over to check the level in their pitcher, and ran for a refill. The Harpers in the square struck up a tune. Robinton recognized it as a sea chantey Numa taught him during their first contest. He hummed a little of the refrain. Some of the others paid the musicians their whole attention. A few drained their glasses and went off to see what there was to see in the stalls and booths. Robinton watched them go. He took a small sip of his wine. It wasn't a Benden, nor any other vintage that he'd had the privilege to taste in the past, but it was pleasantly fruity, not so sweet as to be cloying.

It occurred to him that he should soon make himself known to the Ista Hold Master Harper, and volunteer to take a Harper's turn during the festivities. But if he did that, he'd likely miss all of the Gather. The smells wafting over from the baker's stall certainly warranted investigation. Breakfast was just long enough gone that he was beginning to think about lunch. Perhaps if he saw the Gather first, then approached the Master, that would serve just as well.

If Robinton decides to go directly to the Istan Harper, turn to section 27.

If he decides to see the Gather first, turn to section 38.

* 40 *

The angry man punches out, putting his weight behind his fist. Robinton notices, almost impersonally, that he is sighting at his midsection and whisks himself out of the way in time to avoid the blow. Overshooting his mark, the Holder strikes the wall with his fist. A scream of frustration and pain echoes between the stone walls as the man clutches his bruised hand by the wrist.

By now, Robinton has his own fists up, and swings a right uppercut at the other man's jaw. He connects, but it is not a solid blow. The Holder shakes his head and works his jaw uncomfortably; obviously Robinton's punch has done a little damage.

Once again, the two men circle, each looking for the best opening. The onlookers are cheering on their favorites. Robinton can already feel the unfamiliar heat beginning to affect him. Sweat is running down his temples and into his eyes. He blinks it away, not daring to move one of his hands out of guard. The Holder strikes out, a quick one-two with his fists, feinting to the head with the first blow, and catching the younger man in the stomach with the second.

Breath explodes out of Robinton as he folds around the other man's punch. He cries out involuntarily. The world swims in his eyes. He tries to raise his hands to defend himself, but his arms have suddenly gone weak. Backing away to avoid the Holder, he discovers he is once more standing against the stone wall. It feels good to slump against it. Somewhere inside him, he finds the strength to pick up his hands.

Another blow hits him, this time in the ribs. Gritting his teeth, he flings himself away from the wall, swinging at his opponent. One of his flailing hands strikes the out-thrust jaw. The Holder roars with rage and pain. He shoulders Robinton to the wall, beating a tattoo on his stomach and ribs with his fists.

Almost of its own volition, Robinton's right arm comes up in a powerful right cross toward the blurry image of the Holder's chin. The man throws himself backward several steps to avoid the blow. Both men raise their hands. Robinton strides ponderously forward. The Holder assumes a defensive crouch, waiting. One step. Two steps. Three. The last picture in Robinton's mind before it goes black is the Holder's astonished expression, watching him fall flat on his face.

Turn to section 39.

* 41 *

"Nine marks for that brown?" Robinton asked, narrowing his eyes slightly and peering at the smaller runner. It was a skinny creature, probably not over four Turns old. It twitched its ears engagingly at him. "Well, I wouldn't pay over six and a half for it at home. But I don't want to do you in the mark. Seven."

"Well, perhaps nine is a bit over," the man admitted. "Eight and a half."

"Oh, I couldn't go over seven and a half."

"And I can't go under eight."

"Seven and three-fourths?" Robinton asked, displaying the wooden marks enticingly.

"Done." The man extended his hand, and Robinton covered it with his own. The marks disappeared into a grimy pocket. "He's yours."

"Good," Robinton said, reaching for the lead. "Where are riding pads kept?"

The man affected an innocent face. "Oh, you want tack for the beast too? That wasn't in our bargain, Harper. Three marks for used tack, six for new." He folded his enormous arms, looking satisfied with himself. "You Harpers always have more money to spend than a hard-working Holder might, though we owe you the honor."

For answer, Robinton reeled in the hide strap and led his runner toward the door. Behind him, the master chuckled. "Very well, journeyman. An extra mark and a half, and it's yours."

"Done," Robinton said, turning back with a smile.

He settled himself as best he could on the pad, which was old and nearly flat. At least it served its purpose, which was to protect his bottom and the beast's back from one another. The bony runner moved at a brisk trot which would have been painful otherwise.

He stopped only once before leaving Nerat Hold, to secure provisions for himself. As he had predicted, the cost left his purse almost flat. The runner, he was assured, would find ample fodder on the road. Which road? Well, there was only one toward Benden Hold, and that one not very direct. But since he was on a runner, not a dragon, he'd have to do the best he could.

Remove eleven and a quarter marks from his record sheet.

Record the addition of the runner beast and two sevendays' worth of provisions.

Turn to section 48.

* 42 *

"Both are a bit more than I can spend," Robinton said. Sadly, he gathered up his baggage and left the cavern.

After asking directions from a Holder woman, he purchased a half mark's worth of provisions and set out on the road to Benden. Within half an hour on the twisting path, he was winded and exhausted. There were bruises on both his sides from all the instrument cases banging into him at every pace.

Flinging his bags to the ground, he sat down to take a stone out of his boot. He noticed that there was a hole in the upper just under the toe. Since it hadn't been there this morning, he must have torn the boot on some rough obstruction while walking. There was more sand inside the boot. Pushing sweat-soaked hair out of his eyes, he looked around for a cot, or any other sign of humanity. Nothing. He sighed.

"I'll feel like a fool," he said to himself, "but I'll have to walk back to Nerat and buy a runner." Shouldering the bags again, he set out the way he had come.

Robinton arrived back in the beast-cavern just as a holder was leading the bony brown runner away. That left only the big beast available for purchase.

Turn to section 53.

* 43 *

He made sure that the waterskin was intact before he drank from it. After all the trouble he'd been through for fresh water, it would be a nasty irony to drink it flavored with snake venom. No, it was unpunctured.

It was now quite dark out, and he had to guess where he was going. Step up, no, that was too high to be right. He felt around to his left for a lower crest than the one he was attempting to climb. B, not D. Glissando down to a dell, skirt the bushes, two major thirds up to the next crest. It wasn't a perfect system of mapping, but it seemed to be working. He could hear an animal moving around up ahead.

"Twitch?" he called. "Good boy, is that you?"

A whicker answered him. It was a runner, anyway. He hoped that it was his. He moved toward the sound.

With his arms kept out in front of him, he didn't run into any trees, but he tripped on a root or two scrambling up toward his camp. The stars over the little clearing picked out the outline of his bundles on the ground and a runner beast pulling anxiously toward him.

Robinton felt his way to his pack and found his bowl. He filled it several times with water for Twitch, and had a cupful himself to keep the animal company. The runner drank noisily, and whinnied when it had finished. It snuffed at Robinton's tunic, looking for treats. He handed it away, pulling up a handful of grass to satisfy it. Patting Twitch on the cheek, he went to light a fire and prepare a meal for himself.

He had a quantity of salted meat, a cheese, some bread and some redfruit in his supply bag. No klah. He sighed.

Section 43

There wasn't any way to fool himself that he was having fresh roast meat, but if he heated the salt meat over a fire, and toasted some cheese for his bread, that would be as good as a feast.

With some difficulty, he managed to get a fire going. When the first sparks jumped out, he heard scurrying sounds in the brush very near him. There had been animals here watching him. They were afraid of the fire. By the time his fire had grown enough to see by, there was nothing in the clearing beside Twitch and himself.

One of his logs was too green, and it spat and complained all evening long. Twitch nickered softly at him before going to sleep standing up. His baritone wheezes reminded Robinton that he'd had a long day, too. He tended to his wounds, and then curled up to sleep with his head on the runner pad and his back to the banked fire.

If he uses numbweed, subtract 1 D6 damage for one use, 2 D6 for two uses.

If he uses it up, erase it from the record sheet. Subtract one day's food every morning.

If he was stung from behind by the snake, turn to section 57.

If not, turn to section 50.

* 44 *

Vanris and Junos stopped and sat down next to him on the deck in the shade cast by the cabin. They both seemed uncomfortable, but Junos looked more angry than upset, his fair skin flushed with unaccustomed blood. He glared from Vanris to Robinton and back again.

Vanris looked at his foster brother, chidingly. "You said you'd let me handle it."

"All *right!*" Junos snarled and fell silent.

"It's a delicate matter," Vanris began. "I don't wish you to take offense at what I'm about to say, but you're one of the few that we've told . . ."

"Get to it!"

"Be silent!" Vanris spat. It was clear something was straining the relationship between the foster brothers. The young Harper sat up straighter and gave Vanris his whole attention. The seaman ducked his head in embarrassment. "I told you about the ship that Junos and I hope to buy someday."

"The *Misty.* Yes, you did. I remember."

"We've been saving marks for Turns now, and we had a fair amount already put by. You," the seaman stopped and swallowed, struggling to get the unfortunate words out, "you wouldn't have gone looking for them, would you?"

Robinton was aghast. "No, of course not. Your marks are gone?"

"Every last one," Vanris admitted.

"But why ask me?"

"We asked everyone else already."

"You're the only landsman on board," Junos said, as if that explained everything.

"But . . . Do you know, you're not the only person missing something of value? I haven't been able to find my tenor pipe, and Ritolon assured me he put it on my cot. Tarosi lost some necklaces he meant to sell in Ista. There are other examples, though yours is the worst of all I've heard."

The two seamen exchanged glances. Junos looked surprised and somewhat abashed. "But why should we trust your word on this?" he asked.

"You don't need to. I'll go to Elaus and lay the problem out for him to judge. I should have all along, but it's a serious thing to cry theft when you have no proof."

"Indeed it is," Vanris said, pointedly looking at his friend. Junos locked eyes with him for a moment, then extended a callused hand palm up to Robinton.

"Please accept my apology."

Robinton covered the hand gratefully. "Let's go," he said.

Turn to section 34.

* 45 *

It was fully a man's height in length, and its long sharp teeth showed in its open mouth. His heart skipped a beat. This snake was easily twice as long as the dead tunnel snakes which occasionally triumphant drudges brought out from the kitchen caverns. He wondered if it was poisonous.

He knew he couldn't run away from it; it was already coiled to strike at him. In the fading light, he couldn't be sure of hitting it with his thrown belt-knife, so he was left with only his staff for a weapon. As he backed away from the beast, his foot struck something which sloshed. The waterskin! It might make a second defense for him. He lifted it in one hand, moving slowly and carefully, watching the snake.

It angled its head around and hissed at him again. Hefting his stick, he swiftly thrust the long end into the snake's face, and turned to run. Just as quickly, the snake struck at him.

With a grimace, he swung the waterbag around under the reptile's chin.

Roll 3 D6.

If the value rolled is less than or equal to Robinton's value for Dexterity, turn to section 47.

If greater, turn to section 56.

* 46 *

Robinton is surprised by Gurner's attack, and only jumps out of the way by sheer reflex. He knows that he's no match for the burly seaman, and wants to avoid being struck if at all possible. Numa tries to catch Gurner's arms, but the man's fury gives him an extra burst of strength, and he breaks free. Vanris recovers from his surprise at Gurner's outburst, and runs toward the forepart of the ship, calling for Elaus.

Robinton raises his fists. He is backing away from Gurner but is unwilling to leave his guard down. His best defense is his agility, and best weapon guile. The short seaman has skin like old wherhide stretched tight over bones as tough as ship's ribs. Robinton's main strength is that his wiles aren't clouded by anger, like Gurner's.

Gurner reaches out for him with one hand, aiming a blow with the other. Robinton twists toward the reaching hand, and out of the path of the punch. With his victim just out of his grasp, Gurner swipes at the empty air, and turns his head from side to side like a maddened herdbeast, searching. Robinton dashes behind him, clasps both hands together, and swings a hard blow at the back of the man's head. Gurner's momentum carries him forward, sending him stumbling to his knees.

Numa steps between them, then, trying to put a stop to the fight. He beckons Robinton forward, and then Gurner. Robinton stands behind Numa, smiling at Gurner to show that there were no hard feelings for the attack. Panting, the subdued seaman walks to them, but when he's a few paces away he dives over the mate, catching Robinton in the jaw with a wildly swinging punch.

The Harper staggers backward, and sits down on the deck. His head is ringing. He feels around the place where Gurner's fist struck. No blood, but it hurts. He moves his jaw around, making sure it isn't dislocated, only bruised. Numa has managed to restrain Gurner for the moment, but it's clear he is going to need help. A dirty kick from the thieving seaman makes Numa let go of him to clutch at his own leg. The enraged seaman dives for Robinton.

A twist to the left, and Robinton flips over onto his belly, trying to crawl away from the fight. He misjudges the direction, however, and has the breath knocked out of him as Gurner lands on his back. His long legs shoot out from under him. In this helpless position, Robinton has no choice but to take the blows the angry seaman delivers to his back and head. Numa, limping and furious, tries to pull him off, but Gurner doesn't even notice him. He growls like a madman, and Robinton feels a tremendous blow strike him in the back of the head, shoving his face into the floorboards. Gasping, he tries to roll and upset Gurner's balance. In reply, the seaman picks up Robinton's head by his thick hair and slams it against the deck. The Harper can hear footsteps running toward him. He tries to cry out, but his head is jerked backward once again and slammed down. A loud red pain explodes behind his eyes, and all is dark.

When Robinton comes to, Gurner is being held firmly by two crewmen, and Elaus is glaring at him.

Go to section 58.

* 47 *

The snake, with an abbreviated hiss, tumbled through the air. It landed against a rock, wrapping itself backward around it in anger and self-defense. Robinton shot forward, jamming the waterskin against the snake, trapping it between the skin and the rock. He dug the end of the staff into the pebbled bank, and propped it so that the snake would be able to work its way out, but not too quickly.

Backing away from the furious creature, he moved off into the twilight. Give it a half of an hour, and he would be able to reclaim his property after the snake left. Especially his other boot.

Turn to section 43.

* 48 *

A noise caught his attention, far, far away. There was nothing in the distance any way he looked which would make such a sound: huff-swish! huff-swish! like giant brooms sweeping the air. The air? He searched the sky. Yes, there it was, a dragon! A . . . a bronze! Robinton watched it fly with a smile of pure delight on his face. It was an amazing creature. How effortlessly it swam the sky. The light shone through its delicate wings, making it look like it had been painted on crystal. It flew a sweeping circle high above Nerat Hold once, twice, and then vanished. It had gone Between! How beautiful it was.

Robinton closed his eyes and imagined that he was on the back of a dragon, one he had Impressed at its hatching. He felt the wind rush past him as his dragon soared through the air. And even the cold of Between didn't frighten him, knowing that his dragon would keep him safe, only holding them Between for as long as it took him to cough three times and then they were—anywhere they wanted on Pern. They would be together forever. He had heard the story—as who had not?—at Harper Hall about how C'gan had come to Impress Tagath. If it could happen once that a Harper Impressed a dragon, why not twice? But it would never happen to him. He let out the breath he'd been holding with a sigh.

The runner answered him with a whicker and a twitch of his ears. Robinton laughed and gathered up the fallen reins. What a marvel that it was dragons—mighty, gentle, firebreathing dragons—that Pern was beholden to. It was more satisfying than, say, being beholden to runners. Honor the Stable and the Runner-riders, he thought, starting to formulate another humorous song, then was abashed at his boldness. What rude thoughts! Though there was no one to see him, he blushed bright red.

"If I can't curb my tongue even in private," he told the runner, "then it's just as well I won't be near anyone for a while."

The animal twitched its ears, then its muzzle, and for good measure, its tail. Robinton scratched it between the tall ears.

"You need a name, my dear runner. I can't call you wherbait, though that's what the beastmaster said you were, so I guess it'll have to be Twitch, since that seems to be your most outstanding characteristic."

Twitch. Twitch. Twitch.

"Well, that's settled." He gave it a flick with the reins and headed for the only road to Benden. Just once more, he searched the sky, hoping the bronze had returned. No, not his luck. Someday, he would ride on a dragon. Not his own dragon, of course. But any dragon would do.

The world was breaking out of the shell of the long Cold very slowly, to Robinton's point of view. He sang all the spring songs he knew as he rode, breathing in great draughts of air. Here and there, trees and bushes were already in full blossom. There were still others that had decided that spring had only just begun, leafing out with tiny fresh green buds and foliage. No fruit fit to eat stood on any tree yet; all he found were hard pippins the size of his fingernail with skirts of blossom still clinging to them.

The forest through which he rode was clear enough that he could see for quite a distance. To right and left were stands of trees and brush so thick that there was no light on the ground between them. He shivered faintly. All that green was, well, not obscene, but uncomfortable for a Harper who had spent his life learning that it was safest to have less of that about. Green, growing stuff attracted Thread. Not that Thread had fallen for nearly 400 Turns now, but one's earliest Teachings stayed with one longest.

In spite of the pad his tailbones were getting very sore. The more painful they became, the more compressed his voice was getting as he slouched over to ease them. He reined Twitch over and tied him to the low-hanging branch of a needle-leaf. It was time for a meal anyway. He ate lightly, offering the runner the core of his dessert fruit. Twitch accepted it with a shake of his head and a loud whicker which Robinton took to be an expression of gratitude. He was reasonably well pleased with the brown beast. In spite of his inexperience, he seemed to have secured a good mount.

Long before night fell, Robinton was looking for a place in which he could sleep. He did spot a place where someone had made camp within the last few sevendays. The stone ring for laying a fire was still filled with charred wood.

Tethering Twitch to a tree surrounded by tall grass, Robinton unloaded his belongings. While the runner tore up mouthfuls of plants, he undid the pad and gave Twitch a brisk rubdown. He'd never actually thought what he'd do on the road about currying and caring for his animal, so he ended up using the bath sheet from his pack. He'd have to dry in the sun after his own baths from now on.

Water was also becoming important to his mind. He recalled from the Hall maps that there was a river a few lengths to the northeast of where he'd made his camp. After seeing that Twitch was as comfortable as possible, he set out in search of the river. He took his small waterskin and picked up a long stick to use as a staff.

He debated while walking if he should drink what remainded in the skin, or keep it until he found the stream. A few sips widely spaced assuaged his thirst, which was not so fierce now that the sun was going down. He walked faster, knowing that he was not experienced enough in woodcraft to find his way back to his little camp in the dark.

It took him longer than he expected to find the streambed. The land was folded into creases, each of which had stands of bushes and marsh plants in it. He was very much afraid of losing his way. An idea struck him: why not assign a musical note to each level of land? That way he'd be sure he was going the right way, if the score matched the terrain. He whistled to himself as he walked, rehearsing his mapping tune.

Finally, he heard the sound of running water very close by. He followed his nose down a slope, and stopped when his torn boot toe filled with water. The stream smelled good enough. He recognized the flora on the bank as freshwater reeds and flowers. A cautious cupped handful assured him that he had found a potable source. Emptying the stale water out on the bank, he filled the skin again and set it aside. He scooped up more for himself, splashed it on his hands and hot face. The skin stung enough where the cool water touched to let him know that he had gotten a bit of sunburn. If it continued springlike over the next few days, he'd gradually get a tan, but if it became blisteringly hot, he'd be lucky if he didn't go red and peel.

The water felt so inviting that he decided to risk the dying light and have a short swim. Discarding his clothes next to the waterskin, he waded in and splashed around. Now he had to be very careful to keep his sense of direction. The stream was fast-flowing and very deep. He dove under the surface, angling so that he would stay parallel to his mark on the bank.

The coolness numbed all the places sore from his day's ride. He discovered ridged blisters where his boot tops rubbed against the insides of his legs. If he was this sore now, by the Shell, how much worse would he be when he reached Benden?

Feeling much refreshed by his bath, Robinton climbed out and sat down on the pebbles to dress. He picked up a boot and tried to put it on. Oops, wrong foot. He flung that boot absently to one side and picked up the other.

From where the boot landed, he heard a hiss. Alarmed, he grabbed for his staff and scrambled to his feet. The sound came again. Definitely a hiss. He could see the creature who had made the sound not a leg away from him. He'd hit a river snake with his thrown boot. It was coiling up now to strike, looking annoyed as only snakes can.

If he chooses to run away from the snake, turn to section 55.

If he chooses to trap the snake, turn to section 45.

If he chooses to fight the snake, turn to section 52.

* 49 *

He couldn't remember whether it was true that snakes had poor vision and found their way by smell. Well, if pressed, perhaps it wouldn't stop to sniff. He moved the waterskin gingerly forward and away to the side. Yes, the snake's head followed its movement, ignoring him. Just a bit farther. Steady. Steady.

He thrust it forward into the snake's face and swung at the reptile with his staff. It bounced off the waterskin and fell to the ground. As it wound into a protective bundle, he hit at it again, shielding himself behind the heavy bag. It coiled up again, drawing its head back. He interposed the waterskin again, readying the stick.

It struck, catching its teeth in the strap of the water

carrier. Drawing its body up in a bundle, it tried to wind around to find its real enemy.

Robinton dropped the bag on top of the snake. When it stuck its head out from under, he slammed the staff down. With furious strength, the snake tossed the bag off, and coiled its body around its wounded head, hissing. The Harper did not wait for it to recover. He slammed the snake again and again. After the ugly head was flattened the body still struggled and wiggled around, but it was dead. He drew his boot carefully to him, and put it on, watching the reptile die. Guilt welled up in him. He hated killing things, even when it was necessary for his own survival.

Turn to section 43.

* 50 *

When he woke, Robinton ate some bread and redfruit and drank some water. As before, he offered a small piece of the fruit to Twitch, who accepted it gratefully and then went back to cropping grass. The Harper slapped the pad on his mount's back, and began to fasten the bags and cases to it as on the day before. Twitch ignored anything that was going on behind his ears, and continued to pull up plants contentedly.

Robinton elected to keep his gitar over his shoulder instead of fastened into his case. If he held on properly with his knees, he should have no trouble playing while he rode. He estimated that he was three days out of Half Circle Sea Hold. His food should hold out easily until then.

Turn to section 67.

* 51 *

Robinton is surprised by Gurner's attack, and only jumps out of the way by sheer reflex. He knows that he's no match for the burly seaman, and wants to avoid being struck if at all possible. Numa tries to catch Gurner's arms, but the man's fury gives him an extra burst of strength, and he breaks free. Vanris recovers from his surprise at Gurner's outburst, and runs toward the forepart of the ship, calling for Elaus.

Robinton raises his fists. He is backing away from Gurner but is unwilling to leave his guard down. His best defense is his agility, and best weapon guile. The short seaman has skin that looks like old wherhide stretched tight over bones as tough as ship's ribs. Robinton's main strength is that his wiles aren't clouded by anger, like Gurner's.

Gurner reaches out for him with one hand, aiming a blow with the other. Robinton twists toward the reaching hand, and out of the path of the punch. With his victim just out of his grasp, Gurner swipes at the empty air, and turns his head from side to side like a maddened herdbeast, searching. Robinton dashes behind him, clasps both hands together, and swings a hard blow at the back of the man's head. Gurner's momentum carries him forward, and he stumbles to his knees.

Numa steps between them, trying to put a stop to the fight. He beckons Robinton forward, and then Gurner. Robinton stands behind Numa, smiling at Gurner to show that there were no hard feelings for the attack. The subdued seaman walks to them, but a few paces away he dives over the mate, catching Robinton in the jaw with a wildly swinging punch.

The Harper staggers backward, sitting hard down on the deck. His head is ringing. He feels around the place where Gurner's fist struck. No blood, but it hurts. He moves his jaw around, making sure it isn't dislocated, only bruised. Numa has managed to restrain Gurner for the moment, but it's clear he is going to need help. A sly kick from the thieving seaman makes Numa let go of him to clutch at his own leg. Gurner dives for Robinton.

A twist to the left brings Robinton out of the way of the dive, but Gurner grabs his leg, keeping him from escaping. The young Harper struggles, his lanky legs feeling as if they're being smashed flat under the weight of his assailant. In a moment, the weight moves, and he tries to crawl away again. Instead, he chokes from the pressure of his own laces against his throat, as Gurner hauls him up by the back of his tunic. Robinton grabs for the seaman's free arm and twists. With a surprised gasp of pain, Gurner lets go, his head bowed forward to ease the pressure on his arm. Robinton releases the arm, and delivers another two-handed chop to the back of the seaman's head. Gurner falls flat on his face to the deck.

As Robinton raises himself to his feet, panting, Elaus and Vanris come running.

Turn to section 58.

* 52 *

Now he was in trouble. He couldn't run away from it; it was already coiled to strike at him. In the fading light, he couldn't be sure of hitting it with his thrown belt-knife, so he was left with only his staff for a weapon. As he backed away from the beast, his foot struck something which sloshed. The waterskin! It might make a second defense for him.

RIVER SNAKE
To be hit: 11 To hit Robinton: 14 Hit points: 5
Bite does 1 point of damage. Also, each time it bites successfully, roll 3 D6 against Robinton's value for Constitution. If the roll is higher, take 1 D6 extra damage for effect of poison.

If Robinton wins, turn to section 49.

If he loses, turn to section 54.

* 53 *

"Twelve marks," the beastmaster said, scratching the runner between its ears. The ears twitched with pleasure, and the beast shifted from foot to foot. Robinton eyed it. It did look strong and healthy, give it that. Well, might as well get it over with. There was no choice.

"Done," Robinton said at last.

"Done," the man echoed. He extended his palm. Robinton placed his hand over it in the traditional seal of a bargain.

"Good," Robinton said, reaching for the lead. "Where are riding pads kept?"

The man affected an innocent face. "Oh, you want tack for the beast too? That wasn't in our bargain, Harper. Three marks for used tack, six for new." He folded his enormous arms, looking satisfied with himself. "You Harpers always have more money to spend than a hard-working Holder might, though we owe you the honor."

For answer, Robinton reeled in the hide strap and led his runner toward the door. Behind him, the master chuckled. "Very well, Journeyman. It's yours."

"Done," Robinton said, turning back with a smile.

He settled himself as best he could on the backpad, which was old and nearly flat. At least it served its purpose, which was to protect his bottom and the beast's back from one another. The bony runner moved at a brisk trot which would have been painful otherwise.

He had but half a mark's worth of provisions in his pouch. The runner, he was assured, would find ample fodder on the road. Which road? Well, there was only one toward Benden Hold, and that one not very direct. But since he was on a runner, not a dragon, he'd have to do the best he could.

Subtract twelve and a half marks from the record sheet. Record the addition of a runner beast and four days' worth of provisions.

Turn to section 48.

* 54 *

He couldn't remember whether or not it was true that snakes had poor vision and found their way by smell. Well, if pressed, perhaps it wouldn't stop to sniff. He moved the waterskin gingerly forward and away to the side. Yes, the snake's head followed its movement, ignoring him. Just a bit farther. Steady. Steady.

He thrust it forward into the snake's face and swung at the reptile with his staff. It bounced off the waterskin and fell to the ground. As it wound into a protective bundle, he hit at it again, shielding himself behind the heavy bag. It coiled up again, drawing its head back. He interposed the waterskin again, readying the stick.

Snap! The snake straightened out like lightning striking, straight for his bare ankle. Too late, he remembered the discarded boot which had started the whole argument. He batted at the snake with the staff and bag, but he could feel himself becoming more ill. The bite venom was starting to have an effect on him. Abruptly, his bare foot folded up under him, and he fell to one knee.

The snake was as startled by his fall as he was, but made one last thrust before it fled. It flew at his face. He moved up one hand to shield his eyes, and felt the sharp fangs puncture his skin. Robinton stared at the hand, expecting the two oozing holes to mean something to his spinning brain. He looked around for the snake, fearing another attack, but it was gone. How kind; it had left his boot behind for him. The flesh where he had been bitten felt as though it was swelling, making his whole body inflate. He couldn't see his hands anymore, but perhaps that was because it was night. He ought to sleep.

The ground rushed up and struck him hard in the cheekbone.

Turn to section 29.

* 55 *

It was fully a man's height in length, striped in green and black, and its long sharp teeth showed in its open mouth. His heart skipped a beat. This snake was easily twice as long as the dead tunnel snakes which occasionally triumphant drudges brought out from the kitchen caverns. He wondered if it was poisonous.

It angled its head around and hissed at him again,

©1986

flicking the end of its tail back and forth in a threatening gesture. Hefting his stick, Robinton swiftly thrust the long end into the snake's face, and turned to run. Just as quickly, the snake struck at him.

"Aaagh!" Caught most definitely from behind, Robinton had to turn to swat at the deadly reptile. He promised himself that he'd tend to his damaged dignity after he had dispatched the snake.

Take 1 point of damage, and roll 3 D6 against Robinton's value for Constitution.

If the total is less than or equal to his Constitution, turn to section 52.

If greater, turn to section 59.

* 56 *

The snake's leap carried it over the waterbag. It snapped its teeth into Robinton's forearm, and then dropped to the ground. Angrily, it coiled up and hissed warningly. The snake was prepared to strike again. Robinton backed away as slowly as he could, preparing to defend himself.

He felt a little weak and sick. The snake's bite was poisonous!

Take one point of damage. Roll 3 D6 against Robinton's value for Constitution. If the roll is higher, take 1 D6 extra damage for the effect of poison.

Turn to section 52.

* 57 *

When he woke, Robinton ate some bread and redfruit and drank some water. As before, he offered a small piece of the fruit to Twitch, who accepted it gratefully and then went back to cropping grass. The Harper slapped the pad on his mount's back, and began to fasten the bags and cases to it as on the day before. Twitch ignored anything that was going on behind his ears, and continued to pull up plants contentedly.

Robinton elected to keep his gitar over his shoulder instead of fastened in his case. He could play as he walked, and take his mind off the tedium of the trip and the unfortunate pain in his backside. He estimated that it would take an extra two days before his wound healed enough that he could sit a runner comfortably, so he was four or five days out of Half-Circle Sea Hold. In the meantime, Twitch would carry only his baggage.

Subtract two days' worth of food from the record sheet.

Turn to section 67.

* 58 *

Elaus, fists on hips, regarded Gurner sternly. Vanris and Junos stood by, explaining the situation in whispers to the other seamen as they joined the little group by the galley.

"Why did you thieve, Gurner?" Elaus asked, trying to make sense out of his man's actions. "Were you in some need we didn't know? You had only to ask, and any of us would have aided you."

Robinton stood nearby, feeling horribly uncomfortable. He ached with an empathy for the man, knowing how he would feel if he had been accused of such a crime. But his feelings were wasted on the angry seaman. Gurner stood sullenly silent. With a heavy sigh, Elaus turned away from him. "So be it. You know our custom. Numa?"

Out of a heavy sea-chest, Numa drew a set of metal manacles. That they had not been used in Turns was evident by the rust and grime encrusting the chain. The mate brushed at them with the edge of his sleeve, and then gave the job up as hopeless.

"Oh, no, Captain," Gurner pleaded. For the first time since he'd been caught, the anger broke, and there was shame in his eyes. He stood between Tarosi and Dolgi, shoulders slumped, defeated.

"You won't have them on long," Elaus assured him, coolly. "Just until we make land. They will remind you that you have abused our trust."

The chains were fastened on Gurner's wrists, and he was led below. The crew dispersed silently, slipping away like ghosts. In a moment, there was no one left but Elaus and Robinton. The young man was chewing unhappily on his upper lip, turning the recovered pipe over and over in his hands. "Somehow, I feel that all of this is my fault," he blurted out.

Elaus eyed him, not without sympathy. "Most of the time you're a level-headed young man. Try to see it in perspective. He thieved quietly. He seems to have taken only small items which would not be immediately noticed. For some time now things have gone missing, and my men thought that their possessions were merely lost overboard or left ashore, common on any ship. You leave that which you must not lose back in the home port. This is the first time that I know of that a guest had

anything taken. He was careless, and you were perceptive enough to find out where your property had gone. So, you were in the right."

"It's not often," Robinton said with rueful humor, "that I hate being right."

The weather was fine and warm over the next few days, but Robinton couldn't enjoy them. The situation with Gurner had spoiled a lot of the fun he was having on board the *Sea Dragon*, and he was still burdened with guilt as to the man's fate. A few times, he found himself pausing outside the hold, where Gurner had been chained with a rush bag for a bed. What would he do if he actually went in? The seaman had made it clear that he didn't want company, least of all Robinton, whom he blamed for his exposure and humiliation. The young Harper felt as though he should make some amends to Gurner, though the others told him that he had no reason to do so. The man was a thief, and as such deserved any doom that he earned.

Robinton hadn't touched the pipe since the day it had been recovered. It wasn't a valuable instrument by any means, but now it would remind him of this voyage forever. He sighed, picking out a gloomy melody on his gitar in the shade of the jibsail.

Junos had made many an apology for suspecting Robinton of the theft of his money. All the marks but ten or eleven were found under the pads in the lookout basket, and this trading expedition would more than replenish that amount. He and Vanris had let Robinton know that he would be welcome anywhere they went, in Hold or on the *Misty*, when they had her. He was grateful for their kindness, but he still felt depressed.

Soon, Nerat Tip came into view. Elaus issued orders, and the *Sea Dragon* steered north by northeast until it was only lengths from land. They dropped anchor while still in deep water, and shipped the sails. The *Sea Dragon* rocked gently against her tether.

Gurner was brought up on deck, still in chains. Elaus unlocked them and let them drop with a clank, leaving Gurner to rub at his wrists. Over his shoulder, Elaus nodded to Numa. The mate stepped forward. He had collected all of Gurner's belongings, and set them now between the gunwales of a small boat already bobbing in the water. Gesturing that Gurner should precede him, he climbed down a rope ladder into the skiff and rowed it to land.

"But there are no Holds anywhere around here," Robinton observed, scanning the shore.

"That matters little," Elaus said, shortly. "There is an unwritten law of the sea, that no man betrays the trust. If he does, he is outcast, no longer welcome on boat or ship or in Seahold. We will pass the word among sea folk. He'll never be trusted again."

Robinton said nothing more, but watched the little boat as it moved slowly toward the shore. In a short time it returned, but only Numa was in it, rowing solemnly back alone.

The next day was as bright and sunny as a summer day. Robinton did a little counting in his head, and determined that it actually was nearly summer. He should have fine weather for the remainder of his trip to Benden Hold. The thought cheered him up quite a bit. In fact, the good weather contributed to improving moods all through the crew of the *Sea Dragon*.

Numa calculated that the next day would bring them to Nerat Hold. He declared one final song contest in Robinton's honor.

"I don't deny it's for all of us, lad," the mate said, clapping the young Harper companionably on the back. "I don't think any of us have had so musical a voyage in

Turns. We'll miss you, that's sure. A pity it is that you are not to be in a Seahold. It's a long way inland to Benden. It's a wonder the poor little grapes aren't all worn out by the time they reach us," he grinned slyly, holding up a new cask of wine.

Robinton threw back his head and laughed. "Why on Pern weren't you a Harper, Numa? You're as good a singer as many apprentices I know in the Harper-crafthall."

"There was never a question of it, boy. The sea is a part of me, and I of it. Did I spend as much time as it needs to become a Harper, I'd dry right out." In response to that thirsty thought, Numa took a long draught of wine.

Robinton pointed at the empty glass. "That means you start," he said.

It was a workday when the *Sea Dragon* drew into Nerat Hold harbor. Robinton's possessions were taken off along with the cargo. As the net hit the dock, he felt a lump in his throat. He'd be sorry to leave the ship behind. It had indeed been a jolly trip. One by one the seamen came over to say goodby. Even Elaus interrupted his bargaining for best harbor rates to bid him farewell and a safe journey.

Arloc was the last. He embraced the lad heartily, and handed him a small covered pot. "Because you're always getting into scrapes, you might need this."

Robinton did not even need to open it to determine the contents. The noxious odor announced itself. "Numbweed." He wrinkled his nose.

"Aye. It's foul, but think where you might be without it. Take it to remember us by."

"Thank you, Arloc. Good trading." And, assembling the raft of straps across his shoulders, Robinton turned away.

Add one pot of numbweed to the list of Robinton's possessions. It may be used twice before it is gone. Return all his hit points to full strength.

Nerat Hold was a cross between Fort and Ista Holds. As the farthest southeast of all the major Holds, and surrounded as it was on three sides by water, it was as full of traders and fishermen as was Ista. Yet the Hold was much farther back from the shore, and it had the same sounds and odors as Fort Hold. Robinton grinned to himself. It was funny that the thing which should remind him most of his home Hold here was the smell of farm beasts.

The buildings nearest the dock all seemed to have to do with the trades of the sea. They were rough, sturdy buildings hewn out of rock and mounted on pilings just like the piers. A row of ships in drydock announced that this was a repair facility as well as a working port.

Since anyone Holding here could expect nearly half the Turn to be filled with storms, Robinton could easily understand why the living quarters were so far inland. It would make any Holder reluctant to open his door if he knew on the other side was a wash of salt water. By the sound (and the smell), Robinton guessed that the beast cavern was just northwest of the harbor, and not too far away, either. It was where he was bound now, to find himself a runner beast for the last half of his trip to Benden. He also hoped to get accurate directions from the beastmaster. He counted his marks. Thirteen. He'd spent two at the Ista Gather. No matter how many times he recounted them they still totaled thirteen. He was unlikely to get much of a runner for that, especially if he held out for provisions.

The beastmaster was a tall, dark-skinned man with arms nearly as thick as Robinton's legs. When Robinton entered the cavern, he was holding up a newborn runner, trying to help it get its balance as the mother lay nearby, looking on trustingly. At last, the tiny thing was able to take a few steps by itself, and the mother rewarded it by hoisting herself to her feet and letting it nurse. That taken care of, the beastmaster had time to greet his visitor.

"So, bound for Benden, are you?" he asked, leading Robinton to the stalls of runners for sale.

"That's right."

"Something's not happened to Harper Evarel, has it?" the man asked with real concern. "He's a fine man. I sold him a beast, oh, two Turns ago, at a Half-Circle Gather."

"No, nothing like that," Robinton assured him quickly. "I'm to be his assistant."

"Quite an honor for you. Lord Raid is a good Holder. Knows his duty."

"We've met," Robinton said dryly, remembering Ista Hold's Gather.

"Ah. Well, here we've a couple of beasts. D'you know much about runners?"

"Enough," Robinton answered, hoping that he didn't look the total novice.

"Ah," the man said again. "Well, this big one's twelve marks, and this little brown one's nine. The first's the stronger animal. I see you're carrying a lot of baggage."

Robinton tallied his money again. He could dicker, but the truth was, he *didn't* know very much about runners, and so far as he could tell, the prices were cheap. The big runner did indeed look stronger than the other, but so tall he might need to stand on something to mount it. It looked as if it could easily take the trip through the mountains to Benden. The other was a more reasonable size, though it didn't look as though it would be too happy to have to carry all his baggage, and him, too. But appearances weren't everything. Both animals had firm muscles under their coarse pelts. No stones or injuries in their feet. Legs sound enough, with no visible sores or bowed tendons. Beyond that, he wasn't very sure.

If Robinton should choose the big runner, turn to section 60.

If he should choose the other, turn to section 41.

If he should decide he can't afford a runner at all, turn to section 42.

* 59 *

He began to feel a little weak and sick to his stomach, in spite of his violent activity. The snake's bite was venomous!

Take 1 D6 points of damage for poison effect.

Turn to section 52.

* 60 *

"I'd like the big runner, I think," Robinton said. Too late he realized he should have started a dicker before he chose, but the words were already out. He decided to try, anyway. "But twelve marks is too steep for me. I'll give you nine for him."

"For nine you can have the skinny brown," the beastmaster said.

"But it's the other I wanted."

"Then it's twelve marks."

Sighing, he thought of how sad his purse would feel if it was flat and empty.

If he should purchase the big runner after all, turn to section 53.

If he decides to take the brown, turn to section 41.

* 61 *

Robinton circled, not turning his back on Twitch. The runner acted as though it didn't know who he was. He kept talking to it, trying to calm it down.

"Come on, Twitch. Good fellow. Come back up to the road, and I'll give you half a redfruit. You'd like that, wouldn't you?"

The runner stuck its nose out, sniffing at him suspiciously. Robinton eyed the dangling lead under its jaw and lunged for it. Just as quickly, Twitch bit his wrist. Somehow, he kept a hold of the lead and threw himself against the runner's side. It lowered its head and tried to nip at his feet just as Robinton put his foot in the stirrup and boosted himself up. He had to stop the runner attacking him; and it was too strong to hold off for long. Perhaps Twitch couldn't attack Robinton on the runner's own back.

Twitch sidled against a tree, scraping him off. Robinton fell to the ground with one foot bent underneath, twisting his knee painfully. The runner backed up, seeking him, and one foot struck him in the side of the head. With an explosive pain, all consciousness fled.

Turn to section 29.

* 62 *

Robinton handed back the puzzles and reached for the little box again. He stroked the fine grain of the wood, and played with the lid. "How much would you ask for this?"

"Oh, two marks for you, Harper. It's made of the wood of a fruit tree that fell not far from my cothold. See how pretty the wood looks? I used a natural transparent wax to polish it. That's the original color, that reddish tone."

"Two marks? Would you take a mark and a quarter?" Robinton asked, boldly, then regretted his outburst. It was worth far more, but—

"A mark and a half, my final offer," Danol said, suddenly.

Robinton considered the price. It sounded fair, and the box was very handsome.

If Robinton has the money, subtract it from the record sheet and note the addition of the wooden box. Turn to section 85.

If he has not, turn to section 64.

* 63 *

Unable to stop his fall, Robinton tumbled down the slope head over heels. The gitar made one *clangg!* of protest before the strap slipped over his head and fell off.

He clutched at bushes, trying to slow down. Little stumps and roots stuck into his ribs as he rolled over them. Berry canes whipsawed in protest at his intrusion. He was full of scratches and thorns by the time he landed in a flowering yellow bush two thirds of the way down the hill. Ouch! It was full of thorns, too.

He picked himself up, and clambered slowly back up the slope to retrieve his gitar. Only one of the strings was broken, and the wood wasn't scratched at all. He strummed the remaining strings as he stumped down the hill, to reassure himself that it and he were intact. There were extra strings in his bag, should he ever manage to catch up with his runner. Robinton discovered how lucky he was to have been stopped, even by a thornbush. This was a river valley, and both sides of the streambed were loaded with big rocks. Fortunately, it was the source end of a river, so it was easy for him to pick his way across the shallows. A bit wiser, he kept an eye open for snakes.

There was a myriad of tiny scratches all over him from the thorns and twigs. He went through contortions to feel the hard-to-reach ones, but pronounced what he could see as harmless. Also, he'd be walking a little stiffly for a while; the bumps and jostles he had received were responsible for that. It was a miracle he wasn't badly hurt.

Robinton receives one hit point of damage from the fall. If this brings his total to zero, turn to section 29.

If not, turn to section 69.

* 64 *

"No, thank you," Robinton said, at last. "Your work is very fine. I'm sure you'll sell everything at Nerat, but I have so much to carry already. I'm not sure how your work would fare knocking around in one of my cases."

Danol was cheerfully philosophical. "If you were meant to have any of my little toys, you'd take it. I'm not insulted by a refusal. The look on your face was high praise, indeed. I think more adults buy my toys than do children. Of course, that's natural, prices being what they are." He put away the wooden goods, repositioned the pack.

Turn to section 78.

* 65 *

He sprang at the runner, hand reaching out to snare the lead. Twitch, in white-eyed frenzy, tried to bite him. Robinton succeeded in catching the rope. He hauled in on it, bringing Twitch up short, and nearly knocking himself off his feet.

The beast spun around in surprise, and promptly tried to bite Robinton on the arm. The Harper clouted him over his sensitive nose, and the runner backed off, snorting. It laid its ears back and bared its teeth.

TWITCH
To be hit: 12 *To hit Robinton: 13* *Hit points: 9*
(see below)
Bite does 1 D6 points of damage.

Robinton will only try to evade and calm the beast, not attack. Twitch will make three attacks on Robinton which can succeed.

If Robinton runs out of hit points, turn to section 61.

If he doesn't, turn to section 79.

* 66 *

He sat under the path, waiting. Sooner or later, the runner would tire itself out, and then he could catch it easily.

It seemed like hours until the beast's pace started to slow down, and then it wasn't long before it stopped moving entirely. Robinton began to feel very hungry. It was long past the time when he would have stopped for a meal. He poked his head out from under the edge of his hiding place and took a look. Twitch was standing head down just a little distance away from him, sides heaving. Moving very slowly, Robinton stood up.

"Good Twitch," he said, almost cooing the phrase. "There's a fine fellow. Come to me." The runner seemed to pause, then looked up at Robinton. The Harper went on chatting to it as though it was a Holder child who had fallen down. "Don't be frightened. I'm your friend, you know that. Come to me. Good Twitch." He held out his hand and began to sidle toward the runner.

There was a clump of grass growing at the edge of the path. He was tempted to pull some up and use it for bait, but he worried that the sudden movement and noise might spook the animal again.

If he decides to pull up some grass, turn to section 77.

If he decides not to, turn to section 80.

* 67 *

It was a lovely, warm day. The air was so moist it was almost like being back on the sea except for the lack of salt smell. This road stretching from Nerat Hold to Half-Circle was ancient and well kept but not, to Robinton's eye, heavily traveled. There were the ruts from the wagons which had passed about the same time as wood had been burned in last night's campsite, but no mark since, and none before then for quite a long time. Nerat did most of its trading north by ship.

He went along singing to his gitar. Because it was so humid it really was more comfortable to walk than chafing on the backpad. Twitch followed him happily, only occasionally pulling at the lead rope looped over Robinton's shoulder. When the road widened out, they walked side by side, the Harper playing and the runner sniffing at the gitar, trying to decide if music was edible. It was so quiet. The jingle-clip-clop of Twitch's ambling walk was the only thing beside his playing and singing breaking the silence. There was no wind, no other animal sounds that he could hear. He had never felt so . . . so isolated. There were always people around wherever he was. He was lonely alone.

Section 67

He talked to Twitch when his throat got too dry for singing. "Have you ever been to Half-Circle? Or Benden? It's a great honor for me, you know."

The runner blew through his lips in answer. Robinton laughed. "You sound like a Holder. They wouldn't care either. In fact, there's a cotholder in Fort Hold who looks like a runner beast. Gregor has got long teeth and a bony face—is he a relative of yours?"

Twitch tossed his head, neither confirming nor denying.

Robinton called a halt so they could both have a drink of water. The waterskin was still full enough that he judged they could last the rest of today and the next day on what was left. A lock of his own hair fell into his eyes. It always grew fairly quickly. He'd be in need of a haircut before he reached Benden, or he'd look as shaggy as his runner. He combed the wavy dark mass back with his fingers, willing it to stay put. "Or you'll be gitar strings soon, see if you won't," he threatened. More hair had to be lifted out of his shirt collar. Great Shells, what must he look like?

Twitch, assuming that Robinton was speaking to him, snuffed at his face and hand, looking for a treat. He pushed the beast away and stood up. "We can't rest any longer. Let's go!"

The sun was sparkling through the new leaves hanging over the road. Robinton filled his lungs, and exhaled with a happy shout that echoed down the road. His runner caught his mood, and whiffled contentedly as they walked. Twitch didn't require being led any longer to stay within a pace of so of Robinton, so the lead rope hung slack under his chin as he trotted.

There was a log or a heavy beam of some kind dropped on the sun-drenched path up ahead. It wouldn't hamper their passage, but Robinton determined to move it if he could, for the safety of future travelers. It looked to be half again man-height, not unmanageable. Twitch followed him curiously, as he approached the log.

When they were within just a few paces of it, the "log" raised a hideously ugly head and snarled. Robinton jumped back. It was a wild wher, sunning itself. Twitch, screaming in terror, galloped around it and up the road. The giant reptile crouched back as if it would leap after Twitch.

"My music!" Robinton cried, racing after the runner. The wher, surprised, turned its head toward him but didn't lunge. Whers were blind in daylight, and so it was unable to judge the size of its opponent. Robinton was lucky; they could both have been killed.

His gitar bounced up and down on his back as he ran. He couldn't see Twitch anymore. A break in the foliage on the side of the road and thrashing noises off to the right told him that the runner had fled in there for cover. He pushed his way in, arms held crossed in front of his face to ward off branches that whipped at him.

"Twitch!" he called. "Twitch, stop!" He could hear frightened whinnies and more crashing up ahead. He thought he saw a brown tail disappearing around a stand of bushes. Pressing on faster, he strove to catch up with the frightened runner. At least in here the beast couldn't move ahead at full speed, but neither could he. "Twitch!" He spat out flowering twigs that somehow got around the sheltering arms, and kept running. He had to keep in sight of the runner before the green and brown undergrowth swallowed it up.

Suddenly, the ground sloped sharply away under his feet. He windmilled his arms, trying to keep his balance.

Roll 3 D6.

If the total is greater than Robinton's value for Dexterity, turn to section 63.

If less than or equal, turn to section 76.

* 68 *

Robinton decided to make camp that night in the curve of an enormous bend in the road. As soon as the bundles were unloaded from his back, Twitch fell to on the tall plants. He was so interested in his dinner that Robinton didn't need to tether him immediately. The Harper laid out his camp and began to look for firewood.

Just then, something flashing overhead caught his attention. Dragons! Another patrol of dragons! He was seeing them fly by more often as he went farther north. He supposed the Weyrleader had them practice more to the south over the Nerat peninsula than over the more heavily populated western Holds. Shading his eyes, he watched them maneuver. A wing formation of three bronzes hovered slowly in midair, their great wings fully open to the glide. Out of Between, a trio of browns, also in formation, appeared to their port flank, and one to the starboard as well. He waved to them with both arms, but they didn't acknowledge him. It was unlikely that they could see him in the forest below. He was proud of them for keeping the ancient traditions, even though no Thread had fallen for hundreds of Turns.

Robinton watched in fascination as they went through complex actions like the weaving of a dance. Weyrleader F'lon—it must be he!—on the leading bronze raised a hand, and the whole wing went Between. Robinton was excited. He could hardly wait for his first visit to the Weyr, to see these wonderful creatures close up.

He gathered up his sticks from where he'd let them

drop. It must have been raining earlier that day or the day before, because Robinton was unable to find more than a few sticks dry enough to light. In fact, the ground itself was more saturated the farther northwest he went. He knew from the maps that there was a lot of marshland on the east side of Nerat Bay, and the sides of the shallow canyon shed a lot of water onto the road every time it rained. As a result, wherever he placed his cloak, intending to settle down for the night, the ground oozed gritty mud or dirty water all around him. At last, he took the damp sticks that would not light and lined them into a comparatively dry, albeit uncomfortable, mat to sleep on. He tied Twitch's lead to a sapling and ate a light meal before he lay down.

When he woke up, the sun shone green-yellow through a thick, waist-high haze that extended for dragonlengths in every direction, laying in the hollow. Hills rose out of the mist like land over a waterfall pool. Plants and shrubs wore drops of dewlike jewels. The landscape seemed unreal. He untied Twitch and they waded through the sea of eerie fog in a curiously silent world. The marsh dwellers sang an isolated note here and there, the bigger ones making a noise like breaking sticks, but for long minutes there was no sound. Even Twitch's hooves seemed to be silenced on the softer ground. He ate quietly, wondering at the dreamlike quality of his surroundings.

Subtract one day's food from the record sheet.

As the sun climbed, the mist burned slowly away, leaving the last wisps to dance in the damp places. Robinton saw white twists of cloud skating across the surface of a pond they passed.

A gentle clip-clopping joined the sound of their own passage, getting louder. In a moment, a big gray runner beast appeared around the next bend, breasting the mist as if it were swimming. On its back was a grizzle-haired man, flanked by heavy bags tied to the rings on the backpad.

Robinton's heart nearly leaped out of his chest when he saw the figures of runner and rider appear out of nowhere. As soon as his eyes sorted out reality from fancy, he recognized a beast with a human on its back. He started forward eagerly to greet the other man. It had been days since he'd spoken to another human being, and he was lonely.

"No offense, Twitch," he apologized to the runner, "but I'm sure you'd sooner listen to one of your own kind than me, too." He raised a hand, hailing the rider.

The man on the gray had already spotted him, and was riding forward, a smile on his face.

"Well, well, well! I didn't think I'd see anyone else on this road in this season. Where are you bound?"

"Half-Circle," Robinton said. "On my way to Benden Hold. Have you come from Half-Circle?"

"No, no," the man protested, resting an elbow on his runner's neck. He broke into a spasm of coughing, which prevented him from answering for a time. "I'm a Smithcrafter. I work in wood. I have a little Hold of my own some lengths from here on the marsh's edge. I see you're a Harper. Danol's my name."

"I'm Robinton." A suspicious thought crossed his mind, remembering what he'd seen in Ista Hold. "Do you make doors?"

Danol laughed in surprise, which set him coughing again. His cheeks had a pinched, unhealthy look, though the brown eyes above them were bright and clear. "What? They'd not last ten Turns on the marsh, and why waste the wood? I don't make anything I can't use myself. If it doesn't sell, I have to keep it or destroy it."

©1986

He sighed, counting to himself. "There was a lot of expensive firewood last season. I hope I'll do better this time."

"What do you craft?"

Danol was already rummaging in one of his packs. "I've made a lot of these. I'm on my way to Nerat. Hoping for a Gather this restday. Here, have a look." He put a small box into Robinton's hands.

The box had been crafted out of a smooth-grained wood of a ruddy hue. Instead of opening on a hinge, the top slid through two fine grooved lips protruding up from the long sides. The inside had been divided into four equal compartments with thin pieces of wood. "It's very well made," Robinton said critically, turning it over in his hands. Master Liesult had not instructed the apprentices to make anything like this. It would be very useful for storing coiled gitar strings, or tuning keys. Wooden boxes like these would be rare and much sought after, he knew.

"I've also got these." "These" were wooden puzzles, the outline shapes of which included dragons, men, runners, ships, cotholds and fish. Each one disassembled into a handful of little pieces which looked absolutely nothing like the whole from which they came. "They can be put together in several different ways, but there's only one right way. I use wood instead of bone, and it carves much easier. A great favorite with bright children as well as adults. I've a lot of time on my hands. Don't get around as much as I used to. I used to work in metals, but I think my lungs were damaged by the fumes. Time was when I made beautiful things out of bronze and copper and silver. Wood is not a bad substitute. Easier to work, but it breaks far more readily." Robinton turned over a handsomely painted fish puzzle, marveling at the glossy silver paint, picking out the scales. "Would you be interested in any of my wares, eh?"

If Robinton is interested in buying a box, turn to section 62.

If he'd like to buy a puzzle, turn to section 74.

If he is interested in buying both, turn to section 82.

If he is not interested in making a purchase, turn to section 64.

* 69 *

High above him on the other side of the small valley, he could see Twitch running frantically back and forth, trying to find a way through the thick growth at the top of the ridge.

Robinton scrambled up the slope, keeping low, so the runner wouldn't see him. There was nothing he could do about the noises he made climbing. He could only hope that the runner would think it was the river bumbling away down here, or another animal.

He reached a place just under and out of sight from the dead-end path where Twitch was pacing. Pushing himself into the overhang, he could observe the runner unseen until he could decide what to do. Besides, he was exhausted. Above him, Twitch neighed furiously and turned to run a dragonlength or so the other way again.

He'd seen this behavior in animals before, especially vermin who were cornered in dead-end tunnels. They never turned back to the direction they came from. Instead, they would keep dashing to and fro, expecting an escape route to appear. What should he do? If he tried to catch Twitch in this mood, the runner might attack him. But if he didn't capture him soon, he might get away, and Robinton couldn't count on another lucky dead end.

If he should try to herd Twitch into running back down the hill toward the road, turn to section 81.

If he wants to try to catch hold of the lead rein, turn to section 70.

If instead he should try to lure the runner to him, turn to section 84.

If he decides to wait until Twitch calms down, turn to section 66.

* 70 *

Robinton determined that the best way to capture his hysterical animal was simply to leap up and grab for the dangling lead. Twitch was all the way at the other end of his little path. Robinton gathered himself up to pounce. The thundering of Twitch's gallop was nearly over him. Ready . . . jump!

Roll 3 D6.

If the number rolled is greater than Robinton's value for Dexterity, turn to section 65.

If less than or equal to his Dexterity, turn to section 77.

* 71 *

Robinton settled himself on the pad. He counted all the bags and cases. To his relief, they were all still attached. The straps were sound. He made a clucking noise, and Twitch moved down the slope toward the river.

He stopped to have a drink before fording the stream, reminding Robinton that they were both thirsty and hungry. The sun was past its height for the day, but it was still very hot.

With a heave, Twitch crested the last ridge and emerged onto the road. While the young Harper leaned exhausted back on the pad and brushed twigs off his clothes, Twitch turned his head around to nuzzle at him and beg for a treat, as if nothing had happened at all. Robinton reached down automatically to scratch under the runner's jaw. "Stupid beast," he panted affectionately.

Turn to section 68.

* 72 *

When morning came, he rummaged in his pack, thinking avidly of breakfast. He scratched at new bites from insects who had elected to share his cloak with him for the night. Twitch swiveled interested ears toward the sound, remembering fruit rinds and bread. Grinning at the eager runner, Robinton reached farther and farther into the carrysack. Bowl, cup, spoon. Bath sheet, brush, soapsand. Sharpening stone for his belt knife. But there was no food left. Well, he was not a heavy eater. He could do without for one day. But he was hungry.

Twitch, seeing that no treats were forthcoming, went back to cropping grass. Robinton watched him enjoying his meal and wishing he could eat the same stuff. "There's a lot of it wherever you go," he told the runner, "and you never have to worry about its being fresh."

He looked at the sky, where leaden clouds clustered around the sun. There might not be much time to forage, and he wanted to reach the Hold before it rained.

If he decides to go hungry for the day, turn to section 93.

If he decides to seek food, turn to section 75.

* 73 *

White-eyed, Twitch charged past him, veering off and heading downhill. Branches snapped under his feet. Robinton jumped off the path and set off in pursuit of his runner. Every so often, he whipped his crop through the air, creating a sharp whistling sound. Twitch's ears swiveled back every time he heard the sound, and redoubled his pace. The Harper counted the bags on the beast's back, and determined to his relief that none of them had fallen off when Twitch had fled.

The runner trotted through the water at the bottom of the slope, and heaved himself up the other side. The rock path across the stream was slippery. Robinton had to slow down to keep from falling. He had only reached the far bank of the river by the time Twitch was midway up the ridge. The beast's rump disappeared over the edge, and Robinton scrambled up after it, shouting.

As Robinton had predicted, or rather, as he had hoped, when he emerged the runner was standing in the middle of the road looking confused and lost. While the young Harper leaned exhausted against a tree and brushed twigs off his clothes, Twitch walked over to nuzzle at his ear and beg for a treat, as if nothing had happened at all. Robinton reached up automatically to scratch under the runner's jaw. "Stupid beast," he panted.

Turn to section 68.

* 74 *

"I like the puzzle," Robinton said. "The little silver fish. I saw creatures like that from shipboard."

"Ah," Danol said. "You appreciate the accuracy, then. I had a real one to work from. This is the tenth fish I have made. All the others were sold like that!" He snapped his fingers. "And I ask only half a mark. There's real silver in the paint. Not much, I admit, but that makes it costly to do. I sell them for a lot more at Gathers, but I think you really appreciate the skill it takes to make them."

"Half a mark?" Robinton considered, thinking of the contents of his purse. He did like the toy, and the price was fair.

If Robinton has the money, subtract it from the record sheet and note the addition of the fish puzzle. Turn to section 85.

If he has not, turn to section 64.

* 75 *

He decided to risk searching for something to eat. It wasn't the season for berries, or any other big fruit, but nuts should be easy to find, likewise tubers, since he knew what the plant looked like growing. He thought longingly of roast wherry, but he hadn't seen any flocking nearby, and he didn't have time to cook one if he did manage to catch it. It had better be fruits and vegetables.

Roll 3 D6.

If the total is between three and eight, turn to section 90.

If nine or greater, turn to section 97.

* 76 *

Breasting the air like a swimmer pushing through water, Robinton managed to propel himself backward, stopping the forward momentum of his run. He sat down hard, scraping his legs against a small stump that was just exactly where he'd have stepped next. He could have been catapulted clear into the river he could see at the bottom of this valley. This slope was steep!

He made his way carefully down, one hand out for balance, and the other holding the gitar back, keeping it from swinging around in front of him. Both sides of the broad streambed were loaded with big rocks. Fortunately, this was the source end of a river, so it was easy for the young Harper to pick his way across the shallows. A bit wiser, he kept an eye open for snakes.

Turn to section 69.

* 77 *

"Good boy," he said, moving slowly toward the runner. Twitch stuck his head out toward the Harper, putting its ears back. The sudden baring of the long yellow teeth gave Robinton pause, but he continued to press confidently toward the beast. "Easy. Easy. Good Twitch."

He caught hold of the lead with one hand, held up the other for Twitch to see, and then caressed the ears and the side of Twitch's jaw. Offering the runner a mouthful of grass, he continued to talk slowly and calmly. Gradually, the runner relaxed. Its ears swiveled around again, and it nickered to him.

"Of course I forgive you. That was a big scary wher, wasn't it, boy?" Robinton said, stroking the soft nose. "Come on. I want some lunch, and I'll wager you do, too."

Turn to section 71.

* 78 *

"I hope you will have good weather in Nerat," Robinton said, reluctant to end his contact with the craftsman. It felt good to talk to another human again. He'd been very lonely. "It was very fine when I left."

Section 78

"That's a wonder," Danol said darkly. "This is the time of the seasonal rains. I'm afraid that you have much worse weather to look forward to. From here on," he gestured behind him, "you have thick swamplands and wetlands, all the way to Half-Circle. It's not so bad when the road is cut as deep as it is here, but here and there it will be exposed to the strong winds off the sea. You've got another day's travel, maybe a little more." A hacking cough interrupted him again. "Maybe I'll see the healer in Nerat. Ah, I never seem to have time when business is good. Well, good journey to you, Journeyman!" He flicked the reins, and the gray runner ambled off.

Robinton waved to him, and set off in the opposite direction.

The ground was damper as they rode on. Twitch's hooves became caked with stiff mud which fell off in clumps when it got too heavy. Robinton gave up, dismounting to clear the runner's hooves, since they only collected more mud before they'd gone a few dragonlengths. Twitch stepped heavily, snorting at the mucky road.

A layer of clouds wrapped about the sun, darkening the sky. Robinton had to unpack his cloak and heavier tunic. The light one he'd been wearing was no longer warm enough. It felt as though it might rain. He rode on all day, watching the sky. No rain had fallen by the time he made camp.

The smell and the sound of marsh-dwellers told him that he was on the edge of the swamp, and probably not far from Danol's hold, if he only knew where to find it. As it was, he was set for one more night in the rough. Tomorrow, they would reach Half-Circle for sure.

If Robinton is out of food, turn to section 72.

If he still has supplies, turn to section 83.

* 79 *

Robinton circled, not turning his back on Twitch. The runner acted as though it didn't know who he was. He kept talking to it, trying to calm it down.

"Come on, Twitch. Good fellow. Come back up to the road, and I'll give you half a redfruit. You'd like that, wouldn't you?"

The runner stuck its nose out, sniffing at him suspiciously. Robinton eyed the dangling lead under its jaw and lunged for it. Just as quickly, Twitch bit his wrist. Somehow, he kept a hold of the lead and threw himself against the runner's side. It lowered its head and tried to nip at his feet just as Robinton put his foot in the stirrup and boosted himself up. He had to stop the runner attacking him. Twitch sidled against a tree and attempted to brush him off. Robinton flung his leg over the beast's back. He then plunged his heels into the beast's side. Startled, Twitch broke into a trot. Robinton regained his seat, and steered him along the narrow path. Before too long, the runner was reacting normally.

Turn to section 71.

* 80 *

"Good boy," he said, moving slowly toward the runner. Twitch stuck his head out toward the Harper, putting its ears back. The sudden baring of the long yellow teeth gave Robinton pause, but he continued to press confidently toward the beast. "Easy. Easy. Good Twitch." The runner eyed him suspiciously, sniffing.

He caught hold of the lead with one hand, held up the other for Twitch to see, and then caressed the ears and the side of Twitch's jaw. "Yes, you're a good boy. Easy does . . . ow!"

Twitch had inspected the hand holding the lead, and found it to be empty. In disgust, he bit the back of Robinton's hand.

The flesh started to turn purple right away. Robinton stared at it for a moment, then became aware that Twitch was still watching him. He bent and pulled up a handful of grass, which he offered to the runner, continuing to talk slowly and calmly. Gradually, the runner relaxed. Its ears swiveled around again, and it nickered to him.

"Of course I forgive you. That was a big scary wher, wasn't it, boy?" Robinton said, stroking the soft nose. "Come on. I want some lunch, and I'm sure you do, too, if you're trying to eat me."

Take one hit point of damage for the bite.

If his total of hit points falls to zero, turn to section 29.

If not, turn to section 71.

* 81 *

Robinton chose a stick as much like a riding crop in weight and flex that he could from the debris scattered around his hiding place. At least in theory, if he could appear as a figure of authority, he could overmaster

Twitch and herd him back toward the road. By the time they'd reach it, the runner would have calmed down.

He smacked the stick into his palm for effect, then stood up so Twitch could see him. "Here, now," he pronounced ponderously, trying to sound as much as he could like the Lord Holder of Fort. His Lordship had an expression which could halt unruly apprentices in their tracks. Robinton had reason to remember how effective it was. "We'll have none of this unsuitable behavior. Calm down." He swatted the makeshift crop into his palm again. Twitch was just turning around for another run toward him. "You'll be quiet, and we can resume our journey. Do you understand?" Smack. He got up on the path and stood directly in the runner's way, preparing to steer him down the hill. Smack!

Roll 1 D6.

If the number rolled is 1 through 4, turn to section 73.

If it is 5 or 6, turn to section 65.

* 82 *

"How much for this and the box?" Robinton asked, holding up the fish puzzle.

Danol rubbed his lips with the back of a knuckle, considering. "I'll tell you what, Harper. Since we're not at the Gather yet, I don't have pitch prices to pay. Two and a half marks for the both of them. You won't find a better price in Nerat nor Benden. Holders can pay for craftsmanship like this."

If Robinton chooses to buy both, subtract the money from the record sheet and note the addition of the box and the fish puzzle. Turn to section 85.

If he chooses instead to buy only the box after all, turn to section 62.

If he decides to buy only the fish puzzle, turn to section 74.

If he wants neither, turn to section 64.

* 83 *

When morning came, he rummaged in his pack, thinking avidly of breakfast. Twitch swiveled interested ears toward the sound, remembering fruit rinds and bread. Grinning at the eager runner, Robinton reached into the carrysack and drew out crusts for Twitch and a whole breadroll for himself. He tapped the roll with a fingernail. It was hard. There was only one piece of fruit left, and it had been bruised on one side, but it smelled sweet and inviting.

Twitch whickered over his treat, and then went back to cropping grass. Robinton watched him over a bite of his redfruit. "If I could eat what you do, my friend, I wouldn't have to carry a pack! And I'd never have to worry about its being fresh. All of my bread is stale now." He broke the roll into several sections. He had no preserves or sweet spreads, but if he drizzled redfruit juice onto it, it would be soft enough to eat.

A square of cheese finished his meal, and he was ready to go on.

Turn to section 93.

* 84 *

He reasoned that it would be better to lure Twitch to him than frighten him further out of his limited wits. He rose slowly to his feet and saw that Twitch was wheeling to gallop back toward him from the other end of the path.

"Good Twitch," he said, cooing the phrase. "There's a fine fellow. Come to me." The runner seemed to pause, then continued its headlong gallop past Robinton. The Harper ignored the runner's hysteria, chatting to him as though he was a Holder child who had fallen down. "Don't be frightened. I'm your friend, you know that. Come to me. Good Twitch." He held out his hand.

The runner shied at the hand, rearing up on his back legs in surprise, but he stopped. Robinton spoke comfortingly to it, waiting for it to calm down. He stepped forward, his hand held out.

Turn to section 77.

* 85 *

Robinton put his purchase away in the bag with his clothes and personal goods. He felt satisfied with his bargain, though his purse was lighter. So apparently did Danol, who hummed a little as he repacked the rest of his wares.

Turn to section 78.

* 86 *

Robinton felt concern for the unhappy runner. If Twitch was having trouble walking, perhaps there was something caught in his foot. There had been big thorns and sharp stones all the way along the road since Nerat. Guiltily, he remembered that he hadn't examined the runner's feet since the weather had turned bad.

He pulled back on the leads. Twitch stopped with a snort, looking back over his shoulder at his young master. Robinton patted the wet mane and scrambled off the pad, awkwardly now because of the gitar. With a little persuasion and brute force, Robinton contrived to lift Twitch's foot and examine it. Yes, there was a sharp object wedged in the sensitive single toe. He pried it out with his belt knife and peered at the foot. It was bleeding slightly. He blotted at it with the edge of his cloak and applied a little numbweed to it from the jar in his pack.

Twitch gave him a grateful nudge as the anesthetic properties of the salve took effect. As soon as the numbweed hardened, Robinton let go of the foot. He decided to lead the beast rather than ride it, lest he irritate the sore hoof to infection. It wasn't far now to Half-Circle.

Turn to section 99.

* 87 *

"Don't try to confuse me," Teer said, angrily. "You talk too much."

"Shut up," Daro growled, lunging at Robinton.

DARO
To be hit: 11 *To hit Robinton: 12* *Hit points: 5*

TEER
To be hit: 10 *To hit Robinton: 13* *Hit points: 7*

All three men do 1 D6 non-fatal damage with their fists.

Robinton may strike only one opponent with each hit. The seamen will continue to fight until both (or Robinton) are unconscious.

If the seamen win, turn to section 105.

If Robinton wins, turn to section 95.

* 88 *

"Stop!" Orelia cried, managing to get between Robinton and the seaman's next punch. "He's a Harper! You must never attack a Harper. All Pern knows that."

Her beau, startled by her intervention, as if he was hearing her voice for the first time, stopped short. He regarded his friend, and looked again at Robinton. His hand dropped.

Orelia caught hold of the young Harper's arm and drew him to a chair. His lip was puffy and bleeding, and there were other bruises starting. She shot a reproachful look at the two young seamen and left the room. When she returned in a moment with a jar, they both looked expectantly at her, but she ignored them.

"It's numbweed, Harper." Orelia dabbed a little on the lip and facial bruises. Immediately, the injuries stung and then went dead. Robinton accepted the jar from her and withdrew to the room assigned to him. While he anointed the sore places of his body with the healing salve, he could hear her voice, getting louder and louder, in the main room.

When he returned, the two seamen were sitting in their former seats, not looking at her or each other.

Daro spoke first. "We owe an apology to you, Harper," he said, uncomfortably. "We have broken an ancient tradition. I'm sorry."

"I, too," Teer said. "Are you badly hurt?"

"No, not at all," Robinton said, amiably. He sat down cautiously, but the numbweed had done its work well. He didn't feel a thing. His fingers described a short run on the gitar strings. "Come, shall we begin again? I have recently taken a long journey by ship, and I learned many Sea Holder songs from the crew. Perhaps I know one of your favorites?"

"Oh, yes." Orelia, eager to end the discomfort, clapped her hands. "Do you know this one?" She began to hum, and Robinton recognized the tune. He picked it out, and then played the chorus. "Yes, that's the one."

He began again, playing the introduction to give the seamen time to sit down and make themselves comfortable. They relaxed, and were soon singing along with Robinton and Orelia.

Roll 1 D6 for hit points regained by use of numbweed.
Turn to section 92.

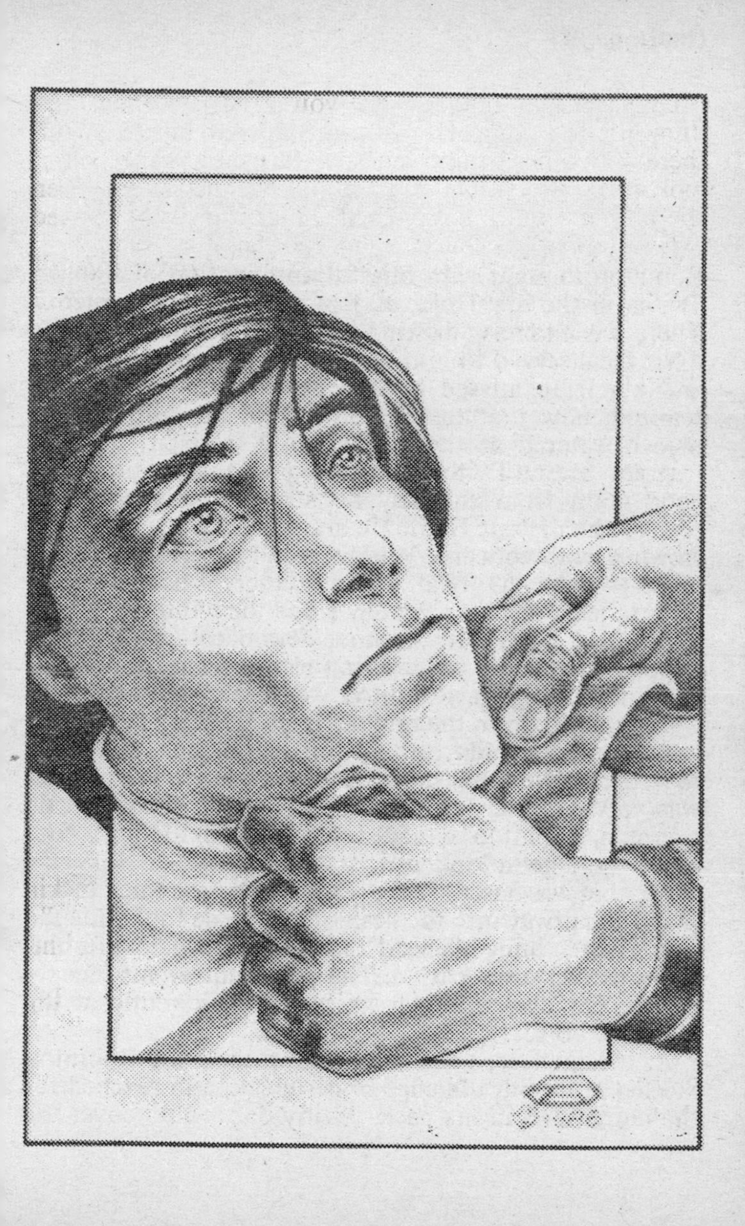

* 89 *

Robinton thought with blissful anticipation of stabling Twitch in the dry Hold, and putting on dry garments. There was a fantasy drifting through his mind of having a hot meal served to him by a pretty girl, and a hot fire, and klah! He missed his morning cup more than he realized; now that the custom might be resumed, his mouth watered at the remembered taste of the rich, fragrant brew. Twitch snorted, probably anticipating good grain from the way he stretched his neck out toward the distant Hold. He stumbled again. Robinton frowned with concern. Was the road deteriorating that much in the rain? By all accounts there'd been a downpour at least once a sevenday since the winter's end.

No, that wasn't it. Another few paces, and Twitch tripped again, this time falling to one knee, and struggling upright again. Robinton was nearly unseated and exposed his gitar to the rain again as his cloak flew open.

Pulling the folds around his shoulders, Robinton tugged on Twitch's leads and dismounted. The runner was very definitely favoring one foot. With some little coercion, Robinton managed to get Twitch to lift the foot so he could get a look at it.

Ah, that was nasty. There was a stone, or a thick thorn, plunged halfway into the flesh of the single toe inside the hoof. Twitch hung his head and rubbed it against Robinton's back in supplication. The youth cursed his inexperience, but drew his belt knife and dug gently at the intrusive object.

As it came free, a gush of blood washed out. Robinton blotted at it with the edge of his cloak, and reached for the numbweed in his pack. A tiny dab would cover the wound. It could do little at this point but ease the pain. Possibly the foot was already infected. He shielded it from the rain and waited for the salve to harden.

At last, he picked up the lead and started again toward the Sea Hold. The gitar was transferred to his back, making the cloak gape open in the front. He was thoroughly wet now, and mud was coming in the hole in the toe of his boot. Twitch followed him, keeping his head lowered. He seemed not to care where they were going. Robinton kept a gentle pull on the lead, but took great care not to tug on it suddenly.

Without warning, the runner stumbled, knocking Robinton off his feet. The Harper measured his length in the slippery mud. Spitting out dirt and bits of gravel, Robinton climbed back to his feet. He turned, brushing himself off, to berate Twitch for his clumsiness, but stopped. The runner was back on one knee, and the pained look in his eyes said that he wouldn't be able to go on much longer.

One by one, Robinton lifted his baggage off of the runner's back. Free of burdens, Twitch was able to stand on all four feet again. The two of them tottered slowly through the rain toward the Hold.

Turn to section 99.

* 90 *

The trees around him had only little curled leaves and buds. What he wanted were old nut trees. This year's growth would be side by side on the branches with last year's. Moving off the path, he sought the boles of trees he knew in Fort Hold. There was a thick old gentleman of the forest; one which produced a round, tan nut the shells of which children made play spoons. Ink was made from the bark, as was a deep shaded dye for hides and cloth. An altogether useful tree. He collected some whole nuts from the ground, and from the branches which he could reach easily. Those went into the carrysack.

Next, he found a tuber plant. A heave freed the oblong vegetable from the ground, and he used his belt knife to trim off the shoots. His father had explained that the plant above the tubers could be poisonous to humans, so he was careful to get rid of all of it. Of the two fist-sized tubers, one had a black hole deep into one end. Robinton didn't want to guess if it had a creature nibbling away at it, or if it had simply rotted in the damp ground. The other was healthy, though smaller. He'd tuck it into the embers of his fire for a while, risking the rain. Tubers were no good raw.

His last find was a double discovery. Under the branches of another nut tree stood a smaller gnarled tree, with wizened fruit hanging among the new buds. He found a few which were sound, and packed them away. He went back to his camp to cook his tuber. He'd have to set out soon. The sky was darkening fast.

Turn to section 100.

* 91 *

Daro is not aware that the slimmer Harper's strength is nearly equal to his own. Robinton relaxes his stance, trying to look resigned to the beating Daro raises his massive fist to deliver. Then, just at the last moment, the Harper dives forward and down.

Daro's fist smashes into the wall. More falling than diving forward, the journeyman is barely able to control his motion, but he manages to ram a shoulder into Daro's stomach. Daro's cry of pain is cut off as his breath *whoosh*es out of him.

Knowing he has to take the slim advantage he has gained, Robinton wraps an arm around the breathless seaman and uses his legs to drive him backward across the room. Just before they reach a large waist-high table, the young Harper pulls hard up and lets Daro continue to fly over it.

Breathless and off balance the confused seaman sprawls backward. Disoriented, he lets the force of his momentum carry him over the table and head first onto a bench which splits and spills him to the floor.

He lands with such force Robinton is briefly concerned that he may have broken the man's neck or cracked his skull. He takes a step forward. Daro groans loudly. For a moment he looks confused, as if remembering the Harper's earlier admonitions on who his true rival was. Then his head drops to the ground again.

To his own amazement, Robinton finds himself breathing in gasps, but standing triumphantly next to Orelia. Teer stares at Robinton, and begins to move toward him purposefully.

Belatedly, Jumerti came to the head of the stairs and yelled, "What's going on down there?"

Turn to section 88.

* 92 *

Robinton's journey with Numa aboard the *Sea Dragon* had done him much good. He was able with only small reminders to play nearly everything that his hostess and her two friends wished to hear. He also sang for them new songs from the Harper Hall, but it was clear from their expressions that they would rather listen to songs they knew, though they heard him out politely.

Teer was a baritone, as he himself was, Orelia a high soprano, and Daro a pleasant though untrained tenor. Measuring their voices, he struck the opening chords to the "Ballad of Moreta's Ride." The three regarded him curiously. He sang the opening for them. It suited his baritone range, and he nodded to Teer to join him. They smiled at him in comprehension, waiting for the parts they knew they could sing. When they faltered, he would nod to them, singing the words until they picked up the line. It was the smallest chorus he'd ever performed with, but the gusto with which they sang forgave any inadequacies in their voices.

The ballad forced Orelia to sing both the main part and the ending descants as solos, but she had ceased to look self-conscious. Robinton could tell that she was not going to be able to hit the highest notes, so he transposed the key before she began the last section. They all knew the ballad well. It had been a part of the traditional Teachings for hundreds of Turns, and as they approached the tragic ending, their faces grew solemn. Orelia stopped her voice from cracking until she ended the song. Robinton played a final gentle coda and laid his hand over the strings of his gitar.

There was a long moment of silence. Teer sighed, nodding approval to Robinton. Orelia rose from her chair and slipped out of the room. She was back in a moment with a bottle and a tray of glasses. She poured wine for them, and passed it out, prettily presenting Robinton's glass to him. He took a grateful swallow, identifying the sweet, smooth liquid as Benden wine.

Thus fortified, he began to play again. His audience seemed content just to let him play whatever he liked. He sang sagas and comic songs, Weyr ballads and love songs. Teer and Daro smiled at him, forgetting that they had ever had an argument. Orelia listened from her chair for a while, and ended up sitting at his feet.

Her two admirers never noticed her shift in position until Robinton came to the end of his song. Orelia sighed, resting her head on one hand and gazing limpidly up at the Harper. He smiled at her as he took a sip of wine.

A sound alerted him to look up at his other listeners. Teer and Daro were trying hard not to glare, but there was marked disapproval on both their faces. Robinton began to think of what best he should do, when Orelia laid a gentle hand on his knee.

"Oh, Robinton, play me a sea ballad. Please?" He couldn't help but notice how pretty she was, or how her eyes shone in the light of the glows.

He glanced up again. The two men began to shift in their seats.

If Robinton should agree, turn to section 98.

If he should refuse, turn to section 101.

* 93 *

Today he should reach Half-Circle Sea Hold by the afternoon. With anything like luck, the rain would hold off until then, but Robinton doubted it. A heavy curtain of clouds stretched from west to northeast. Twitch sniffed the air doubtfully. He sensed a storm. He looked over his shoulder at his master, wondering why they were not in a quiet, warm cavern instead of walking right into bad weather.

Robinton urged him on. "That's where we're going, silly beast. You don't expect me to build a shelter around you, do you? We'll be warm and dry soon, if you get moving along. I'd like a hot meal myself."

Twitch snorted, but didn't balk again. He plodded on, blowing disgustedly through his lips.

Turn to section 100.

* 94 *

Teer stood back, blinking stupidly. "I have no quarrel with you," he echoed.

"Then get out of my way, fishguts!" Daro shoved past him and lunged at Robinton.

DARO
To be hit: 11 *To hit Robinton: 12* *Hit points: 5*

Damage with fists: 1 D6 of non fatal damage. Reaching zero points is being knocked out.

If Daro knocks Robinton out, turn to section 104.

If Robinton knocks Daro out, turn to section 91.

* 95 *

Neither seaman is aware that the slimmer Harper's strength is nearly equal to their own. Robinton relaxes in Teer's grip, trying to look resigned to the beating Daro raises his massive fist to deliver. Then just at the last moment, the Harper dives forward and down.

Daro's fist smashes into Teer's chest and the second seaman is thrown backward into a chair, protesting indignantly. He loses his grip on the Harper who is already straining to pull free. More falling than diving forward, the journeyman is barely able to control his motion, ramming a lucky shoulder into Daro's stomach.

The blow is augmented by the larger seaman's own forward motion and his breath rushes out in a painful *whoosh!* Knowing he has to take the slim advantage he has gained, Robinton wraps an arm around the breathless man and uses his legs to drive him backward across the room. Just before they reach a large waist-high table, the young Harper pulls hard up and lets Daro continue on alone.

Breathless and off balance, the confused seaman sprawls backward. Disoriented, he lets the force of his momentum carry him over the table and head first onto a bench, which splits and spills him to the floor.

He lands with such force Robinton is concerned that he may have broken the man's neck or cracked his skull. He takes a step forward, and then Teer's rough hand on his shoulder spins him around.

The second sailor's face is livid with rage. A purple bruise is already beginning to discolor his chin. Screaming, the man rains a series of wild blows against the arms Robinton instinctively raises. Taking a step back the Harper gains a momentary respite from the battering.

Remembering his one advantage over the larger and stronger man is his greater speed and wit, he begins dancing backward through the tables and chairs, taunting the larger man to follow him. Concerned only with catching the elusive Harper, Teer leaves an opening and Robinton aims a blow at him. The Harper lands a powerful uppercut and discovers the man has a jaw of stone. Fearing he might break his fingers before he could knock Teer out, Robinton passes up several opportunities to land further blows on Teer's jaw. Instead he continues to harass the larger man with jabs to his face. The enraged man seems hardly to notice the punches. The journeyman's arms are becoming harder and harder to swing with any force behind them.

Finally Teer stops and turns when Daro groans loudly. For a moment he looks confused, as if remembering the Harper's earlier admonitions as to who was his true rival.

Realizing it is not very sporting but unwilling to give Teer another chance to strike him, Robinton uses the distraction to grab the handle of a large pitcher off a table. Swinging the heavy clay pot he crashes it into the side of Teer's head. The big seaman collapses amid a wash of stale water and shards.

To his own amazement, Robinton finds himself standing triumphantly next to Orelia. She favors him with an admiring glance.

Moving as steadily as he can, he sits down in his chair again and picks up his gitar. As the two seamen stagger to their feet, Teer bemusedly dripping water, Robinton gestures them both to be seated. Realizing that they've had the worst of the fight, they sit down, looking sheepish. The journeyman smiles beatifically on them, and tunes a string on his gitar.

"And now, my friends, what may I play for you?"

Turn to section 92.

* 96 *

"Listen, Harper," Teer said, holding a fist under his nose. "You stay out of this. If you are a guest of the Hold, mind your own business."

"Good gentleman," Robinton said soothingly, "I had no intention of minding anyone else's. There is no need for us to quarrel." He played a little run on the gitar strings.

The sound seemed to irritate Daro, who grabbed at Robinton's wrist. Daro was very strong, but Robinton's arms and hands were like steel wire from years of playing. He concentrated on not alarming the seaman by moving out of his grasp too quickly.

Daro gave his arm a little shake, as if challenging him. Robinton jumped back, raising his other hand to ward a blow from his face. The seaman appeared to think that constituted acceptance of the challenge and thrust the Harper backward. He assumed a fighting stance.

Robinton saw the action coming, and prepared to defend himself, he hoped, without shedding blood. His or the Holders'.

"Are you starting a fight, Harper?" Teer asked. Clearly, he had missed the silent confrontation, and only noticed when both of the other men had their hands raised.

"Stay out of this, Teer," Robinton ordered, trying to sound authoritative, keeping his eyes on Daro.

"Sea Holders stick together," Teer said in flat tones as if reciting a lesson, moving to catch hold of the young Harper's arms. Robinton backed away from them. He could see Orelia out of the corner of one eye, her knuckles to her mouth, eyes open wide. She must not have realized what a hive of feelings she had stirred up. Orelia hadn't any command of the powers she wielded. He felt sorry for her.

The next thing he felt was the wall pressed against his back.

"Why are you helping your rival?" Robinton asked quickly. "I've done nothing to offend you."

Teer seemed to hesitate.

Roll 3 D6.

If the total is the same or less than Robinton's Charisma minus 2, then turn to section 94.

If the total is greater, turn to section 87.

* 97 *

The trees around him had only little curled leaves and buds. What he wanted were old nut trees. Last year's growth would be scattered on the ground, little affected by the Cold. Moving off the path, he sought the boles of trees he knew in Fort Hold. There was a thick old gentleman of the forest; one which produced a round, tan nut the shells of which children made play spoons. Ink could be made from the bark, as could dye for hides and cloth. He searched through the fallen leaves at its foot and found plenty of the empty shells, but none at all that hadn't been cracked by beasts or bored by insects.

He found a few tuber plants, but they had no roots of decent size. His mother had shown him how small tubers were green inside, and not fit for human beings to eat. The one of eating size which he did find had a blackened hole in it, probably from rotting in the wet ground.

There was a wizened fruit tree under the shelter of a taller nut tree. It was just breaking into bud. Standing where it did, it couldn't take advantage of the sunlight. Probably it couldn't produce much fruit even in season.

The nut tree yielded among the leaves on the forest floor a mere handful of the smooth, egg-shaped nuts. He pocketed those greedily, knowing that the small offering to his stomach would make him more ravenous than ever later.

He went back to find Twitch. The sky was darkening fast.

Turn to section 100.

* 98 *

He smiled at her. "All right." His fingers began to weave the delicate music of a ballad he'd heard while on board the *Sea Dragon*. It described how men felt about the sea: not as a tyrant or an obstacle to be overcome, but rather as a lover sees his mistress, to be wooed. Orelia moved gently to recline against his knee, still watching him adoringly.

"I've never heard it sung like that before," she said, when the last notes died away.

"Surely Kender has played that for the Hold," Robinton protested. "I was told it was a very well-known song."

"Oh, he's played it for the Hold," she pouted. "But not for me." She picked up the end of her braid and brushed it back and forth across the back of his hand. "That was lovely." Robinton felt himself reddening with pleasure and embarrassment.

A wordless growl reminded him that he had more

audience than one Sea Holder girl, however beautiful and attentive.

"Gentlemen, and mistress," he said, recovering himself and speaking with the utmost formality he could muster, "I had a long and tiring journey today, and I begin another early tomorrow. Sleep would do much to restore me." He rose from his chair and bowed to the others, whose expressions did not change. "It has been an enjoyable evening." He started toward the door, but the two young Holders headed him off.

Deliberately misreading their motive, Robinton extended his hand to Daro. The seaholder glanced at it without interest and returned his glare to Robinton's face.

"The lady has better prospects than you, Harper. It'd be better for you if you backed off from where you're not wanted. She knows more than to waste her time on worthless types like you."

Robinton was provoked, but he didn't let his face show his reaction. He wanted to make a retort that would wipe the smug look off the man's face, but he didn't know if he dared. If word got back to the Harper Hall that he was brawling! Or worse, to Benden! On the other hand, he didn't know if he should let an insult go unanswered.

If he should take offense at the remark, turn to section 102.

If he decides not to, turn to section 111.

* 99 *

Robinton and Twitch caused quite a sensation appearing at the doors of Half-Circle Sea Hold. A bedraggled, obviously lame runner beast and a wringing wet, shock-haired, long-shanked boy laden with bundles like a fruit tree in autumn were not what a respectable Sea Hold expected to find on its steps during a rainstorm.

Fortunately, the Holders were prepared to care for runner beasts. Twitch was taken away, limping and complaining, by a thick-armed, heavyset man who reminded Robinton of Numa, toward the Dock Cave, a vast natural, flooded cavern in which the people of Half-Circle actually docked their fishing boats and kept their few runners and burden beasts. Robinton watched his beast being led away until he was dragged bodily inside the huge metal doors.

"Well, look at you." A short, plump woman with sparkling black eyes looked him up and down, her glance coming to rest on his many cases. "And where did you come from, Harper? You are a Harper, are you not?" For the first time, the confident tone dropped. She wiped off the crafthall patch on his shoulder.

"Yes, my lady," Robinton said. "Journeyman Robinton, at your service."

"Katoras, wife of Sea Holder Mitran." She made a little courtesy, which Robinton returned, causing his bags to clash together. "Welcome, Journeyman Robinton. You're absolutely soaked. Doesn't the Harper Hall teach its folk to shield against bad weather?"

"My runner went lame," he said, clearing his throat. Thank goodness he didn't seem to have taken cold. "I think we'd have been here before the rain, if not for that and a few other adventures we've had."

"I'll wait to hear it until you're dry and fed." Her eyebrows went up as he began to set down his bundles. "Why, there's nothing to you but a lot of sticks, child. When was the last time you had a meal?"

He began to explain, holding up his supply pack, but she waved it away impatiently. "A real meal. Ah, not for a long time, eh? Where are you from?"

"I've just come from Nerat, but I have traveled all the way from the Harpercrafthall in Fort Hold."

"Ah. A long journey. Which ship?"

"The *Sea Dragon.* Captain Elaus."

"Is that so? Pern's a small place after all. He's my blood brother. Wait until I tell Mitran; he'll be amazed. I came from High Reaches, but the Sea Holder courted me to come here as his wife. Well, come along. We'll see you dried off, then introduce you to the Hold Harper. Do you mind guesting in a family's cot? I'll find accommodation for you while you visit Kender."

"Thank you," was all that Robinton could get in now and again, as Katoras, chattering, led him through smooth stone passages to a bathing room.

Once he was supplied with cleansing sand and a fresh bath sheet, Katoras made off with his pack and wet clothes, saying that she'd see they were washed and decently mended. He had to admit that they showed the wear of his journey. In fact, they seemed quite shabby by comparison to the crisp clothes of the Sea Holder's lady and her drudges.

He sank deep in the hot tub of water. Every muscle was slowly unlocking, and it felt wonderful to him. All he needed now was the pretty girl with klah. Ah, footsteps. As if on cue, a girl appeared, bustling in with a laden tray. She smiled timidly at him, and set down her burden. She wasn't especially pretty, but there assuredly was klah in the pot she carried. He could smell its aroma as she poured a generous serving into a heavy mug.

"My blessings on you," Robinton said, accepting the cup and inhaling the fragrance blissfully. "And on your mistress."

"Thank you, sir," the girl replied, shyly. "Um, I'm also to cut your hair." When Robinton gave her a shocked look, she hastened to explain. "I thought you'd requested one, sir. Katoras said it should be done. I'm very careful, sir. I never cut the skin."

"It's all right," Robinton said, reassuringly. "Forgive me. I must be shaggy as a beast by now. Please go ahead."

She indicated that he should sit with his back to her. He was impressed with the gentle dispatch with which she brushed out his thick dark mane and clipped off the long ends. "There," she said, finally. "It's done."

Robinton smiled at her. "And you didn't cut me. Thank you."

She glanced at him wistfully as she took the shears and the empty tray away. He slid farther into the bathing tub and wrapped both long hands around the cup, sighing with pleasure. The chill was gone from his bones, and the hot liquid melted the ice in his throat and stomach. "I could die happy right here," he said aloud, sinking neck deep again, with only head and hands out of the water. He took a sip of klah.

Loud laughter startled him into splashing bolt upright. Klah splashed out over his hand. He sputtered, brushing at the hot liquid. The intruders stood in the doorway, hands on hips, grinning from ear to ear at his discomfiture.

"Mustn't die in the bath," the larger of the two said, still chortling. He was a big, fair man with wind-weathered features. "Inconsiderate behavior."

"Harper Robinton?" the other, a sharp-featured redhead, said, waving the large man to silence. "I'm Kender, Hold Harper to Sea Holder Mitran." He bowed, deferring to his companion.

"How do you do, gentlemen?" Robinton answered, blushing.

"A bit better than you, by all accounts," the Sea Holder said. "My good wife is turning the Hold upside down setting things in order for you."

"Sir, I don't mean to be any trouble. . . ."

"You are none. Katoras loves company. Why do you think there are no guest rooms available in this Hold today? All are filled with guests! None empty for wandering Harpers who arrive drenched during a downpour. But we'll have fine fishing on the morrow. The schools are well stirred up in a gale like this one. We'll see you in the morning, then?"

"Yes, of course," Robinton spluttered. "I mean, I'd be honored."

"Good. You're welcome here. Good night." Mitran withdrew, leaving his Harper behind to chat with Robinton.

"So," Kender said, sitting down on the side of the bathing tub and helping himself to klah, "give me the news. Where's a Harper going from Nerat?"

"Benden Hold," Robinton answered. "It's my first assignment outside of the Harper Hall." He took a sip of what was left of his drink.

Kender cocked his head to one side, peering at Robinton. "You must be something else, then, me boyo. First-timers don't go to Benden. They go to Hold Gar or Lewis."

"Actually," Robinton said, pretending abashment, "I think it was the Apprentice Master's idea. He always said he wanted me as far away from him as possible."

"Master Morshal?" Kender laughed. Robinton nodded. "Is he still teaching? I thought he was a hundred Turns old."

"Oh, at least." Robinton squeezed his flexible features into a flawless imitation of the sour-faced Master. "When I was an apprentice, I had more respect for the Teachings of my elders than you have apparently ever learned. Or ever will!"

Kender hooted. "That's old Marshface to the teeth! He didn't catch you doing that, did he?"

"He did."

"My apologies, Journeyman. You *are* something else." He threw a bath sheet to Robinton. "Go on, get dressed and I'll take you to Jumerti's house. It's almost time for the evening meal."

A line of small houses stretched along the inside of the curve of Half-Circle Harbor. Jumerti and his family occupied the fourth one to the east of the Hold. Robinton hurried along in Kender's wake, clutching his gitar and his pack. Katoras had supplied a pair of whole boots, refusing to return the torn and mudstained pair he had removed before his bath.

"I have no idea how you walked so far in those on that wet road," she shook her head at him. "It's lucky to gift a Harper, so you take those and just consider you've done me a favor." He thanked her and followed Kender out of the Hold, enjoying the feel of the new hide around his feet. The soles clicked cheerfully on the stone stairs.

He had to admit the idea of a meal waxed importantly in his mind just now. The interesting smells wafting out of the open doors of the other small houses made his stomach rumble alarmingly but not, he hoped, audibly.

Jumerti's wife, Lian, bid Robinton welcome. It was apparent that Kender was a frequent visitor to all the small houses in Half-Circle. He was obviously well liked. Lian bade them sit down and called to her daughter Orelia to serve them. One of Lian's sons was dispatched to the kitchen to fetch the family's meal. "With food for two more," she called after him.

Orelia proved to be a girl of surprising beauty, with

dark golden hair and wide sea-gray eyes. She smiled prettily at Robinton and poured him a mug of steaming klah. Robinton allowed himself a small smile of his own, remembering his fancy of the rainstorm.

"I'm not on a turn in the kitchen today, thank the Egg," Lian said, bustling around. "There's those run off their feet because of the merchant's caravan."

"They leave tomorrow, Lian," Kender said, trying to sound light.

"They're a nuisance," the woman said, disgustedly. "Tried to sell me some woven goods, but they were just plain shoddy. Shoddy! I wouldn't give 'em a sixty-fourth piece for 'em, I said."

"Well, you'd know good weaving, Lian," Kender told her, soothingly. "No one could fool *you.*"

Jumerti came in, his booming voice filling the small room. "Lian, is the meal ready?"

"I've just now sent Alt for it. Here he is." The boy raced headlong into the room, almost upsetting the heavy pot he held in both hands. He also had a woven basket full of bread under one arm.

"Well, well," Jumerti said, noticing the Harpers. "The drowned boy! Katoras said you'd be guesting with us." He pumped Robinton's hand jovially, and nodded to Kender.

Robinton recognized Jumerti as the Holder who'd taken charge of Twitch. "Yes, sir. Thank you for your hospitality. How is my runner beast?"

The man's face saddened. "The foot's infected. Poor beast. I'll do my best with him, but it'll be a sevenday or more before he's walking again."

"A sevenday! That's too long for me to wait. I'll have to leave before then. I must get to Benden Hold as soon as I can."

"Well, you'll leave without him, then. He can't walk far. He would, but he can't. I'll tell you what, though. I'll buy him from you. He's a good beast. Friendly, willing as can be. We'll work out a fair price."

Robinton liked the way Jumerti sounded. His instincts told him to trust him. "Agreed."

"Good. Then shall we eat?"

After the meal had been cleared away, Kender excused himself and went back to attend the Sea Holder. "There are a few fosterings to arrange, and the merchants have agreed to take the information north for us. Can't waste an opportunity." Robinton was shown to a small room. The cot had a well-plumped rush bag and pillow, and the room smelled fresh even though there were no windows by which it could be easily aired. "I hope you'll be comfortable here, Robinton," Lian said.

"Yes, thank you."

"Are you tired now? Perhaps you'll come out and sing for us. If you know a new one or two, we'd be grateful."

Robinton elected to rejoin the family. By the time he had his few belongings arranged, two strapping young sailors had arrived to visit in the main room of the house.

"Harper Robinton," Jumerti said formally, "meet Daro and Teer."

He bowed to them, and they nodded curtly back. Neither of them appeared to be in a mood to chat. Robinton sat down near Lian and began to tune his gitar, thinking of what songs he knew that might please a Sea Holder. Orelia came sweeping into the room, and the cause of Daro's and Teer's bad moods became obvious. They were rivals for the girl's affections. Fierce rivals. And both here at the same time. An uncomfortable situation, if ever he'd seen one.

He started to strum one of the songs he had learned aboard the *Sea Dragon* from Numa. Lian smiled in recognition of the tune, a traditional sea song, and let herself sway gently to its rhythm. Orelia sat down between her two beaux, seemingly unaware of the ill will they had for one another. Robinton tried not to stare, concentrating rather on the Holder and his wife, who were enjoying his music. Instead, he looked over surreptitiously from time to time

The young men spoke in low tones, occasionally shooting glances at Orelia's father to see if he was listening to them. Robinton gradually discovered that Orelia did indeed know of her suitors' rivalry, and what was more, she was enjoying it.

Daro and Teer abruptly stopped speaking in undertones, and exploded into a loud argument.

"She said she'd be faithful to me! To me, not some undersecond netman's mate!"

"And what do you know about women, or fishing either?"

"I know you don't use the same bait on both, you stupid wherry!"

"So I should talk loudly about prospects I don't have, eh?"

And in the middle of all the chaos, Orelia sat, demurely looking from one brawny young man to the other in pretended shock. When neither noticed her, she let the corners of her pouting pink lips turn up. She liked having them fight over her. She seemed to consider it her due.

"Gentlemen!" Jumerti bellowed. The combatants looked at him and fell silent. "That's better. I am going to bed. Freedom of our house to you. Good night, *gentlemen*," he finished, stressing the last word and holding out his hand to his wife. She rose, thanked Robinton for his playing, and followed her husband out of the room.

Teer and Daro stood and glared at one another over Orelia's head. It was clear that in a moment they would come to blows. Robinton felt nervous about interfering, especially between two men who could take turns tearing him apart without any effort.

The argument had begun again.

"You steered her away from me, you thieving fishgutter."

"Better a gutter than a sack of fishguts!"

"She should know better than to associate with you. There've been rocks in your nets so your catches seem to weigh more. She'd never know when she'd go hungry with you. Can't eat stones."

"Can't think with stones. That's why you can't think!"

Robinton could listen to no more. He bent around his gitar and struck a loud chord, looking as though he was only tuning the instrument. When he raised his head, they were all looking at him. Continuing to strum, he got up and strolled between the two young men.

"Gentlemen, and lady," he bowed to Orelia, "it's too nice a night for fighting. It's a Harper's honor, when hospitality is extended to one of us, to return the kindness as best it can be. May I play a song or two for you?" His hand wandered down the gitar neck, modulating into another key. He struck up the song of the Sea Serpent, looking appealingly from one seaman to the other, as his fingers flew along the strings, enticing them into the song.

Roll 3 D6.

If the total is greater than Robinton's value for Charisma, turn to section 96.

If less than or equal, turn to section 103.

* 100 *

Before too long, it was raining. Robinton rode down the hill, hunched unhappily under his cloak. He could see the humped backs of Half-Circle's cliffs up ahead through the heavy marsh growth. He'd welcome a chance for a hot bath and a seat next to a fire. The gloomy browns of the Sea Hold and the band of purple water beyond it perfectly matched his mood. Gusts of wind blew stinging drops into his face. The rain and the sea roared in his ears.

He was too miserable even to check his bags, to make sure that no water was leaking in on his instruments. His gitar he held clutched protectively to him under the cloak, but even it was getting a little wet, as rainwater trickled inside his hood and down his front.

The yellow dust of the road was beginning to turn into a gluey ochre mud, under which stones sat, waiting for an unwary step. Robinton steered Twitch away from the biggest of them, but those he couldn't see kept pecking against the runner's hooves. Twitch walked with his head well down and his ears back. It was clear this was not the beast's favorite weather. Well, it wasn't Robinton's, either.

Twitch lifted his feet and set them down as if in a daze. He would change his path unconsciously, until Robinton could see that they were heading straight for a tree. Then he would jerk the lead to one side. Twitch would shake his head, dislodging a shower of raindrops from his mane, as if he was unaware why they were going that way, and resume his head-down plodding.

Gradually, Twitch began to peck more often with his

left forefoot. He stumbled several times on the way down the hill, always to that side. At the bottom, his walk smoothed out. It was raining harder than ever now. Twitch didn't stumble again, but he was clearly as miserable as his master. Fortunately, the Hold was straight ahead on a gently sloping road.

If Robinton should dismount and examine the foreleg now, turn to section 86.

If he chooses not to, turn to section 89.

* 101 *

Robinton cleared his throat and drank the last sip of wine from his cup. "Forgive me," he said, shaking his head regretfully, setting down the empty goblet. "I had a hard journey today, and I begin another early tomorrow. Sleep would do much to restore me." He rose from his chair and bowed to the others, whose expressions began to relax. They seemed as relieved as he.

Extending a hand, he raised Orelia to her feet. She stood up very close to him. Her skin was warm and fragrant, and the soft golden locks of her braided hair brushed against his hand. Her smile was the loveliest thing he had ever seen, until he looked into her eyes, in which there was a silent appeal just for him. Robinton was uncomfortably aware that she was attracted to him. He was to her, he had to admit, but it was an inconvenient time with her gigantic admirers just a few arms-lengths away. With much private regret, he bowed over her hand.

"Good night, mistress. Thank you and yours for your most generous hospitality. Gentlemen, good night."

He retreated to the small chamber and settled himself alone into the deep rush mattress.

Turn to section 120.

* 102 *

"I think you wrong the lady," Robinton said, coolly. "She's capable of determining what is agreeable to her and what is not. If she chooses to pay attention to me, it is certainly not a bad reflection on *me.*" The insult, turned back, dawned slowly on the seamen.

Daro caught a bunched handful of Robinton's tunic and slammed him hard against the hold wall. The abused muscles in his back caused him to gasp in pain. "Watch how you talk to *men,* wherry-legs. If you were a man, you'd be doing a man's work, not dandling around with a stringed box." Robinton curled his arm protectively around the gitar but kept his chin high. Teer started forward fists up, angling around Daro to add his own physical reminder. Daro stiff-armed him back. "No, he's had his lesson. Let him go."

Robinton said nothing more, retreating back to his small chamber. He eased his sore back deep into the rush mattress and tried to go to sleep.

Turn to section 106.

* 103 *

The sailors looked at him, then at each other. Daro turned away, and Teer studied his shoes. "We must be presenting a disgraceful picture to you, Harper," he said, uncomfortably. "We apologize."

"No, not at all," Robinton said, amiably. He played a little run on the gitar strings. "Come, shall we sit down again? I have recently taken a long journey by ship, and I learned many chanteys from the crew. Perhaps I know one of your favorites?"

"Oh, yes," Orelia clapped her hands. "Do you know this one?" She began to hum, and Robinton recognized the tune. He picked it out, and then played the chorus. "Yes, that's the one."

He began again, using a repeat of the chorus for introduction, to give the seamen time to sit down and make themselves comfortable. They relaxed, and were soon singing along with Robinton and Orelia.

Turn to section 92.

* 104 *

His muscles complain even as he summons up strength that they have had no real rest today. He begs them to cooperate, steeling himself against the impending battle, the outcome of which he already knows.

While Daro feints a blow toward his face, Robinton

ducks away. Before the Harper can avoid it, Daro's hand catches him in the cheekbone.

Robinton jerks backward, then stands relaxed, trying to look resigned to the beating he is about to suffer. Then, just at the last moment, the Harper dives forward and down.

Daro's fist smashes into the wall, causing him to cry out. More falling than diving forward the journeyman is barely able to control his motion, ramming a lucky shoulder into Daro's stomach. The seaman's shout is cut off with a *whoosh!*

Knowing he has to take the slim advantage he has gained, Robinton wraps an arm around the breathless sailor and uses his legs to drive him backward across the room. Just before they reach a large waist-high table, the seaman twists wildly in Robinton's grasp, pulls hard, and lets Robinton continue on alone.

Breathless and off balance the Harper sprawls backward. Disoriented, he lets the force of his momentum carry him over the table and head-first onto a bench, which splits and spills him to the floor. Shaking his head woozily, Robinton sees Daro starting for him again.

Robinton receives three points of real damage in the brawl. If Robinton runs out of hit points, turn to section 29.

If he doesn't, turn to section 88.

* 105 *

He is badly outnumbered, one cool head against two hot ones. His muscles complain even as he summons up strength that they have had no real rest today. He begs them to cooperate, steeling himself against the impending battle, the outcome of which he already knows.

While Daro feints a blow toward his face, Teer maneuvers around behind Robinton. Before the Harper can avoid either man, Teer captures his upper arms and holds him firmly.

"Hit him, Daro. Hit him good."

Daro looks disgusted with his slow-witted companion. "I don't need fighting lessons from you." He raises a fist.

Robinton relaxes in Teer's grip, trying to look resigned to the beating he is about to suffer. Then just at the last moment, the Harper dives forward and down.

Daro's fist smashes into Teer's chest and the second seaman is thrown backward into a chair, protesting indignantly. He loses his grip on the Harper, who is already straining to pull free. More falling than diving forward the Journeyman is barely able to control his motion, ramming a lucky shoulder into Daro's stomach.

The blow is augmented by the larger seaman's own forward motion and his breath rushes out in a painful *whoosh.* Knowing he has to take the slim advantage he has gained, Robinton wraps an arm around the breathless sailor and uses his legs to drive him backward across the room. Just before they reach a large waist-high table, the young Harper pulls up hard and lets Daro continue on alone.

Breathless and off balance, the confused seaman

sprawls backward. He hits the wall with a smack. Robinton turns away, seeking Teer. The other seaman is standing behind him, swinging at him. Robinton tries to duck, but he is taken by surprise. Teer's fist hits him just under the ear and knocks him sprawling. Everything goes black for a moment.

He feels that he is moving again, though not under his own power. Woozily, he bats at the hands which grab the front of his tunic to haul him to his feet. They belong to Teer, who draws back to punch him again.

Robinton receives three points of real damage in the brawl. If Robinton runs out of hit points, turn to section 29.

If he does not, turn to section 88.

* 106 *

A gentle touch woke him before he remembered that he had actually fallen asleep.

"Who's there?" he whispered. A tiny patch of glows hovered somewhere over his head. He couldn't see who was holding it.

"Orelia. Just lie still. I have some numbweed here. I think you could use it."

Robinton, mentally recounting his injuries, agreed. The icy tingling followed by numbness as the salve touched his skin made him sigh with relief. Orelia laughed at him. He was too grateful to care. Closing his eyes, he relaxed and let her treat his many bruises.

Roll 1 D6 for hit points regained by the use of numbweed. Turn to section 120.

* 107 *

"I want a chance to even up the score," Coron said. "Will one of you ask another riddle?" Keir and Wissa looked at one another.

"I know one," Keir said. "Listen, what has feet and legs and nothing else?"

If Robinton thinks the answer is crawlers, turn to section 128.

If he thinks the answer is stockings, turn to section 127.

* 108 *

"Hmm. Ah, yes, I remember. A bottle has a neck, but no head. Isn't that correct?"

Coron looked miffed. It was evident he considered that to be an obscure and difficult riddle. Robinton had his measure now. He thought of one of his own. But should he verbally trounce this rude lordling, or should he offer him an easy one and keep the contest even?

If he decides to ask a hard riddle, turn to section 110.

If he decides to ask an easy one, turn to section 109.

* 109 *

"Very well," Robinton nodded, thinking. "What's a protection in the air and a danger on the ground?"

"I don't know," Wissa said. "Lightning?" She pointed to the west, where the storm was dropping crackling bolts over the sea.

"I've heard that one before," Coron said. He thought deeply for a moment. "Ah! Greens during Threadfall." Wissa looked blank, and he explained. "Green dragons in the air, and plants near the Hold. Do you see?"

Robinton bowed. "Very good, my lord."

If Robinton and Coron are tied, turn to section 122.

If Coron has answered one correctly and Robinton hasn't, turn to section 125.

If Robinton has answered one correctly and Coron hasn't, turn to section 107.

* 110 *

"Here's a difficult one," Robinton said. Coron was immediately on his guard.

"Well?" he demanded, pugnaciously. "Let me hear it."

"What is the thing that when it corrupts, its error turns to good, and when its qualities are choice, it stirs up mischief wherever it goes? Its only parent is of pure descent, but it itself can be wicked."

"What sort of a riddle is that?"

"A classical one, my lord," Robinton answered, outwardly meek, but inwardly gloating.

"I haven't got the faintest idea. There is no answer."

"I'm afraid there is, and you're familiar with it in its material form. It's wine."

"Wine! Well, I will be damned."

If Robinton and Coron are tied, turn to section 122.

If Robinton has answered one correctly and Coron hasn't, turn to section 107.

* 111 *

He looked from one seaman to the other, measuring. Teer was duller than his shorter and more slender friend, but both were strong and quick on their feet and spoiling for a fight. He decided to preserve the dignity of the Harper Hall at the expense of his own reputation, much though it galled him.

"I do not presume to choose for the lady," Robinton said. He angled around Teer and Daro. Daro caught hold of his wrist as he passed and twisted it sharply. Wincing, Robinton tore his hand loose. Daro stared at him in amazement. The Harper had broken his grip without any apparent effort. The seaman didn't try to stop him this time.

"Good night," Robinton said again. And retreated to his small room. He waited to rub his wrist until he was safely out of sight of the others.

With a rueful smile of regret, he settled himself into the deep rush mattress and settled down to sleep.

Turn to section 106.

* 112 *

Robinton started to open his mouth to say the sun, when Coron said, "The wind."

Wissa nodded, smiling. "That's right, my lord. You've won. Good for you."

"My lord, congratulations," Robinton said.

Coron accepted them with his nose in the air.

Turn to section 134.

* 113 *

"Eight marks seems rather steep," Robinton commented.

"It's less than I'm asking of others who want to travel with me. There's safety in numbers, you know. There are bandits on the road. It's a long way between safe Holds. I've heard of lone travelers being robbed, even killed!"

"It'll take longer than if I travel alone, won't it?"

"A few days, Journeyman. We must go where the carts can pass."

Robinton wrinkled his brows, eyeing Keir speculatively. "I could pay you four marks. That's fair."

"Might take seven, but it'd be less than your upkeep."

"Five, and I'll help out if needed on the road."
"Five and a half, and you help out. What do you say?"

If he decides the price is fair, turn to section 116.

If he decides he'd rather travel alone, turn to section 117.

* 114 *

In a little while, he felt well enough to move. He looked up at the precipice and saw the long face of the little gray beast looking over it at him with puzzlement written on its furry features. It neighed to him, a drawn-out tenor whine very much unlike Twitch's alto whistle.

"Stay there!" he called to it, willing it to understand. Its ears swiveled forward at the sound of his voice. He seemed to remember a switchback not too far behind them on the trail. Staggering to his feet, he thrashed through the sand, his feet obeying him only grudgingly. There was a hope that he'd find the lower end of the path and be able to climb up without having to scale the sheer edge of the bluff. He definitely did not feel up to that.

He discovered it without much trouble. A zig-zag of ochre sand ran down to the beach through a tangle of seabeach plants. Their rough sawtooth edges caught at his clothes as he climbed up. It seemed an endless maze, but at last he reached the top.

If he still has numbweed and uses it, roll 1 D6 for hit points restored. Remove that dose of numbweed from the record sheet.

Turn to section 121.

* 115 *

"Very well," Robinton said, counting out the money. "I've got some things in the Hold. When will we be leaving?"

"As soon as the carts are loaded," Keir said, cheerfully. "Say, a bit before lunch?"

"All right. I'll see you then."

Turn to section 116.

* 116 *

"All right."

The Harper followed Jumerti back to the Hold to pick up his cases. A small child guided him through the main Hold to where Katoras and her women were at work sewing sails. Orelia stood up when she saw him come in, but the Sea Holder's lady scooped him up and escorted him out of the room, talking away.

"Now, I've seen to all your cases. They've been freshly oiled, so they'll be more resistant to water, though Mitran says there are no more storms in the wind for a sevenday to come. How he knows I will never understand, but he's always right. Here they are. Your clothes are clean, but the tunic and trousers are still damp. You might air them later. Come back again someday, Robinton. You'll always be welcome in this Hold. But for the Egg's sake, learn to eat more! You'll starve to death one day."

Between good advice and invitations for the future, Robinton managed to get in a few much-interrupted words of thanks. He envied the Hold that had so industrious a woman to manage it, but he found her very energy exhausting. Katoras saw him on his way along the stone walk, then turned away, busy already with other tasks.

Orelia followed them quietly to the Hold door, and stood in the shadows until Katoras had gone back to the sewing room. Then she slipped outside, looking over her shoulder to make sure the Sea Holder's lady wasn't coming back.

"Robinton," she called over the crash of waves against the seawall. The Harper heard her voice and looked back. "Weren't you going to say goodby?"

He set down his cases and ran back to her.

The caravan set out along the marsh road, backtracking far enough to high solid ground. The two long wagons, pulled by four burden beasts each, were drawn up a shallow ramp cut into the roadside which Robinton had missed the other day in the rain. Keir and his four workers pulled and pushed until they were safely up on the bluff, and then directed the beasts to draw the carts along the palisades above Half-Circle.

"There's no real road north from here, but I like to stop in Half-Circle at least once a Turn," Keir explained to Robinton, who sat beside him on the drover's bench of the lead wagon. "Besides, even if we followed the shore, we'd have to go inland in any case at Bayhead. It's all marsh there."

Robinton nodded. He remembered the configuration of the land from the maps at Harper Hall. The Bayhead marsh was a broad, flat wetland in which nothing lived but reptiles and amphibians and strange plants. He was happy to avoid it. Traveling with the caravan would be a reasonably comfortable journey, always providing that nothing happened to the wagons, which had seen many Turns of service.

There were seven other people traveling with Keir beside himself. Two of Keir's four carters drove the second wagon, and the other two rode runner beasts before and behind the caravan. A stout lady, Keir's wife, and a slim one, his daughter, sat at the back of the lead wagon, chatting to each other. And there was Coron, the fourth son of Lord Holder Raid whom, Keir had told him in an undertone, had become bored visiting Lord Dinesdan on Ista, and obtained passage off the island intending to go home. He joined the party as company for his journey back to Benden, but it was clear he regarded himself as a cut far above his companions.

Lord Coron, riding solitarily next to the caravan, had made no effort to speak to Robinton after Keir introduced him. Already he was treating him as a vassal to the Hold. Robinton, stung, resolved privately to rewrite his Lord Holder song to suit the son, rather than the father, of whom he had a better opinion. He did not bother to point out that Craftmasters were the equals of Lords Holder, and he was still under the authority of Master Harper Aldrem. Coron did spend some time with Wissa, Keir's daughter, the only person in the group to whom he was civil.

Off to the west, Robinton watched a storm gathering. It blew up out in the bay that afternoon, but it stayed out over the water. Nothing but a chill wind came nearer. He was provided with a unique opportunity to see the storm rage without having to get soaked.

The presence of the thunderstorm made Keir apply his lash to the backs of the beasts pulling the wagon. "I don't want to be caught in another downpour," he said, keeping an eye on the rain falling to the west. "We lost a fair quantity of our sweetmeats in the last one. They melted. That was before we stopped at Half-Circle."

"I'm bored, Papa," Wissa's voice came from the back

of the wagon. She crept up between the bales and barrels to sit behind them. "Would the Harper be good enough to sing for us?"

Coron, who was riding nearby, glowered over his beast's mane. Robinton saw the look on his face, and drew back the hand already reaching for his gitar. He didn't want to cause any difficulties on the trip, which in this case meant not taking the center stage for himself.

"I'd be happy to sing later, Wissa, when I can sit toward my audience. It's hard on my voice when I can't sit facing all in one direction." Robinton demonstrated, twisting his body around toward her, which made her giggle. "What about a game? Everyone can participate in a game."

"Oh, yes," she said. "But what should we play?"

"My lord Coron, can you suggest a game?" Robinton acceded diplomatically, fanning the tiny spark of interest he saw in the languid youth's face.

"Do you know any riddles?" Coron asked, but he was looking at the girl.

"A few," she said, without much confidence. "But I'm sure the Journeyman knows many."

Robinton cursed quietly to himself. This peacemaking was not going to work. He forced a smile to his lips. "Why don't you begin, my lord."

Coron puffed himself up smugly and eyed the Harper. "Certainly. See if you can guess this one. What has a neck but no head?"

Robinton tapped his nose with his forefinger. "That's a hard one. Let me think."

Roll 3 D6.

If the number rolled is less than or equal to his value for Intelligence, turn to section 108.

If greater, turn to section 124.

* 117 *

Robinton left Keir and his people loading their wagons.

"It does occur to me," Robinton said, "that I will need some way of carrying all my baggage. If I don't travel with the caravan, that is. They're too much for me on foot."

"Well," Jumerti mused. "There's not another beast of a size you can ride, even as light as you are, but I do have a runner that can carry your bags. This way."

The runner was without a doubt the oddest of its breed Robinton had ever seen. The creature was a gray runner beast, to be sure, but its back was only waist high to the Harper, and its ears as long as his forearm. "He's not too bright, but he's willing." Jumerti patted the beast between the astounding ears. "Four marks, harness and all. What do you say?"

"I'd pay more, if you asked," Robinton said. "Why such a small sum? There isn't anything wrong with the little beast, is there?"

"That's all I want. He's pining shut up in here. He's used to grasslands. It was sell him or set him free. It's far less than his keep has been, and it wouldn't have brought me a thirty-second to set him free. Benden'll be an ideal place for him. You're doing me a favor, my friend."

The Harper followed Jumerti back to the Hold to pick up his cases. A small child guided him through the main Hold to where Katoras and her women were at work sewing sails. Orelia stood up when she saw Robinton come in, but the Sea Holder's lady scooped him up and escorted him out of the room, talking away.

"Now, I've seen to all your cases. They've been freshly oiled, so they'll be more resistant to water, though

Mitran says there are no more storms in the wind for a sevenday to come. How he knows I will never understand, but he's always right. Here they are. Your clothes are clean, but the tunic and trousers are still damp. You might air them later. Come back again someday, Robinton. You'll always be welcome in this Hold. But for the Egg's sake, learn to eat more! You'll starve to death one day."

Between good advice and invitations for the future, Robinton managed to get in a few much-interrupted words of thanks. He envied the Hold that was managed by so industrious a woman, but he found her very energy exhausting. Katoras saw him on his way along the stone Holdway, then turned, busy already with other tasks.

Orelia followed them quietly to the Hold door, and stood in the shadows until Katoras had gone on to the sewing room. Then she slipped outside, looking over her shoulder to make sure the Sea Holder's lady wasn't coming back.

"Robinton," she called over the crash of waves against the seawall. The Harper heard her voice and looked over his shoulder. "Weren't you going to say goodby?"

He set down his cases and ran back to her.

Robinton loaded all of his possessions onto the back of the small gray runner. He led it along the Holdway and up the Marsh Road to the palisade overlooking the sea. There was a narrow path, evidently used often by the Holders in Half-Circle, beaten into the crisp brown and-green grass. He patted the package of delicious-smelling fishrolls Katoras had pressed on him to take, looking forward to sitting down later for a snack.

Humming as he walked along, Robinton sighted the far horizon, planning his route for ease of travel. Not that he was terribly concerned about it. New boots, new haircut, clean clothes, and a night's sleep in the first real bed he'd seen since the Harper Hall had done miracles for his spirits. Not to mention a pretty girl. He felt wonderful.

The seacoast looked very dramatic, drawn in grays and muted dark green, brown and slate. Sunlight not strong enough to draw him a shadow illumined the waves and rocks far below him like a tapestry rather than something real. Running stitches for the waves, and short, choppy stitches irregularly placed for the sand and the rocks. And a solid wall of split-stitched grays and silvers for the sky to the west. It looked like it would rain soon, but Robinton hoped the wind blowing in his face would drive it south of him.

The promised storm blew up out in the bay that afternoon, and did cross back and away from him. Nothing but a chill wind came nearer. He was provided with a unique opportunity to see the storm rage without having to get soaked. The little runner towed him along by its lead rope, stolidly heading north. It was amazingly strong for its size. He trusted it to stay on the path, and watched the storm as he followed the beast along.

He stumbled only occasionally, when the beast made a turn to stay with the trail and he failed to observe the different angle of his lead rope. Once or twice, they crossed over places where the path was cut by natural sluices or narrow switchbacks leading down to the beach. Those began to appear more often as they got farther away from Half-Circle, where the Holdway and pathways were well maintained. The coarse grass was taller, too, making it harder to see the path when he did bother to look down.

His toy thunderheads, for that was how he was beginning to think of them, grew blacker and thicker as he went north and they went south. How large a storm this must be! Rumbles and flashes once more distant erupted under his very nose. The wind grew in velocity, rustling the shoots of grass around him, and he feared that the next wave of clouds might wash over him.

Suddenly, there was a mighty *crash!* and the little runner screamed in fear. A lightning bolt cracked the sky over them, and a frightened wherry exploded from its nest almost beneath their feet.

Roll 3 D6.

If the total is less than or equal to Robinton's value for Strength, turn to section 123.

If greater, turn to section 119.

* 118 *

"Eight marks seems rather steep," Robinton commented. "No, I think I'll travel on my own. I'd like to get to Benden as soon as possible. Thank you."

"I don't advise it, young man. There's safety in numbers, you know. There are bandits on the road. It's a long way between safe Holds. I've heard of lone travelers being robbed, even killed!"

"I should be safe enough," Robinton said. "Good journey."

"Farewell, then." Disgusted, Keir turned away and went back to supervising his men.

Turn to section 117.

* 119 *

The little runner jumped backward to avoid the hysterical bird. He crashed into Robinton, pushing him off his feet. The wherry, shrieking in agitation, flew away into the storm.

Robinton landed on his back near the very edge of the cliff. He struggled to get up, but he felt the sandy soil under the grass eroding, threatening to drop him over the cliff. Clawing at the tufts of grass, he sought a purchase for his fingers. Still, he continued to slide. There was time for one more lunge—the rope! The little runner's lead rope. It was just a few fingertips away. He leaped, trying to reach it, but it was out of his grasp. More sandy soil crumbled under him, and now his legs were hanging out over the precipice.

He made clucking sounds with his tongue, trying to coax the runner within arm's reach. The little creature came over to sniff curiously at him, not understanding that he was in danger. Robinton grabbed for one of its legs, just above the hoof. With a scream, the runner bit at his hand and danced backward. Robinton lost his grip on it at the same time the section of sand and grassroot under his belly slid away, and he fell.

There were no hand- or footholds he could catch to save himself. He flailed at the air until his back hit the beach with a thump. He gasped, wind knocked out of him. His head fell backward to the sand. It was too much trouble to breathe.

Roll 1 D6 and subtract the number rolled from Robinton's hit points.

If he is brought below zero hit points, turn to section 29.

If not, turn to section 114.

* 120 *

His eyes flew open in surprise, but it was completely dark in the room now. The rush mattress rustled and dipped as someone else nestled against him. "What?" he sputtered.

Slim fingers touched his lips in the darkness, and Orelia's fragrant hair brushed against his chest. "It's just me, silly."

"You shouldn't even be in here," Robinton whispered, thinking of her father and two angry young seamen besides.

"Of course I shouldn't, but I do what I want. Don't you want me in here?" Her hands went around him and began to trace the lines of his back.

"Well . . . Yes, I do, but . . ."

She giggled. "I was so surprised when Teer and Daro both decided to visit tonight. I do like them both, but I don't think that I want to marry either one of them. They're so jealous! You're much more interesting than they are. And handsomer, too." Soft kisses traveled along his neck and up to his ear. He gathered her into his own arms and buried his face in her hair, stroking her back gently with his long fingers. Orelia sighed softly and drew him closer, her hands drawing tingling patterns along his spine. She had undone her plaits, and her soft tresses floated over his shoulders and chest as her lips touched his. . . .

Section 120

When he woke up, Robinton was alone. Clattering noises and cooking odors told him where Orelia must have gone. He stretched luxuriously, yawning as he reminded himself that sometimes there were better things to do than sleep.

The curtain over the door swayed as someone in the Hold passed by it. Everyone else must already be awake. He finished his stretch and climbed out of bed, looking for his clothes. The sun was probably already up.

Fortified with a cup of klah and some hot cereal, he wandered down to the Docking Cavern to visit Twitch. Orelia had served him his breakfast, but declined sadly to go with him to see his runner beast. She had chores to do, and then she was needed in the main Hold to help Katoras with sewing. Robinton promised to come over later to say goodby to her. Lian had looked the other way as she kissed him.

Twitch greeted him with a whicker and several happy twitches of his furry ears. His hoof was bound up in stiff bandages which smelled of medicines and balm. He seemed already able to stand comfortably upon it. Twitch went back to munching on a heaping pile of fodder as Robinton examined him and then went off to look for Jumerti.

"Good morning, young Robinton," the Holder greeted him. "Sleep well?"

The ingenuous question flustered Robinton by guilty association. He managed to choke out, "Yes, very well."

"Seen your beast this morning?"

"Yes," Robinton said, moving on to a safer subject. "You did a good job of nursing that hoof. He'll be well very soon."

"Um-hmm, but not soon enough for you, you said." The Holder squinted over at Twitch, happily eating his fodder and ignoring his surroundings. "Where did you say you were headed?"

"Benden Hold."

"Ah. Well, now, what would you say to seven marks for the beast and gear?"

The Harper cocked his head. "I'd say, 'nine.'"

Jumerti laughed. "All right, that tells me. Is it eight, then?"

"Eight would be fine. Treat him well. He's a fine beast."

"Oh, I will." They clasped hands to seal the bargain and Jumerti gave him the marks. "I like runner beasts. Some of my blood folk live in landbound Holds. I might have raised runners if I wasn't needed here. I want to feed this fellow up and see his hoof healed before I put him to work. He's a scrawny one, to be sure."

Robinton bridled defensively, then realized that he'd already sold the runner, and Jumerti was commenting about his own property.

"Well, now. What did you name him?"

"I call him Twitch, because he does. It's as good a name as any."

"Does he know it?"

"He seems to."

The Holder nodded. "Good. Now, let me introduce you to Keir. He leads a merchant caravan that is going up toward Benden. Perhaps you two can do some business."

Keir was deeper in the cavern, overseeing the setting of a new wheel onto the axle of a broad, flat wagon painted with the Valley Hold colors. He was a small man, thin and narrow-shouldered, but with a paunch beginning under the gaudy tunic. His clothing was of rich fabric edged with fancy embroidery. Two men also in Valley Hold colors worked, teeth set, at holding the edge of the wagon up while two more maneuvered the wheel onto the hub.

"Keir, this is the young Harper I told you about. He's bound for Benden Hold. Journeyman Robinton, Mastertrader Keir."

Section 120

"I'm pleased to meet you, young man," Keir said, snapping a glance over his shoulder at the workmen even as he clasped hands with Robinton. "Careful with that, you! I can't afford to replace that axle, too!"

One of the workers shot Keir a dirty look, but the wheel was fastened in place without much more difficulty. The four stopped to wipe their sweaty faces, then began other tasks without speaking.

"We make a long circuit several times a Turn. We trade all the way across Pern. We've just begun our first trip of the Turn, now that the weather's warmed up. It can be a hard life, but you get to meet people, and I like that." Keir turned away from the carters, who were loading the long wagon with bundles.

"So," he said, throwing an arm over Robinton's shoulders. As he was a span or so shorter he had to walk somewhat lopsidedly, but it didn't seem to bother him. "Are you interested in joining us on our way? As you're a Harper, I'll only ask eight marks. That includes your passage, and all meals are paid for out of that, too." Robinton tried to meet his eyes, but Keir seemed to look everywhere in the cavern but at him.

Robinton looked at the Sea Holder, and then back to where they'd been chatting. It wasn't impossible that the trader had heard the details of their bargain, but it certainly was a lucky guess as to what would empty his purse again. Jumerti guessed his thoughts, but he shrugged.

If Robinton decides to go with the caravan, turn to section 115.

If he decides to bargain with Keir on the fee, turn to section 113.

If he would rather travel alone, turn to section 118.

* 121 *

He and the runner made their way along the bluff for a while longer, but Robinton was tiring. The storm had gone long ago, and the sky was darkening now for night. Sea Holder Mitran had been correct in his weather wisdom, for which Robinton was grateful. He looked about for some place more sheltered in which to sleep. All around him, the windswept grass whistled and clattered, but there was hardly a tree within five dragonlengths.

Ahead of him he could see a low line of brush. He made toward that, telling his tired muscles they would be able to rest soon.

The bushes were much taller than he had expected. The whole angle of the land changed as he approached. The foliage was really the tops of trees in a river valley that slanted down lazily toward the beach. He pulled the runner along, and soon had his camp set up under a flowering tree next to the narrow stream. He refilled his waterskin and had a refreshing cold bath. The runner had a drink too, snorting through its nostrils under the surface. Robinton chuckled at it. It supplied a humorous running commentary on everything it did.

There was plenty of dry wood to be had, so he laid a good big fire between himself and the water's edge, banking it so it couldn't spread. The gray runner consumed water plants and shore plants with equal relish. It too seemed happy with his choice of site.

With Katoras's fishrolls inside him, and warmth outside, Robinton fell contentedly asleep.

Section 121

The beach was much broader here than it had been near Half-Circle, so he walked the rest of the way down. The little runner seemed as content to walk on sand as it did on the bluff tops, and plowed along stolidly.

By the time the sun reached its highest point, Robinton was wishing he'd saved a fishroll for his lunch. He was forced to think about looking for food. The longer it took him to forage, the more it would slow him up getting to Benden. If he could find a goodly supply of something, he wouldn't have to stop so often for his stomach's sake.

Down the beach aways he saw some good-sized torguana lizards scuttling among a tumble of rocks. One would supply him with enough food to reach Benden Hold easily. His mouth watered at the thought of roast lizard. The Hall kitchens had a way of spicing it so that the natural flavor was enhanced beyond succulence. He dismissed that thought from his mind. He had to catch one of them first, and that would not be an easy task.

A snare trap would be the easiest to make. Turning his pack inside out, he discovered that he had only a short length of rope with him. Certainly not enough to make a respectable snare. He didn't want to have to hold the end while the stupid thing trapped itself. An idea struck him, and he turned out his gitar case as well. There were two or three spare strings in it. Gut was almost as tough as wire. These would make a splendid snare. He just hoped that none of his gitar's present strings would break before he reached the Hold. Making more took time and skill, and he would hate to be without music for the duration.

Using the strings and twigs and sea plants thrown up on the beach, he managed to improvise a fair trap alongside the brush. Now all he needed was some bait. Torguanas would eat almost anything, he knew.

He searched the beach for anything he could use as bait. The runner trotted obediently at his heels, stopping when he did, and commenting on the proceedings now and again in its nasal voice. He managed to find several dead and decaying fish washed up along the shore. With barely contained disgust, he brought them back to his trap and laid them in the looped string. He tethered the runner farther in the valley to keep it from driving away the lizards, and crawled into the brush to wait.

The hand holding the loop sweated so much that he had to wipe it to keep the string from squirting out of his grasp. He'd made a running noose at both ends, one to trap the lizard, and the other which he tied to the narrow sapling to his left. He held on to the slack in the middle. Sweat ran down his face, but he controlled the urge to wipe it with a hand that reeked of rancid seaweed.

Small insects walked over him, some stopping to crawl inside his clothes. He scratched as best he could with one hand, being careful not to move the noose. He wiggled his legs to dislodge the ones he couldn't reach. The longer he lay still, the more attention he attracted from the little pests.

It took a long time for the lizards to notice the trap. Robinton was seething with impatience before the first one darted over to the heap of decayed fish. It hissed and prepared to feed, but was driven off by a bigger and meaner looking lizard. He silently urged one of them to eat the fish, but they kept bullying one another out of the way.

A smaller one circled around while the two big ones were busy fighting, and wandered into the circle of string. It was still a large creature, about half his height in length. As soon as it was well occupied with the rotten fish, Robinton hauled back on the line, closing the noose around the ugly thing's back feet.

Screeching with exasperation, the lizard tried to run away, only to find its flight halted by the tetherline to the tree. It thumped to the ground. The other two hastily ran away, hissing in agitation. The young Harper scrambled out of his hiding place, belt knife drawn, and circled the lizard seeking where he should strike. It screamed and struggled, flinging leaves and fragments of stinking bait all over him.

TORGUANA
To be hit: 9 To hit Robinton: 11 Hit points: 7
Roll 2 hits per successful attack for the lizard, once for the teeth (does two hit points of damage) and once for the claws (does one hit point of damage).

Robinton's knife does 1 D6 of damage.

If Robinton manages to kill the lizard, turn to section 142.

If he runs out of hit points, turn to section 146.

* 122 *

"By my count," the Harper said, "we are tied. Wissa, will you ask the last riddle? The one who answers first will be the winner of the contest."

"Fair enough." Coron leaned close to Wissa, which made her blush.

"Oh, I don't know what to ask! Well, what is it that goes through the woods but never touches a thing?"

If Robinton thinks the answer is the sun, turn to section 112.

If Robinton thinks the answer is the wind, turn to section 130.

* 123 *

The little runner jumped backward to avoid the hysterical bird. He crashed into Robinton, pushing him off his feet. The wherry, shrieking in agitation, flew away into the storm.

Robinton landed on his back near the very edge of the cliff. He struggled to get up, but he felt the sandy soil under the grass eroding, threatening to drop him over the edge. Clawing at the tufts of grass, he sought purchase with his fingers. Still, he continued to slide. There was time for one more lunge—the rope! The little runner's lead rope. It was just a few fingertips away. He leaped, trying to reach it, but it was out of his grasp. He dug at the soil with his fingertips, hoping to make the rope fall into the depression within his range. More sandy soil crumbled under him, and now his legs were hanging out over the precipice.

He made clucking sounds with his tongue, trying to coax the runner within arm's reach. The little creature came over to sniff curiously at him, not understanding the danger he was in. Robinton grabbed one of its legs, just above the hoof. It screamed in fear and backed up, but he had a firm grip, and it couldn't get free.

When it dug in its little heels and strained at his weight, Robinton took his chance. He scrabbled at the cliff face with his toes, giving himself a slight but swiftly crumbling foothold. Levering himself up, he kicked and clawed until he had a knee on the edge again. Both knees. One foot. The other foot. When at least he was stretched out to his full length on the grassy path, he let go of the runner's hoof. It protested indignantly and galloped a distance up the road, where it stood crying angrily at him.

He ignored it and lay on the ground, panting.

Turn to section 121.

* 124 *

Was the answer a wherry ready for the pot or an isthmus? Robinton couldn't remember. If anything, a Harper should have a large supply of riddles on hand. So much of what their work consisted of was making what was obscure seem easy and vice versa.

With a pleased look on his face, Coron inquired, "Well? Do you know?"

Robinton sighed, ceding Coron the victory. "No, I don't. I can't remember."

"Too bad, Harper. That means I ask you another one." A sly look forecast the delivery of another difficult one. "What has heads but no eyes and eyes but no heads?"

"I know that one," Wissa said, with a relieved smile. "I thought you wouldn't ask any I knew at all. Pins and needles."

Coron bowed to her. "Then, you may ask the next one."

"Papa, do you want to play?" Wissa asked, leaning over her father's shoulder.

"No, thank you very much, my dear. I'd rather keep my ignorance to myself." Keir chuckled and tapped the near burden beast with his crop.

She appealed to Robinton. "You ask one for me, please."

"All right," he said. He looked to Coron, but the young lord was already waiting for the question. He was enjoying himself. Robinton had his measure now. He thought of one of his own. But should he verbally trounce this rude lordling, or should he offer him an easy one?

If Robinton should ask a difficult riddle, turn to section 110.

If he should ask an easy one, turn to section 109.

* 125 *

"My lord," Robinton said, "you're in the lead by one. Do you want best two of three, or will you be content to have been the only one to answer correctly?"

"The best two of three," Coron answered magnanimously.

Keir spoke up. "Here's an old, old one that your great-grandfathers might have puzzled over. What kind of cold have you got when you only cough when you can't see? Think, now."

If Robinton thinks the answer is Between, turn to section 131.

If he thinks the answer is firehead fever, turn to section 133.

* 126 *

Two stretched-hide shelters were raised, one for Keir and his family, and one for the six men. The lord's son immediately took possession of the sheltered wall farthest away from the door curtain, paying no heed to the grumbles of the four men who would have to sleep cramped because of him. Keir pretended not to hear his men's complaints. His lordship was a paying customer, and that seemed to overcome anyone else's objections.

Robinton elected to sleep nearest the curtain, thereby giving the other four more sheltered room to stretch out. The tradesmen gave him grateful looks, knowing that they wouldn't have to deal with his duelling idiosyncrasies. They chatted with him around the fire after the meal, leaving Coron to scowl in silence. Acceding to general clamor, Robinton found his gitar and struck up a tune.

"What's that you're playing?" Keir's wife asked, after listening for a moment, brows furrowed. "I've been trying to place it."

"Oh, a song I learned on my sea journey from Fort Hold," he said, beginning the strum again. This time, he sang the words.

"It's lovely," she said. "I've never heard that before."

"Nor I," Keir agreed.

"I learned it from a seaman. Don't you do business with ship owners?"

"Well, yes, of course. Some of our best customers. But we don't associate with them. They've got their own ways that aren't like ours."

"Oh, there's not that much difference," Robinton said, fingers busy on the gitar strings. "I spent a sevenday on board ship, and except for the smell of fish, I might have been back in Fort Hold."

"Be that so?" Keir asked. Robinton nodded. "Well, then I might see that for myself. I might take a closer look, any road. It always seemed that ship's life was a strange thing, an alien thing. But men live it, don't they."

Coron snorted. "Harpers are stranger things than seamen, Holder."

"I'm not a Holder, my lord. My home's in a Crafthold."

"The real differences between people aren't visible," Robinton commented, dryly. He looked up into pairs of uncomprehending eyes. Smiling ingenuously, he began to play a spry dance tune which had them all clapping in a moment.

There would be no room for the gitar in the hide shelter, so he put it back in its case on the wain. The weather, though cold, was dry. He was sure it and his other instruments would be safe enough where they were.

Men were already snoring in the shelter when he crept in to sleep. He spread his cloak out on the rough floor cloth and rolled himself up in it. To the accompaniment of an irregular chorus of whistles, snorts and wheezes, he fell asleep.

Roll 3 D6.

If the total is less than or equal to the value for Robinton's Wisdom (luck), turn to section 135.

If greater, turn to section 132.

* 127 *

"Crawlers," said Coron.

"Stockings," said Robinton. "I heard that one from the Apprentice Master. He's about a thousand Turns old, just a few Turns younger than that riddle."

Turn to section 129.

* 128 *

"Crawlers," said Robinton.

"Stockings," said Coron.

"My lord is right," Wissa said, almost apologetically. "You've each got one right, I think."

Turn to section 122.

* 129 *

Coron said nothing more, but rode ahead until Keir called a halt for the evening.

"We make camp here," he said. "It's a good place, sheltered from the winds. There's a stream just a little ways down the hill, there. All right, to work!"

Robinton pitched in to get the work done quickly.

Keir's wife was laying a fire to make a meal, and he wanted that delayed as little as possible. The woman noticed his interested gaze as she set light to her fire and laughed. "Not too long. I always make a stew while we're on the road, and it's quick cooking. You look like you could eat the pot empty. Ah, me, it's too long since I had boys to feed." Robinton blushed and went back to work.

Coron ignored the bustle that was going on around him. He stayed out of the way, ignoring everyone but Wissa. After his runner was tethered to a tree with a good supply of fodder, he sprawled himself next to the bonfire site, refusing to do any more. Robinton helped one of Keir's men unload Coron's press from the wagon. The man was grumbling to himself about overprivileged, lazy whelps. The young Harper kept the protests from getting any louder by engaging the man in conversation about himself, his family and his home Hold. He was determined to keep the mood high, though Coron was still showing bored hostility toward him for winning the contest.

Turn to section 126.

* 130 *

"The wind," Robinton said, quickly.

"You win," Wissa said. "That's the right answer."

Coron gave him a dirty look. "I was about to say the same thing."

"But he said it first, my lord. That was the rule."

With his nose in the air, Coron rode ahead in sullen silence.

Turn to section 129.

* 131 *

"I don't know," Coron said, sullenly.

"Could the answer be *Between?*" Robinton asked.

"Yes, dash it," the young lord said. "I should have remembered that one. I've heard it from my cradle."

Turn to section 122.

* 132 *

He woke up, staring into the darkness at the hide roof of the shelter. Something had disturbed him. A nudge? A noise? He listened carefully, tuning out the wheezes of the sleeping men. Outside, there was a shuffling sound, a beast or man walking? He pulled aside a corner of the curtain and peered out.

A man was walking out of the clearing with a bundle under his arm. It didn't look like Keir, and all the other men were asleep behind him in the shelter. Robinton got to his knees, trying to decide who it was.

His furtive movements indicated that his presence was not accidental, so he must be a sneak-thief. Robinton couldn't remember any Holds since they'd left that morning, so this man must have followed them all the way from Half-Circle. The bag under the man's arm clinked. Robinton recognized the clatter of the bag's contents. The thief was stealing his tools! He sprang out of the shadows. "Help! Thief!" the Harper cried. "Hey!"

The man spun, seeking for the source of the voice.

Robinton threw himself after the thief, still shouting.
Without hesitation, the man dashed out of the clearing. The Harper followed. There was a full moon and a crescent, so his quarry was clearly visible. When the man stopped to get his bearings, Robinton leaped on him.

THIEF
To be hit: 9   *To hit Robinton: 12*   *Hit points: 7*
Does 2 points damage with fists.

If Robinton wins, turn to section 141.

If he loses, turn to section 144.

* 133 *

"I think that the answer is firehead fever," Robinton said.
"It's *Between,"* Coron said. "I've heard that one from my cradle. The score is two to nothing."
"You win, my lord," Robinton said, graciously.

Turn to section 134.

* 134 *

Coron rode with his head held at a proud angle. "I haven't forgotten my Teachings. The old Harper taught us all the riddles he knew. I have an especially good memory."
Robinton, cringing inwardly at the shameless display of ego, said, "You're a credit to your father, my lord."

His reward was a fatuous smirk.

Since he had won the contest, Coron was nearly tolerable that evening when they stopped to make camp. He stayed out of the way, ignoring everyone but Wissa. After his runner was tethered to a tree with a good supply of fodder, he sprawled himself next to the designated bonfire site, refusing to do any more. Robinton helped one of Keir's men unload Coron's press from the wagon. The man was grumbling to himself about overprivileged, lazy whelps. The young Harper kept the protests from getting any louder by engaging the man in conversation about himself, his family and his home Hold. He was determined to keep the mood high.

Soon the evening meal was cooking, savory stew, and the work was done.

Turn to section 126.

* 135 *

He woke up, staring into the darkness at the hide roof of the shelter. Something had disturbed him. A nudge? A noise? He listened carefully, tuning out the wheezes of the sleeping men. Outside, there was a shuffling sound, a beast or man walking? He pulled aside a corner of the curtain and peered out.

A man's figure stood near the wain, and began silently fingering the bundles. It wasn't Keir, so it must be a thief! Quietly, Robinton rose to his knees, feeling around in the darkness for a couple of big stones. He crept through the curtain and stood in the shadow of his shelter, measuring the distance between himself and the man.

There was a full moon and a crescent in the sky, both

of them behind Robinton, so he had a good view of his quarry. The man's furtive efforts indicated that his presence was not accidental. Robinton couldn't remember any Holds since they'd left that morning, so this man must have followed them all the way from Half-Circle. "Hey!" Robinton boomed. His baritone sounded sinister enough in the dark. "Who's there?"

The man spun, seeking for the source of the voice. Robinton threw one of the big rocks into the bushes just to the other side of the shelter, making the branches rustle as if someone else stood there. "Look there, Keir, a sneak-thief! We know how to deal with those!"

Without hesitation, the man snatched the bundle nearest to him and dashed for the edge of the clearing. Robinton recognized the clatter of the bag's contents. The thief was stealing his tools! He sprang out of the shadows. "Help! Thief!" the Harper cried. He leaped onto the other man's back, dragging him to the ground. Panicked, the thief hit him across the ear with his own toolbag. He threw the lighter man off and went for his throat.

His shouting roused some of the other sleepers. Keir came out, blinking stupidly at the two men fighting in the moonlight.

THIEF
To be hit: 9 *To his Robinton: 12* *Hit points: 7*
Does 2 points damage with fists.

Keir and the others will stop the fight after two rounds.

If Robinton has run out of hit points, turn to section 147.

If not, turn to section 141.

* 136 *

His nonchalant pose broke the instant Coron jumped toward him. As Coron swung, Robinton's arms flashed open and out, knocking the punch away and cracking the edge of his other hand against Coron's other wrist. Howling, Coron put his head down and charged at him. Unfortunately, the Harper had left himself wide open to an attack like that. He backed up hastily toward a tree. He braced himself, raised a foot and kicked his opponent in the chest. Coron grunted, but grabbed hold of the leg. Thus supported, Robinton brought up his other foot and kicked Coron in the chin. Coron's head flew back with an audible snap, and he fell to the ground, panting. Cautiously, Robinton abandoned his defensive position, and stood over him to make sure he wasn't badly hurt.

When Coron opened his eyes and saw Robinton, instead of the jealous hate in his eyes, there was something like a guarded respect. He shook his head to clear it, felt at his jaw. Struggling to his feet, he caught his runner beast, mounted and sat quietly waiting for the others to take their places. Without a word said, the caravan moved again.

With an eye out for the hanging creepers, Robinton brought out his gitar and played to ease the strain. They all seemed disinclined to talk, so music would be the best thing to raise their spirits without insisting on their participation. He grinned to himself. He would have played anyway. Music was food and drink and even sleep to him. He stroked the gitar lovingly, drawing melodies from its strings. Something brought him to mind of his dream on the beach, and left his fingers reaching for dragonsong even as his mind searched for the memory.

Dragons on tree branches. A Gatherday fancy.

Wissa spoke up, driving the thought away. "That'd sound prettier on this, Robinton. Can you play a harp?"

"Of course I can," he said, turning around and then staring. Wissa held out to him a small harp, a miracle of wood and wire. Awed, he turned it over in his hands, admiring the craftsmanship. The forepillar and frame had been pressed together vertically out of three pieces of wood, the outer ones naturally shaded and the narrow center piece dyed a smooth blue. It had then been carved in the bow of the frame with a little pattern of dragons. It was slightly bigger than a lap harp, but just the same weight. Every edge was smooth, and the sounding board was rounded instead of squared off. A dozen, a thousand times nicer than the one he'd had to leave back in the Harpercrafthall. "This is a Master's work," he breathed. "Does it belong to you?"

"No, not at all," she said, amused. "It's a part of our merchandise for the north."

"What are you asking for it?" He set the curve against his shoulder and plucked out a few sweet chords. Its voice flowed smoothly, for it was so well made that it was still nearly in tune, even after traveling in a jostling wagon for many dragonlengths. He had fallen in love with the little harp, even though it had to be many marks costlier than he could afford. Perhaps something could be worked out over the price. He . . . coveted it, an uncommon emotion for him.

"Oh, that'n's not for sale," Keir said, glancing over at the Harper, who was reverently examining the instrument. "It's a paid commission piece. To be delivered. I'm truly sorry, for I can see that you appreciate it."

Robinton's heart sank with disappointment. He picked out a sad little tune with the highest pitched strings, and put a melodramatic expression of tragedy on his long face. Wissa laughed. "Well, play it anyway," she said. "You can use it until we get to Bayhead."

Section 136

He tuned it and set his long fingers on the strings. After a moment's thought, he smiled. "What better to play on a dragonharp?

> "Dragonmen must fly
> When Threads are in the sky . . ."

Keir and Wissa smiled, and he nodded, about to go on with the teaching ballad. He stopped, having heard a derisive snort from one of the carters. "What's wrong?" Robinton asked him, affably.

The man waved it away. "Why make songs about something that's been gone for hundreds of Turns? My grandad said his grandad never knew anyone who saw Thread fall."

"Are you suggesting that it never happened?" All friendliness was out of his voice now.

"No." The carter seemed to understand that he needed to tread carefully here. "But it'll never happen again. I don't think Pern needs dragons anymore. Anyway, they scare the guts out of me."

Robinton sat up straight and spoke as ponderously as only a fledgling Harper could. "I find your lack of respect for the Weyr a poor reflection on you, and on your employer, who has a greater respect for his Teachings and the safety of Pern than you appear to . . ."

"Just a moment," Coron interrupted them.

Roll 3 D6.

If the total is less than or equal to Robinton's value for Charisma, turn to section 143.

If greater, turn to section 148.

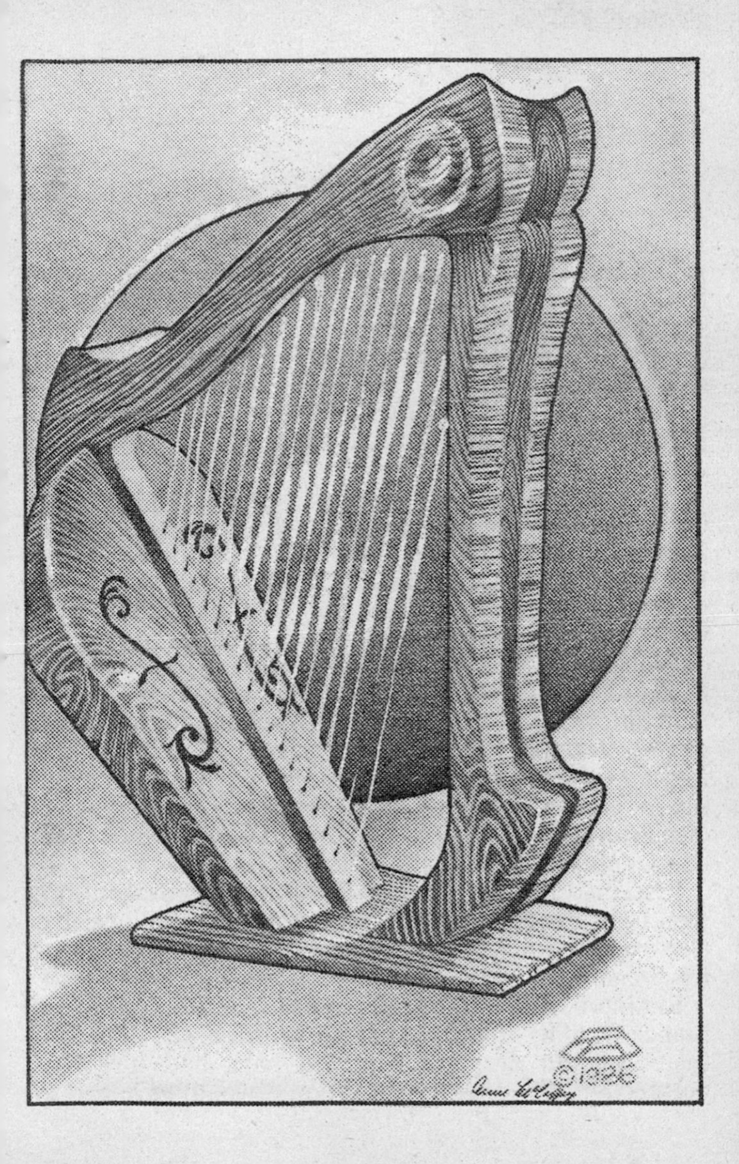
©1986

* 137 *

He chose a spot that was just under the branches of the last trees before the open beach. The sea was very shallow here, and the water waved a warm breeze in his direction. It felt good to him. He intended to bake his sore muscles thoroughly. His cloak was spread out as a ground cloth, and his pack made a somewhat bulgy pillow. Lulled by the roar and crash of the waves a safe distance away, he fell asleep.

And dreamed of dragons. He'd spotted another dragon, a blue, circling high overhead the day before. Their beauty and grace charmed him, these giant protectors of Pern. He felt a surge of pride in knowing that his job was soon to be bringing dragons back to the attention of a world that had nearly forgotten them. A flight of dragons on wings of song. He liked that image. If he couldn't have one of his own, it was the next best thing.

In his dream, a wing formation of each color of dragon danced in the sky, around and around, weaving in and about a fabulous queen dragon, who hovered in the sky like a golden beam of light. With a cry, the wings disappeared, all except a brown dragon, which flew down and perched on a tree branch.

It seemed perfectly plausible at first, this dragon in a tree, until his conscious mind questioned the idea. No tree existed which was large enough to support a roosting dragon. But there it was, as clear as . . . day.

Robinton sat up, looking around. There was the tree branch from his dream, directly over his head. Of course there was no dragon on it. To have had the right perspective, any dragon that sat on it would have had to be less than an armslength long. No, no. He must have seen a small wherry. But he was sure it had had wings and four limbs, not wings and two.

Dreams could play strange tricks on one.

Turn to section 140.

* 138 *

Harper Mettin received Robinton into his private workroom. "It sounds like you have had some varied adventures since you left home, young man." He ruffled Robinton's dark locks, and called out of the door for wine. "A welcoming cup. You won't refuse?"

"No, indeed. I'm parched. It's hot and windy today." Robinton settled himself into the offered chair.

"Is it? I hadn't noticed. Living on the sea, the wind is an everyday nuisance. After a time, you pay no attention to it. And it's summer, so what do you expect? We look to Benden, but our weather comes from Nerat. I have a message scroll I must send to the Harper Hall very soon. Shall I include a note from you? For your father, perhaps? Or your master? To whom were you apprenticed?"

"To Master Harper Aldrem," Robinton said. "I'd be grateful. They'd be happy to know I'm nearly in-Benden."

"All the Harpers hereabout knew to look out for you. Word went to Benden by drum you were on your way, so of course we'd all heard it." The wine arrived and Mettin poured two glasses full, setting a third glass to one side. Robinton sniffed the wine's bouquet. A Benden vintage. He was learning to recognize them. "It's a pleasant surprise to see you, but a surprise nevertheless. When you were announced, I was expecting C'gan."

"C'gan!" Robinton's eyes shone.

"Oh, yes, we're old friends. We were apprentices together, Caigan and I." Mettin pushed a hand through his gray-shot hair. "For two Turns I saw nothing of him after he went to the Weyr, and one day he appears on a blue dragon! He pointed at the astonished expression on my face and said, 'That's how I felt when it happened. They call me C'gan now.' But let him tell you all about it. That's what you're here for, isn't it?"

"Oh, yes!" Robinton exclaimed.

Mettin chuckled. "Dragon crazy. All young people are. I was, too. He'll introduce you to Tagath."

"That would be wonderful."

"My pleasure. Would you like to stay with us for a day? Benden Hold is another three, four days' travel from here. One more shouldn't matter."

"I'd be happy to." Draining their cups, he and Mettin went out to see to the little runner, who was stabled with the other Hold beasts. When Robinton removed the beast's harness, he twitched all the skin on its back from withers to tail and let out a comical noise which sounded like a sigh.

Mettin was amused. "Told you as clear as can be how relieved he is to be rid of it."

"I'll be glad when I'm done with the journey, too." Robinton slipped his disreputably stained shirt over his head, and put on a fresh one from his pack. "That feels much better."

"Mettin?" A tentative voice echoed in the dim cavern.

"C'gan!" Mettin boomed, hastening out into the sunlight to find his friend. Robinton was not far behind him, though hampered with his many bags and cases. He emerged from the cavern, blinking, as Mettin greeted a man dressed from head to toe in wherhide. Mettin gestured him over. "Robinton, meet C'gan."

The dragonrider pulled off his close-fitting riding helmet and grinned at Robinton, who was wide-eyed with excitement. He was of the same age as Robinton's father, some forty Turns, but his face was wind-weathered into lines and creases. His quick light eyes crinkled in amusement as he clasped the young man's hand. "Merelan's son. I'd know the family resemblance anywhere on Pern. So you want to ride dragons, eh?" Robinton blushed. "Yes, it's that obvious. Well, don't worry about it. I don't mind. Come and meet Tagath. Then we can have a cup of wine together and talk."

"You didn't set him down near the herdbeasts, did you?" Mettin asked, rolling his eyes innocently skyward.

"And where else?" C'gan asked in mock amusement, hoisting his bundles to his shoulder. He led the way through the streets. "On a Gatherday every other field in the Hold is otherwise occupied. They'll just have to panic this once. Tagath's already eaten this week."

Robinton mentally catalogued the information. It was part of the Teachings about dragons, but it was nice to know the accuracy of the old traditions.

Down below the meadows there was a large herdbeast enclosure. Every creature in it was at the top end of the field, huddled together, for at the seaward end, a long blue mound occupied the beach just outside the fences. As C'gan approached, it raised its head, eliciting cries of fear from the beasts.

"Come here, lazy. I have some company for you," he called.

Tagath rose to his feet and stretched, opening his wings out so the sun shone through the translucent vanes. He yawned hugely, displaying rows of long, shiny white teeth. The young Harper felt some sympathy for the herdbeasts. But he was utterly arrested by the dragon's eyes.

Section 138

They were sparkling rainbows, gigantic jewels glowing and changing hue as the dragon came fully awake and became curious about the humans approaching. Robinton thought he had never seen anything so lovely in his life. The dragon rumbled in his throat, and C'gan laughed.

"He says, thank you for the compliment." The huge head snaked down, and C'gan scratched between the eyes and around the back of Tagath's ear. "Would you like to have a ride later? I could even take you to Benden Hold."

Robinton nodded vigorously. At C'gan's urging, he scratched around the dragon's eye ridges, too. He was pleased when Tagath rumbled happily at the attentions, but it surprised him when a transparent lid suddenly closed over the jeweled eye. "That means he's relaxed," C'gan explained. "You're an old softy," he chided the dragon, but there was love in his voice.

"He can hear thoughts?" Robinton asked, when they returned to Mettin's workroom.

"Mostly those of other dragons, and mine, of course, but only occasionally other humans. He pretends he can't hear the Weyrwoman, and it makes Jora furious. Almost never people outside the Weyr."

"How long can you stay?" Mettin asked, pouring more wine.

"Not long at all," C'gan answered with regret in his voice. "I came only to pick up some things at the Gather. There's to be a Hatching soon, and it could begin at any time. Fourteen eggs. I have to be there to record the Impressions."

"Oh," said Robinton.

"Don't worry, my lad. You'll get your ride before I go. And you'll be visiting me, remember." He emptied his wine and held his hand up to forestall a refill. "I'd best be going. Farewell, Mettin." He smiled at Robinton, who wished with all his might he could go to the Hatching, too.

Roll 3 D6.

If the value is less than or equal to Robinton's value for Wisdom (luck), turn to section 172.

If greater, turn to section 156.

* 139 *

With an eye out for the hanging creepers, Robinton brought out his gitar and played to amuse the group and to improve his own mood. He felt thoroughly humiliated, and his dignity needed some healing. The others seemed disinclined to talk, so music would be the best thing to raise their spirits without insisting on their participation. He grinned to himself. He would have played anyway. Music was food and drink and even sleep to him. He stroked the gitar lovingly, drawing forth melodies from its strings. Something brought him to mind of his dream on the beach, and left his fingers reaching for dragonsong even as his mind searched for the memory. Dragons on tree branches. A Gatherday fancy.

Wissa spoke up, driving the thought away. "That'd sound prettier on this, Robinton. Can you play a harp?"

"Of course I can," he said, turning around, and then staring. Wissa held out to him a small harp, a miracle of wood and wire. Awed, he turned it over in his hands, admiring the craftsmanship. The forepillar and frame had been pressed together vertically out of three pieces of wood, the outer ones naturally shaded and the narrow center piece dyed a smooth blue. It had then been carved in the bow of the frame with a little pattern of dragons. It was slightly bigger than a lap harp, but just the same weight. Every edge was smooth, and the sounding board was rounded instead of squared off. A dozen, a thousand times nicer than the one he'd had to leave back in the Harpercrafthall. "This is a master's work," he breathed. "Does it belong to you?"

"No, not at all," she said, amused. "It's a part of our merchandise for the north."

"What are you asking for it?" He set the curve against his shoulder and plucked out a few sweet chords. Its voice flowed smoothly, for it was so well made that it was still nearly in tune even after traveling in a jostling wagon for many dragonlengths. He had fallen in love with the little harp, even though it had to be many marks costlier than he could afford. Perhaps something could be worked out over the price. He . . . coveted it, an uncommon emotion for him.

"Oh, that'n's not for sale," Keir said, glancing over at the Harper, who was reverently examining the instrument. "It's a paid commission piece. To be delivered. I'm truly sorry, for I can see that you appreciate it."

Robinton's heart sank with disappointment. He picked out a sad little tune with the highest pitched strings, a melodramatic expression of tragedy on his long face. Wissa laughed. "Well, play it anyway," she said. "You can use it until we get to Bayhead."

He tuned it and set his long fingers on the strings. After a moment's thought, he smiled. "What better to play on a dragonharp?

> "Dragonmen must fly
> When Threads are in the sky . . ."

Keir and Wissa smiled, and he nodded, about to go on with the teaching ballad. He stopped, having heard a derisive snort from one of the carters. "What's wrong?" Robinton asked him, affably.

The man waved it away. "Why make songs about something that's been gone for hundreds of Turns? My grandad said his grandad never knew anyone who saw Thread fall."

"Are you suggesting that it never happened?" All friendliness drained out of his voice now.

"No." The carter seemed to understand that he needed to tread carefully here. "But it'll never happen again. I don't think Pern needs dragons anymore. Anyway, they scare the guts out of me."

Robinton sat up straight and spoke as ponderously as only a fledgling Harper could. "I find your lack of respect for the Weyr a poor reflection on you, and on your employer, who has a greater respect for his Teachings and the safety of Pern than you appear to . . ."

"Just a moment," Coron interrupted them.

Roll 3 D6.

If the total is less than or equal to Robinton's value for Charisma, turn turn section 143.

If greater, turn to section 155.

* 140 *

Wissa came looking for him not long afterward.

"My father would like to get back on the road," she said, apologetically. "We'll be in Bayhead by tomorrow night if we don't lose any more time."

"Of course," said Robinton, trying to put her at her ease. "The earlier we arrive, the sooner he can do business."

Section 140

She seemed grateful for his cheeriness, and led the way back through the thicket to the wagons. He guessed that she had had to find Lord Coron first, and his lordship was still in a sulk. Yes, the Benden Holder was there on his runner, looking bored. When he spotted Robinton, he rode away from the rest of the group.

It was necessary now for the caravan to move due north in order to miss the broad marshes that occupied all the land to the east of Bayhead Hold. The road was easier to find now, because all traffic skirted the marsh. There was no way through it, Keir told him. Anything, anyone even as light as a child, could sink into the mire without a hope of ever getting out. Robinton shuddered, imagining accidentally falling into quickmud. He watched the road under the burden beasts' feet carefully, to assure himself that it was dry and solid.

That night, the stew cooked over dark, peat-smelling wood, and long streamers of moss hung in the trees around the fire. The air, though moist, was warm, and Robinton felt relaxed. After Bayhead, they would reach the Keroon River, where there was a good road leading directly to Benden. He wasn't far away now. He hoped that the message he was carrying for the Lord Warder of Benden wouldn't be long outdated by the time he delivered it.

Coron retired for the night without saying a word to anyone. On his way out of the firelit circle, he kicked a little spray of loose earth at Robinton, who ignored the gesture. The others noticed it, but made no reference to it since Robinton did not. It made no sense to provoke him. They might have to coexist a long time at the Hold. He'd have to suggest a fostering out for Coron to Harper Evarel. Preferably one far distant from Benden.

Keir had made the whole group fill waterskins and bottles before they approached the marsh. Robinton appreciated why the next day. The water and even the very air were flavored with the fetid taint of the swamp.

Marsh-dwellers chirped and croaked in a monotonous cacophony that chipped away at everyone's nerves. Robinton found that every song he tried to play ended up canted to the rhythm of the croakers' chorus.

And the marsh was doing its best to encroach upon the road. The trees and their hanging moss curtained each bend so that it was impossible to see more than a length forward or behind, and the growth to the sides was thick and slimy in texture. The riders stayed in front or behind the wagons, avoiding any contact with the plant life.

Coron rode between the wains, keeping in the exact center of the pathway. Marsh-dwellers and snakes hopped or slithered across the road at intervals, making the runners very nervous.

Robinton had a green stripe on one shoulder of his cloth tunic. Warned by Keir about the moss, he had worn his oldest clothes. He was glad he'd paid heed to the trader. Coron had on a hide tunic which was too hot for the weather, but wouldn't stain. He was uncomfortable, which augmented his bad temper.

There was a loud squeal behind him, and Wissa cried, "My lord! Catch him! Catch him!"

Robinton turned around, in time to see Coron's runner toss him from the backpad and make off in a panic, passing by the wagon. The Harper's hand shot out and snatched at the trailing leads of the panicked animal. He threw himself backward, bracing his feet against the splashboard of the wagon. The runner's speed nearly yanked his arm off, but the shock of the pull on its metal mouthpiece brought the beast to a surprised stop. Keir halted the wagon.

"What happened?" he demanded.

Wissa had already climbed out and was helping Coron to his feet. "A marsh-dweller jumped up right under his beast's nose, Father. Are you all right?"

"Yes, yes," Coron said, impatiently, but pleased to get the attention. He rubbed his back with one hand while gesturing imperiously at Robinton to bring him his runner. The Harper scowled, tired of Coron's lordly behavior. "My runner, Harper. Now!"

"There's no need to speak sharply, my lord," Robinton said gently, extending the leads to him.

Coron slapped his hand away and gathered up the reins himself. "You have no right to tell me how to act, Harper." He made the title a slap. Robinton would have enjoyed wiping that arrogant sneer off Coron's face. But he didn't know if the consequences would be worth it.

If Robinton decides he's been provoked enough, turn to section 145.

If he decides it would cause too much trouble later, turn to section 149.

* 141 *

He leaped forward, bringing the man down. The tool bag flew off. Robinton promised himself he'd retrieve it later, but he had to subdue this wretched fellow and bring him back to Keir. Who knows what else he would have taken if Robinton hadn't heard him? He aimed a punch at the thief's jaw, only to miss when he was flung off onto the ground. His lighter weight put him at a disadvantage. He clambered to his knees, trying to recover himself, and put his hands up to guard his head. The other seized a stick and brought it down across Robinton's back.

He dropped face down to the brown leaves on the forest floor. The thief brought back a foot to kick him, but Robinton grabbed his leg and threw him forward. He landed with a thud, and the youth twisted the thief's arm up between his shoulder blades. He snaked a foot out and caught the strap of his tool bag, then forced the man to his feet.

Keir's men, half-asleep, received the struggling thief with grim smiles. Two of them held him while the caravan's master grabbed his jaw and wrenched it from one side to the other. The man cowered, his eyes rolling in fear. Keir slapped his cheek with a palm.

"So, a sneaker, eh? We like to catch such as you, don't we, lads?" The men assented in growls. "Thieving could get you killed, you know. Or lose an arm. How would you like that?" Keir seized the thief's right wrist, only to have it snatched out of his grip. "Got some fight in you. Good, it'll be a more even contest. Teach him a lesson, lads, then fling him out. But I'll take his knife first, so he doesn't try to add murder to his crimes." Keir slid the belt knife out of the man's sheath and threw it into the bonfire. He turned away as his men dragged the thief off.

"Journeyman, I owe you a great deal. I have some valuable merchandise with me, much more than I care to lose to a night thief. Thank you. You're a brave man, taking a chance like that."

"I should have done it in any case," Robinton said, displaying his tool bag. "But I had a special incentive. He was stealing my property, too."

Keir laughed. "Well, public minded or self-interested, I'm still grateful. I might offer you a reward . . ."

"No, I can't accept a reward. Thank you all the same. I'd consider it more of a favor if I could go back to sleep."

"I insist. Your travel fare returned." Keir saw the temptation in Robinton's eyes though it was quickly supressed. "Part of it, then. Four marks?"

The young man gave in. "Thank you, Keir. It's generous of you."

If Robinton still has numbweed and uses it, roll 1 D6 per application and restore that number of hit points to his total. Remove from the record sheet if it is used up.

Turn to section 153.

* 142 *

The torguana, correctly judging that Robinton was responsible for its predicament, snaked its ugly mouth out and bit him. He dropped back, trying to circle around behind and stab at it. It wheeled and hissed furiously. Its feet were bound tightly together, making the stupid thing fall over again and again. It struggled at the end of its rope, trying to attack him. He threw up his arms to fend it off, receiving a slash on the forearm from its claws which might have hit his face. His heel slipped in the sand and he fell down.

The lizard lunged at him, dropping again, neck outstretched to the ground. Robinton drew both legs up and brought his heels crashing down on its head. As it lay stunned, he held it down and slashed through its neck. The blood spattered him as he sat on the sand panting.

Turn to section 151.

* 143 *

"It has been the duty and the pleasure of my family to Hold in Benden for many generations. I think, Harper, that this sort of chastisement is best left to me." Robinton stopped, surprised. Coron nodded to him politely, then rounded on the unfortunate carter. "In my family's Hold there are Records of the names, long Records, of the dragonriders who died to save Pern for your grandad, and your grandad's grandad. If a Harper," he indicated Robinton, "chooses to remind you of your duty, you ought to thank him. You lack respect. Robinton." The Holder addressed him by his name for the first time. "Will you continue to play?"

"Of course, my lord."

"Coron. Just Coron, all right?"

Robinton's eyebrows climbed. "Coron." The harp sang a glissando.

> "From the Weyr and from the Bowl,
> Bronze and brown and blue and green,
> Rise the dragonmen of Pern,
> Aloft on wing; seen, then unseen."

The Lord Holder's son nodded, listening critically. Robinton watched his face, until Coron met his eyes. "That was a sound trouncing you gave out. I won't tell my father if you won't."

"Agreed!" Robinton said, heartily.

Turn to section 138.

* 144 *

He leaped forward, bringing the man down. The tool bag flew off. Robinton promised himself he'd retrieve it later, but he had to subdue this wretched fellow and bring him back to Keir. Who knows what else he would have taken if Robinton hadn't heard him? He aimed a punch at the thief's jaw, only to miss when he was flung off onto the ground. His lighter weight put him at a disadvantage. He clambered to his knees, trying to recover himself, and put his hands up to guard his head. The other seized a stick and brought it down across Robinton's back.

He dropped face down in the brown leaves on the forest floor. The thief brought back a foot to kick him, but Robinton grabbed his leg and threw him forward. He landed next to the Harper, but he was prepared. He flipped over on his back and brought a heel down hard into Robinton's stomach. The youth's breath exploded out of him and he collapsed. He heard the jingle of the tool bag as the other man picked it up and ran away.

If Robinton has lost all his hit points, turn to section 29.

If not, turn to section 150.

* 145 *

"Someone ought to," Robinton said, folding his arms. "You've been rude and uncooperative throughout this journey. No one's dared to say a word to you about it because you're a Lord Holder's son. That doesn't excuse you from behaving with common courtesy."

"What?" Coron turned purple. "What do you think you're saying? Who do you think you are?"

"I'm a Harper," he answered calmly, "and I'm telling you the truth about yourself: something you're hearing possibly for the first time in your life."

Coron, teeth clenched, advanced on Robinton with his fists up. They were fairly evenly matched. Coron was stockier but Robinton had the advantage of reach and agility over the shorter boy. The Harper was prepared to meet him, cost what it may.

CORON
To be hit: 10 To hit Robinton: 11 Hit points: 10
Each does 1 D6 damage with fists. Neither is attacking to do permanent damage. Whomever is reduced to 0 hit points is knocked unconscious.

If Robinton loses, turn to section 154.

If he wins, turn to section 136.

* 146 *

The torguana, correctly judging that Robinton was responsible for its predicament, snaked its ugly mouth out and bit at him. He dropped back, trying to circle around behind and stab at it. It shrieked, switching its tail furiously. Its feet were bound tightly together, making the stupid lizard fall over again and again. It scrambled at the end of its rope, trying to attack him. He threw up his arms to fend it off, receiving a slash on the forearm from its claws which might have hit his face. His heel slipped in the sand and he fell to his knees just within the lizard's range.

The torguana lunged at him, snapping furiously. Its teeth made a lucky jab at his upper arm. It must have hit something important, damaging the bicep, rendering the whole arm useless. His hand shaking, Robinton dropped his knife and rolled away from the beast. Tearing a strip off the hem of his shirt, he did his best to bind the wound so it would stop bleeding. Pain made him clumsy, and he judged that he had lost too much blood by the time he got the cloth tied, using one hand and his teeth. The lizard screamed in his ears. He felt dizzy. The best thing for him to do was to lie down and rest. With the lizard's hisses in his ears, Robinton lapsed into unconsciousness.

Turn to section 29.

* 147 *

Keir's men, half-asleep, pulled the struggling thief off of Robinton's chest. Two of them held him while the caravan's master examined the young Harper.

"He's hit you hard, young one. No, don't try to move." He looked around for his wife, who had disappeared back into their shelter. "She's getting some numbweed. You need more than that, but it's all we have with us."

Robinton tried to speak, but it hurt too much to get words out. Pain. Pain in his back and throat.

"Just relax, Journeyman. You'll be all right. We'll get you to a healer as soon as we can. We owe you a lot. This miserable thief will go to the Warders in Bayhead. Relax."

With a sigh that sounded more like a groan to the traders, Robinton willed himself to relax. His eyes closed.

Turn to section 29.

* 148 *

"It has been the duty and the pleasure of my family to Hold in Benden for many generations. I think, Harper, that this sort of chastisement is best left to me." Robinton stopped, surprised. Coron nodded to him politely, then rounded on the unfortunate carter. "In my family's Hold there are Records of the names, long Records, of the dragonriders who died to save Pern for your grandad, and your grandad's grandad. If a Harper," he indicated Robinton, "chooses to remind you of your duty, you ought to thank him. You lack respect. As for you, Harper, you ought to understand your place. When we reach Bayhead, I intend to bespeak the Hold Harper and see you sent home until you understand where your authority lies and where it does not."

Robinton kept silent, knowing that speaking out now would only worsen his case. The beautiful harp lay forgotten in his arms.

"Brawling! And speaking out in front of me, presuming to take my place in instructing a surly wretch who has forgotten his gratitude toward dragonkind . . ."

The Bayhead Harper, a brown-haired giant of a man with a surprisingly gentle manner, interrupted Coron mildly, "But it is a Harper's duty to instruct in the Teachings, Lord Coron."

"Fighting, then! He struck me. Me, a son of the Hold."

"And you, you did not strike him back? His reaction was unprovoked?"

"Someone needs to teach him his place." Coron fixed Harper Mettin with a gaze calculated to put fear into the recipient. Mettin smiled patiently at him.

"Youthful spirits, my lord. Neither of you was seriously injured, I trust?"

"No, but . . ."

"Then let the Harper Hall take care of its own. Good day, my lord, and good journey. Remember me to your father." Mettin hustled Coron to the door and out. He turned back to Robinton when the door closed. "I think you had better go home for a time, young one. At least until that hot-headed bundle of conceit forgets the slight. You won the fight, didn't you?" It was more a statement than a question. Robinton nodded, head down. "A most important part of our job is diplomacy. It appears in many forms, some most unpalatable to the diplomat. I also agree that you had to speak out against disrespect to the Weyr. We are in a difficult position today on Pern. Time was, many, many Turns back, when Harpers were much more respected than they are now. We tread cautiously. We must. Well, I will explain it to the Masterharper. It is for your own safety, you do understand that?"

"Oh, yes," Robinton said in a low tone. "I do understand."

Turn to section 29.

* 149 *

Robinton swallowed his angry words. If he said anything at all, especially what was on the end of his tongue, he'd be involving himself in another brawl, something he must avoid. He was by no means ready to go home to the Harper Hall in disgrace, so he bowed coldly and took his seat again in the wagon. Keir looked uncomfortably from the journeyman Harper to the Lord Holder's son, but kept silent. He took the reins, and the caravan moved again. Robinton sat beside him, clenching his fingers together in frustration.

Go to section 139.

* 150 *

He limped back into the camp, where Keir and his men, groggy but awake, were waiting for him. The caravan master eyed the bruises and stains Robinton was sporting.

"What happened, lad?"

"A sneak-thief. I saw him going through the wain, and I ran after him. He stole my instrument-making tools," Robinton added, dejectedly.

"Did he take anything else?" Keir asked anxiously.

"No. I chased him away before he could try."

"You were brave to tackle him by yourself, Journeyman. You have my thanks. I should offer you a reward."

Robinton waved the idea away. "No, thank you."

"What?" Coron said from the doorway of the shelter. He had finally made an appearance, and the carters eyed him with barely concealed contempt. "Pay him for losing his property? Rewards for stupidity, eh? Bad business, trader."

"For trying to save the caravan, my lord," Keir corrected him with careful patience.

"Oh." Coron yawned. "Is that all?" Stretching theatrically, he went back to bed.

Turning away from Coron, the others hastened to

congratulate Robinton on what they considered a laudable feat. Keir made further attempts to have him accept a reward.

They agreed finally that Robinton would accept four marks. With that matter settled to everyone's satisfaction, they all went back to bed.

If Robinton still has numbweed and uses it, roll 1 D6 and restore that number of hit points to his total.
Turn to section 153.

* 151 *

"I did it!" he crowed. "Look at that, Twitch, I killed it!"

The little gray runner answered him from its hiding place in the bushes. Robinton peered around the branches. "Oh, that's right, you're not Twitch," the young Harper said, getting to his feet and walking over to him. "I never did give you a name, did I? Well, I'm used to it, so you can be Twitch Too. It's a tradition-honored name, you know." The little beast nuzzled his hand, uncomprehending. Robinton stroked the soft gray nose, then ripped a strip off his old bath sheet to bind up his forearm.

He went out to retrieve the dead lizard. Blood was still pouring in a sticky red stream from the severed neck. He untied his gitar strings, and bound its feet with the short piece of rope. He let the carcass swing from the ring on the gray's harness. He'd roast it later that evening and have a feast.

The blood ceased to drip in a fairly short time, and Robinton poured some water on the stains it left on Twitch Too's coat. He rubbed the ruddy marks out, leaving the gray coat damp and matted but clean. The runner didn't seem to notice or mind what he was doing.

Robinton camped that evening under the shelter of a natural sea wall above the narrowed beach. He paced out the lines which marked high and low tide, and judged that he would have a slight but acceptable margin if the tide did come in while he was there. A considerable amount of floating wood had come ashore within a few lengths of his camp, and he roasted his lizard over a roaring bonfire. It took him hours sitting on a pile of driftwood to skin the enormous lizard. Robinton had renewed respect for the Hall kitchen drudges who were able to prepare so much food in a single day.

The aroma of cooking aroused his hunger long before the lizard was ready to eat. He had time to climb up the nearest switchback and pull enough grass and plants for Twitch Too to eat. It was quite dark before the lizard was done. He fell to with good appetite, cutting portions off the carcass with his belt knife.

Broad leaves made acceptable packaging for the remainder. Cooked meat would last a good long time, even in the heat. He promised himself he'd remember to purchase extra provisions in Bayhead. Hunting was difficult for someone of his inexperience, and he couldn't count upon being lucky.

After his meal, he curled up in his cloak to go to sleep. The fire was dying down, and the waves washed soothingly up and back on the beach.

Sometime during the night, Twitch Too whinnied in fear. Robinton was instantly alert. He heard growling from more than one direction. He turned his head from side to side, trying to guess how many wild beasts, and what they were. He peered out of the circle of fire. Glowing eyes stared back at him. Too tall for whers. They must be wild canines. He'd heard that they roamed in packs, carrying off young flock animals and eating carrion. And they smelled the blood from Robinton's lizard. Another frightened cry from Twitch Too, and then hoofbeats on the sand as the runner fled. The canines closed in. Their teeth gleamed in the firelight as they growled and slavered at him.

If Robinton should try to run away, turn to section 152.

If he decides to fight them, turn to section 158.

If he runs behind his campfire, turn to section 161.

* 152 *

Robinton fingered his knife, but it gave him no confidence. He might use it as a last defense, but it couldn't help him much against three large hungry animals. The cooked meat wouldn't satisfy them. They'd eat that, and then begin on him and Twitch. They stood just outside the firelight waiting for him to move first.

He decided that the best thing to do would be to get away and let them have the torguana meat. If they moved toward the pack, he could escape past them and hide somewhere until they went away. The biggest one snarled at him. He stretched out his hand for the pack full of meat, flung carelessly to the ground by the fire. The canines growled, and he drew back.

Another attempt, moving slower than before. The beasts kept their eyes on him. His hand touched the strap. He curved his fingers around it, still not making any sudden moves. Lifting it toward him, he noticed the canines' eyes go to the pack.

In a sudden explosive movement, Robinton swung the

pack in an arc and let it go flying. It landed in their midst, startling them, and he dashed off across the sand, hoping he could escape.

Contrary to his prediction, the canines followed him. And they moved faster than ever he had expected. He ran south, trying to find the nearest stream in the dark. If he could cross the water, they might lose his scent.

Once he was out of the firelight, however, the animals were upon him. The big leader sank its fangs into his calf, and he tripped. The other two prepared to spring at him. Somehow he staggered to his feet. He wiped at the blood and sand on his cheek. The canines moved toward him.

LEAD CANINE
To be hit: 9 To hit Robinton: 10 Hit points: 6
Teeth do 1 D6 damage.

CANINES (TWO)
To be hit: 9 To hit Robinton: 11 Hit points: 4
Teeth do 1 D6 damage.

The Lead Canine and one of the other two will get one attack on Robinton.

If Robinton runs out of hit points, turn to section 29.

If not, turn to section 158.

* 153 *

Beginning the next morning, the carters treated Robinton with an additional measure of respect. When he made an effort to help break camp, one or another of Keir's workers took the bundle out of his hands, or took over a task that he had begun. At last, he conceded, and sat on the bench of the wain, practicing on his gitar and chatting with Keir's wife.

Coron had decided to remain abed long after everyone else had risen. As a result, no one was able to strike and pack the hide shelter. Anyone who tried to suggest to his lordship that it was time to get up was treated to an earful of invective. At last, the carters appealed to Keir, who went in to talk with Coron. In a very short time, the Lord Holder appeared, bad-tempered and inclined to be obstructive. Somehow, even with his interference, the caravan was on the road within an hour. Robinton was curious, but he didn't dare ask Keir what sort of lever he'd used on Coron to get him out of bed.

The caravan master was in good spirits that morning. He too treated Robinton well for having saved his property. Even when his wife reminded him to pay the Harper the promised four marks, he still maintained his good humor.

Robinton pocketed his reward money with some reluctance. He didn't consider it to be fair to benefit from an action which anyone would have performed. Nobody in the train begrudged him, since he still bore the marks of his confrontation with the thief, but he still felt a little awkward. Keir's wife coaxed him out of his tunic, and mended the three-cornered tear in the sleeve which he hadn't noticed himself.

The young lord showed all the signs of being jealous of the attention Robinton was receiving. He remained coldly aloof all day long, ignoring all attempts to draw him into conversations, songs or games. His attitude even reached to Wissa, who was hurt and disappointed by the loss of her admirer. She turned her attentions to the Harper, who kept her amused, but made no effort to pay her the same sort of compliments.

They rested that afternoon in a valley with a sandy bottom that descended all the way to the bay. A shallow stream bubbling with fresh water emptied into the salt water bisected a narrow wedge of beach. Most of the others elected to stay in the shade, but Robinton thought it would be more agreeable to nap in the sunshine.

Turn to section 137.

* 154 *

His nonchalant pose broke the instant Coron jumped toward him. As Coron swung, Robinton's arms flashed open and out, knocking the punch away and cracking the edge of his other hand against Coron's other wrist. Howling, Coron put his head down and charged at him. Unfortunately, the Harper had left himself wide open to an attack of that kind. He backed up hastily toward a tree. He braced himself, raised a foot and kicked his opponent in the chest. Coron grunted, but grabbed hold of the leg. With a vicious twist, he tossed the Harper to the ground and kicked him in the ribs before stooping to pummel with his fists. Robinton tried to fend off the attack, but Coron's punches were hitting several spots which had been much abused on his long journey, and he was fast losing strength.

Section 155

He saw the last punch coming toward his face with a sort of detached interest. And then he saw nothing at all.

Coron backed up from the Harper's prone form. "Well, you all saw! Brawling! My father will have something to say about that!"

The others paid no attention to him, but gathered up the pathetic sprawl of limbs and settled Robinton comfortably in the lead wagon. It was clear they agreed completely with what the Harper had said before. Wissa sat down next to Robinton to wash the blood off his face. He didn't stir.

Turn to section 29.

* 155 *

"It has been the duty and the pleasure of my family to Hold in Benden for many generations. I think, Harper, that this sort of chastisement is best left to me." Robinton stopped, surprised. Coron nodded to him politely, then rounded on the unfortunate carter. "In my family's Hold there are Records of the names, long Records, of the dragonriders who died to save Pern for your grandad, and your grandad's grandad. If a Harper," he indicated Robinton, "chooses to remind you of your duty, you ought to thank him. You lack respect. As for you," he rounded on Robinton, "you ought to understand your place. When we reach Bayhead, I intend to bespeak the Hold Harper and see that he instructs you in a Harper's place, for which you ought to thank me. I could recommend you go home, but I know more than to interfere with crafthall disciplines."

Dismayed, Robinton kept silent, knowing that speaking out now would only worsen his case. The beautiful harp lay forgotten in his arms. He worried all the way to Bayhead whether Coron would fulfill his threat.

When the caravan came to a stop in the merchant's quarter of the Hold, Coron had evidently forgotten all about his grudge against the Harper. Courteously, he helped Wissa down from her seat, and they went off together to see the Hold. Robinton wiped imaginary sweat from his brow, and set off in search of the Bayhead Harper.

He was a brown-haired giant of a man with a surprisingly gentle manner, who listened sympathetically to Robinton's recital of his woes. "I agree with you," Harper Mettin said at last. "I don't think he'll come in search of me now, but you must be more careful. A most important part of our job is diplomacy. It appears in many forms, some most unpalatable to the diplomat. I also agree that you had to speak out against disrespect to the Weyr. We are in a difficult position today on Pern. Time was, many, many Turns back, when Harpers were much more respected than they are now. We tread cautiously. We must. Well, enough of that. Come with me."

Turn to section 138.

* 156 *

C'gan made a little bow at the door and disappeared down the stone hall. Robinton watched after him for a moment, then took a deep draught of wine. "I wish I could see a Hatching," he said wistfully.

"That's a bold request, young man. No one outside of the Weyr attends Hatchings."

Robinton looked a little ashamed. "I suppose that I'm

taking the Master Harper's assignment too seriously. I don't mean to behave improperly. My only intention is to learn as much as I can about the Weyr, so that I can help to spread the knowledge."

"Well spoken, journeyman. I've been so hidebound in my own assignment for so many Turns I don't recognize a new idea when I hear it, and that's a sad pass for a Harper." The big man strode to the doorway and bellowed, "C'gan! C'gan! CAIGAN!"

Far away down the hall, a diminished voice called back. "What is it?"

"Come back here!" Mettin grinned conspiratorily at Robinton. "You're forgetting your passenger."

Turn to section 176.

* 157 *

The knife hit the snake's back just behind its head, pinning it to the ground. It was probably already dead, but it continued to thrash around as if it were still alive. The runner continued to dance on it until he had flattened the head and a good portion of its body into a bloody tatter. Twitch stood over it panting as Robinton came over to pet and soothe him.

"We make a good team, little fellow. If I ever decide to give up being a Harper, we could go into the snake-killing business."

Twitch just brayed.

Turn to section 173.

* 158 *

Drawing his knife, Robinton let go a loud growl, trying to intimidate his attackers. The big animal seemed taken aback, but the two smaller ones jumped forward, aiming for his throat. He was knocked down. Striking about him with his knife, he tried to regain his feet. The leader charged forward, its fangs shining in the moonlight, and made a grab for his knife hand. He brought it up and away just in time, but it left his guard open. The canine growled and leaped for him. The other two bared their teeth at him, waiting.

LEAD CANINE
To be hit: 9 To hit Robinton: 12 Hit points: 6
Teeth do 1 D6 damage.

CANINES (TWO)
To be hit: 9 To hit Robinton: 13 Hit points: 4
Teeth do 1 D6 damage.

The Lead Canine and one of the other two will get one attack on Robinton.

Robinton must kill all three of them.

If he loses, turn to section 167.

If he wins, turn to section 160.

* 159 *

As the snake struck out, Twitch reared up and brought his small sharp hooves down on the beast's head. Robinton rose and drew the pack from behind him. Hefting his knife, he threw it at the snake's body.

Roll 3 D6.

If the total rolled is less than or equal to Robinton's value for Dexterity, turn to section 157.

If greater, turn to section 171.

* 160 *

He snapped a kick at the throat of the nearest canine. It staggered back. Imitating their growl low in his throat, Robinton crouched, knife extended. He backed toward the campfire, trying to keep the canines from getting behind him. The leader dove at him. He slashed at it, knife point drawing a black line through the coarse yellow fur. It jumped back, and all three snarled at him from the darkness.

One of the smaller canines crept forward, growling. As he turned to confront it, the other sprang at him. Spinning toward the assault, he plunged his knife into the canine's belly. It dropped, dragging his knife hand with it. He pulled back, but the lead animal had come forward to sink its teeth into his arm. Sacrificing the pain to expedience, Robinton yanked the beast forward, jumping over a protruding corner of the bonfire. His clothes steamed that close to the blaze. The canine fell into the center of the fire, yelping.

As he emerged from the fire, one of the surviving canines went for his throat. He flung up his empty hand to guard it and stabbed out with his knife. The beast howled its agony. He jerked the blade upward, and the animal fell dead at his feet. The last canine circled him, unwilling to get too close. Robinton grabbed a burning branch from the fire and thrust it into the creature's face. It howled, and fled off into the darkness.

In the morning, Robinton woke up with something tickling his nose. He sneezed and opened his eyes to find he was dusted with the charred remains of his driftwood fire. He stripped and ran into the sea to bathe away the smell of ash.

Presently, Twitch trotted up to him. He looked bedraggled and miserable. Robinton curried him with a brush, and soon the little runner seemed to recover his usual good mood. He nickered away in his odd little voice while Robinton made his own toilet.

Turn to section 168.

* 161 *

Robinton fingered his knife, but it gave him no confidence. He might use it as a last defense, but it couldn't help him much against three large, hungry animals. The cooked meat wouldn't satisfy them. They'd eat that, and then begin on him and Twitch. They stood just outside the firelight waiting for him to move first. It was clear they were afraid of the fire. That gave him the basis for a plan. He stretched out his hand for the pack full of meat, flung carelessly to the ground by the fire. The canines growled, and he drew back in alarm. The growling subsided as soon as he stopped moving.

Another attempt, moving slower than before. The beasts kept their eyes on him. His hand touched the strap. He curved his fingers around it, still not making any sudden moves. Bringing it toward him, he noticed the canines' eyes go to the pack.

In a sudden explosive movement, Robinton swung the pack in an arc. The canines jumped back in fear, and the Harper scurried around the fire to the other side. Now he had the seawall behind him, and only two open sides to guard.

Unwrapping a chunk of cooked meat, he flung it as far as he could into the darkness. The three pairs of eyes blinked out, and he heard growling and yelping as they fought for the scrap of torguana. In the interval, he kicked, dragged and pushed firewood to close off one side. He balanced a burning brand atop the heap, and waited for it to catch.

Too quickly, the canines were back. They circled the blaze, hunting for the meal they knew to be there. Robinton threw another piece of meat, and followed it with another chunk off in the opposite direction. The beasts raced after it, fighting for the prize. He pulled more wood back until it touched the seawall, and set it alight. Now Robinton was surrounded by a ring of fire, and safe from the canine pack. If he didn't run out of fuel. The howling went on in the darkness. He sat down to wait.

In the morning, Robinton woke up with something tickling his nose. He sneezed and opened his eyes to find he was still seated upright against the cliff foot. The charred remains of his driftwood fire had blown cinders all over him, and his sleeves and the ends of his hair and eyebrows were slightly singed. He stripped and ran into the sea to bathe away the smell of ash.

Presently, Twitch trotted up to him. He looked bedraggled and miserable. Robinton curried him with a brush, and soon the little runner seemed to recover his usual good mood. He nickered away in his odd little voice while Robinton made his own toilet.

Turn to section 168.

* 162 *

Bending his knees just a fraction, Robinton flung his hands up and leaped for the branch. He missed it by just a fingertip, and bent to try again. But the snake wasn't giving him a second chance. It slithered forward and sprang at him.

SNAKE
To be hit: 11 *To hit Robinton: 12* *Hit points: 5*
A bite does two points damage plus injects venom. On any successful hit, roll 3 D6 against Robinton's value for Constitution. If you roll a total greater than that value, subtract three additional hit points for damage for the poison.

If Robinton kills the snake, turn to section 169.

If he runs out of hit points, turn to section 174.

* 163 *

He closed his eye and concentrated on staying relaxed. Disciplining his nerves and muscles not to twitch was difficult with the buzzing of the snake's tail incessantly reminding him of the penalty for sudden movement. He was aware of every knob and bump of the carrysack digging into his back, and every pebble and damp patch of mud under his bottom. With deliberate detachment, he sensed a blood-sucking insect land on his wrist and plunge its stinger into his skin. It itched furiously, and he knew there'd be a mark-sized red bump, but it was better than a snakebite.

Some of the insect's friends flew by to have a snack, too. The hardest one to tolerate was one which landed on his cheekbone. Abruptly, the snake stopped rattling its tail. It slithered heavily across Robinton's legs, and he was horribly frightened that it was going for his throat, but it kept moving over and off. Amazingly, he heard Twitch, returning from his browse, neigh a fierce warning. The snake hissed back.

Robinton opened his eyes and stared. The snake had coiled itself up, and was threatening the little runner beast. Twitch's long ears were laid back on his neck, and he had one hoof raised. The serpent feinted toward the runner, and he stepped one pace backward. It rearranged itself a little closer. Twitch screamed at it.

If Robinton should try to help the runner, turn to section 159.

If he doesn't move, turn to section 170.

* 164 *

Bending his knees just a fraction, Robinton flung his hands up and leaped for the branch. In a moment, he had scrambled onto the limb, just over the hissing snake. He jeered at it, relieved to have made his escape.

In a short while, the reptile tired of waiting for its prey to return to attack it, and slithered off. Robinton waited until it was long gone before creeping toward the bole of the tree. He could see Twitch meandering up and down the road, looking for things to eat. With one hand, he pushed away the leaves and vines from the crotch of the tree, so he could put his foot there.

One of the "vines" rose up and hissed at him. It was another snake, sleeping draped over the tree branch. Robinton flung himself backward away from it.

Roll 3 D6.

If the total is less than or equal to Robinton's value for Dexterity, turn to section 166.

If greater, turn to section 175.

* 165 *

It wouldn't make any sense to lie here and wait for it to decide. The snake continued to sway back and forth. In a lightning movement, he rolled over and over to the left, away from the snake. It struck out, luckily hitting only his upflung boot heel. Kicking it away, he leaped to his feet and drew his knife. The snake, recoiling and winding itself up again, hissed furiously at him.

It was farther away than striking distance. Robinton wondered whether he should take the chance on running away now, or trying to kill it. He looked around for weapons. There were none. He was too far from his pack to shield himself with it, and all the stones nearby were bigger than he could easily throw.

No, wait! There was a low tree branch over his head. He could just reach it. If he climbed up, he would be safe.

Roll 3 D6.

If the total is less than or equal to Robinton's value for Dexterity, turn to section 164.

If greater, turn to section 162.

* 166 *

He grabbed the branch and did a neat somersault out of the tree, dropping to the ground on his feet. Backing away hastily, he scanned the branch for signs that the snake might be following to attack him. No, not yet. He listened for the rattling. Probably the creature had just gone back to sleep. Thank goodness.

Twitch trotted over to find out what he was doing. He sniffed curiously at Robinton's tunic. The Harper laughed and scratched the beast's furry ears. "Let's go to Bayhead, little one."

Turn to section 173.

* 167 *

He snapped a kick at the throat of the nearest canine. It staggered back. Imitating their growl low in his throat, Robinton crouched, knife extended. He backed toward the campfire, trying to keep the canines from getting behind him. The leader dove at him. He slashed at it, knife point drawing a black line through the coarse yellow fur. It jumped back, and all three snarled at him from the darkness.

One of the smaller canines crept forward, growling. As he turned to confront it, the other sprang at him. Spinning toward the assault, he plunged his knife into the canine's belly. It dropped, dragging his knife hand with it. He pulled back, but the lead animal had come forward to sink its teeth into his arm. Sacrificing the pain to expedience, Robinton yanked the beast forward, jumping over a protruding corner of the bonfire. His clothes steamed that close to the blaze, but the canine let go.

As he emerged from the fire, the leader went for his throat. He flung up his empty hand to guard it and stabbed out with his knife. The beast howled its agony. Its surviving packmate jumped for Robinton before he could ward it off, its teeth tearing the side of his throat. He felt the searing pain and wetness running down over his collarbone. His knife slammed home in the animal's belly. It fell dead. Robinton stood panting. He was exhausted.

The lead canine still lived, though marked and bleeding from the Harper's slashes. It attacked him, biting again and again. Robinton seized a burning faggot from the fire and thrust it into the animal's face. Baying, the wounded canine fled into the darkness. The Harper dropped his branch. His knife fell unnoticed from his other hand. Blood dripped from his fingers. He raised his hand to look at the dark streams, and dropped to one knee without intending to. The world spun. He was aware of agony in his neck and shoulder and arm. He felt his cheek hit the sand. His back was warmed by the blazing bonfire.

Turn to section 29.

* 168 *

Robinton made haste under the sun, chewing some of his much-defended torguana meat while he walked. The little runner snatched its meals on the march as well, often yanking its lead out of Robinton's grasp when he tried to pull it past especially delectable-looking plants. But on the whole it seemed to understand his impatience to move on.

He climbed to the top of a bluff and shaded his eyes with a hand against the bright cloudless sky. Instead of the interminable water, there appeared at the end of the bay a wide dark sliver. Land! That must be where the shore curved westward. If he had been long enough in the eye, he'd have been able to see Bayhead Hold and the swamp on its eastern border. He was within two days' journey of them.

By afternoon, he was walking asleep on his feet. He had reached a small strip where the beach was bisected by a stream running down from a patch of forest. He elected to take a nap in the sun and bake his sore muscles. There was no place to tether Twitch, so he took the little runner farther into the wood and tied him near plenty of grass.

He chose a spot that was just under the branches of the last tree before the open beach, well within hearing range if anything frightened Twitch, but not close enough to listen to the runner's industrious chewing. The sea was very shallow here, and the water waved a warm breeze in his direction. It felt good to him. His cloak was spread out as a ground cloth, and his pack made a somewhat bulgy pillow. Lulled by the roar and crash of the waves a safe distance away, he fell asleep.

And dreamed of dragons. He'd spotted another dragon, a blue, circling high overhead the day before. Their beauty and grace charmed him, these giant protectors of Pern. He felt a surge of pride in knowing that his job was soon to be bringing back to them the attention and respect of a world that had nearly forgotten them. A flight of dragons on wings of song.

In his dream, a wing formation of each color of dragons danced in the sky, brown, green, blue, bronze, weaving around and about a fabulous queen dragon, who hovered in the sky like a golden beam of light. With a cry, the wings disappeared Between, all except a brown dragon, which flew down and perched on a tree branch.

It seemed perfectly plausible at first, this dragon in a tree, until his conscious mind questioned the idea. No tree existed which was large enough to support a roosting dragon. But there it was, as clear as . . . day.

Robinton sat up, looking around. There was the tree branch from his dream, directly over his head. Of course there was no dragon on it. To have formed the correct perspective, any dragon that sat on it would have had to be less than an armslength long. No, no. He must have seen a small wherry. But he was sure it had had wings and four limbs, not just wings and two.

Section 168

Dreams could play strange tricks.

His rest that night was not disturbed by wherries, wild beasts or dragons that sat in trees. He was glad of his fire, for it was especially cold. He bundled up in both tunics and his cloak, and slept in a ball on the leeward side of the flames.

He followed a trail in the morning that had been cut by the wheels of many wagons and carts. Everything around him smelled musty, and hanging moss decorated nearly every tree. Marsh-dwellers sang their monotonous chorus in a slow march beat. Robinton played marches, and then improvised counterpoint to their song.

Whimsically, he pretended Twitch was a child of Teaching age, and dutifully played teaching ballads for him. Twitch swiveled his long gray ears to listen, and commented occasionally. He performed the Lord Holder song, changing a nuance here, a phrase there. If he was going to have to perform it in Benden, he wanted it to be flawless.

The hanging trees meeting over the path made him think he was walking down a long green tube. Mottled shadows changed patterns on the road as the branches swayed hypnotically in the slight breeze. Marsh-dwellers, lizards and snakes hopped or slithered across before and behind him. He stopped to put on his oldest shirt, because streamers of green would drop unexpectedly out of the trees, and he didn't want stains on his best clothes.

Snakes dropped out of the trees, too. The first one startled him into jumping, but he soon got used to it. When he saw a long shadow begin to descend, he'd bet himself whether it was a snake or a rope of moss. The air was thick and moist, and as the day progressed, it got hotter, until he was virtually gasping for air through the humidity. The little breeze teased him by whisking a tiny zephyr past him through a gap in the wall of plants, stirring up a little cool air. He could see reeds waving beyond the road on both sides. No wind strong enough to dispel the miasma ever penetrated the green corridor.

A big marsh-dweller hopped out into the middle of the road and creaked threateningly at them. When they ignored it, it puffed up its neck until it looked ready to explode, still creaking imperiously. Its bulgy eyes and solemn expression made Robinton think of a fat Holder about to lose his temper. He imitated its stance, puffing out his own chest, arms akimbo, but it was his laughter ringing in the silence that drove it away. The marsh-dweller gave one final croak of disapproval and threshed off into the bushes.

The road was opening up as it turned toward the east. Off to his right, Robinton could see irregular avenues of broad-boled trees marching toward the north. The land dipped into a flat river valley, and he had to ford his way across the wide, sluggish stream which no doubt fed the marsh itself.

He sat down to enjoy some lunch now that there was cool air to breathe. The big trees to his left still were dressed in their sad streamers of green. The gray runner placidly tucked into the grass and young reeds on the roadside. Arranging his pack behind him as a pad against the tough bark, Robinton rested under a tree, long legs crossed at the ankle. He tuned his gitar, then decided he'd rather nap than play it. Folding his hands on his stomach, he let his eyes droop closed.

Hiss!

Cautiously, the Harper cracked one eye. Coiled next to his outstretched legs was a snake, a big green snake, the end of its tail vibrating in a threatening gesture. It must have plopped out of a tree. Remembering his unfortunate experience with the river serpent above Nerat, he was disinclined to move hastily. He kept the eye half open, watching it undulate as it decided what to do about him. The snake's tongue flickered in and out, a faintly disrespectful gesture. Praying that he didn't smell edible to it, Robinton considered his options. Should he pretend to be asleep? He couldn't remember if snakes attacked things which did not move. Would he be able to kill it before it poisoned him?

If Robinton decides not to move, turn to section 163.

If he chooses to move, turn to section 165.

* 169 *

He kicked out at the snake, catching it on the chin with the toe of his boot. It landed across the road, recoiled and slid back toward him all in one swift action. Leaping high, it fastened its teeth in his collarbone. With a yell, he reached down and caught hold of its tail. He dragged it off and whipped its head against the ground. It went limp. He had broken its back. Weak with relief, he fell back against the tree, blotting at the blood.

Twitch trotted over to see what he was doing. When he saw the snake, he let out a fierce whinny and brought his front hooves down on the corpse. The runner continued to dance on it until he had flattened the head and a good portion of its body into a bloody tatter. Twitch stood over it panting as Robinton soothed him.

"What a big fierce fellow you are. Where were you when I needed you?"

Twitch just brayed.

Turn to section 173.

* 170 *

As the snake struck out, Twitch reared up and brought his little hooves down on the beady-eyed head. He stamped and bit at the thrashing body which whipped around in panic. Soon, the snake's body ceased its twisting, and unrolled in a long line on the road. The runner continued to dance on it until he had flattened the head and a good portion of its body into a bloody tatter. Twitch stood over it panting as Robinton came over to pet and soothe him.

"There, there! What a brave fellow you are. I owe you my life, you know. I should write a song in your honor: 'Twitch the Snake Killer.' What do you think of that?"

Twitch just brayed.

Go to section 173.

* 171 *

The knife hissed to a point just between Twitch's front hooves. Panicked, the runner tottered backward, giving the mortally wounded snake a chance to coil up. The tail vibrated again.

"Sorry, old fellow!" Dismayed by his bad aim, Robinton dashed to the roadside and picked up the biggest rock he could carry. Staggering over to where the snake's attention was still fixed on his runner, Robinton dropped the rock, crushing the reptile underneath it. Twitch came over to stamp and bite at the portions of the snake sticking out from under the boulder. Robinton soothed it.

"Let's go to Bayhead, my brave little fellow."

With a final kick at the snake's remains, Twitch followed him.

Turn to section 173.

* 172 *

C'gan stood for a moment, as if deep in thought. He nodded, appearing to have come to some sort of inner conclusion. "Why not? They can always tell me no. Come with me, lad. What baggage have you got?"

"He's staying here tonight," Mettin explained, slowly.

"Why? I'll take him to the Weyr—I can't stay away longer—and after the Hatching, I'll deliver him to Benden Hold. He'll be there by nightfall."

Mettin looked at Robinton for his reaction. The youth couldn't believe his good fortune. C'gan looked from one to the other. "I guess the answer is yes."

Turn to section 176.

* 173 *

It took the rest of the afternoon to travel the rest of the marsh's perimeter. Robinton was heartily looking forward to speaking with humans again, eating bread, and sleeping on a cot without insects for company.

To his surprise, when he entered the Hold, there was a Gather going on. He walked around staring at everything as though he had been out of civilization for Turns instead of just days.

When he felt he'd sufficiently filled his eyes with Gatherday sights and his ears with conversation, he stopped at a crafter booth and asked directions to the Harper's residence. The tanner gave him instructions that sounded too complex for the tired Harper to remember, so Robinton asked him to draw a map on a scrap of hide.

"No need, young master. Over there's the Warder. He'll take you up to the Hold if you want to go." He pointed to a middle-aged man wearing a heavy hide tunic.

"Thank you," Robinton nodded to him and moved off.

"Hey, there! Harper Robinton!"

He turned in surprise, wondering who in this Hold would know him. In a booth far down one side of the Gather meadow, Mastertrader Keir was waving to him. He hurried over, hauling a resisting Twitch through the crowd.

"Well met, young man, well met!" Keir wrung his hand. "Are you just arriving?" Two women, presumably his wife and daughter, went on doing business. Trade was lively for Keir's wares.

"Yes, I am. How long have you been here?"

"Oh, since last evening. We'd have been here sooner, but my other paying customer caused us a bit of trouble. Lord Holder's son had a punch-up with one of my men. I had to calm them both down. How are you?"

"Tired, bruised and hungry. I've had a few interesting times too since I saw you last."

"It might have been worth the eight marks, you know, Journeyman." Keir smiled, and tapped the side of his nose with his forefinger. "Look, you're an expert in your craft . . ."

"Not nearly," Robinton interrupted, humbly.

"More than I am," Keir said, flatly. "What do you think of this, then?"

The trader held out to him a small harp, a miracle of wood and wire. Awed, he turned it over in his hands, admiring the craftsmanship. The forepillar and frame had been pressed together vertically out of three pieces of wood, the outer ones naturally shaded and the narrow center piece dyed a smooth blue. It had then been carved in the bow of the frame with a little pattern of dragons. It was slightly bigger than a lap harp, but just the same weight. Every edge was smooth, and the sounding board was rounded instead of squared off. A dozen, a thousand times nicer than the one he'd had to leave unfinished back in the Harpercrafthall. "This is a master's work," he breathed. "What are you asking for it?"

He set the curve against his shoulder and plucked out a few sweet chords. Its voice flowed smoothly, for it was so well made that it was still nearly in tune even after traveling in a jostling wagon for many dragonlengths. He had fallen in love with the little harp, even though it had to be many marks costlier than he could afford. He looked in his belt pouch, counting up the pieces in it. Perhaps something could be worked out over the price. He . . . coveted the harp, an uncommon emotion for him.

"Oh, that'n's not for sale," Keir said, ruefully watching the Harper, who was reverently examining the instrument. "It's a paid commission piece. To be delivered. I'm truly sorry, for I can see that you appreciate it."

Robinton's heart sank with disappointment. He picked out a sad little tune with the highest pitched strings, a melodramatic expression of tragedy on his mobile features. "It needs tuning."

"I haven't the skill," Keir said. "Would you oblige me?"

"Certainly."

He tuned it and set his long fingers on the strings to test it. After a moment's thought, he smiled. "What better to play on a dragonharp?

"Dragonmen must fly
When Threads are in the sky . . ."

Reluctantly, he handed the harp back to Keir, who folded a soft cloth around it. "Good fortune to your purchaser, then," Robinton said, his voice filled with regret. "And a good Gather to you."

"It has been already, my young friend. Perhaps we'll meet again in Benden."

"I shall count on it." Robinton extended his hand and Keir covered it.

He found the Warder with no difficulty. The man pointed out the Bayhead Hold Harper, who was leading a group sing in the square. As soon as the song was done, Robinton introduced himself. The Harper, a brown-haired giant of a man with a surprisingly mild disposition, shook his hand heartily and led him back to the Harper's residence.

Turn to section 138.

* 174 *

He kicked out at the snake, catching it on the jaw with the toe of his boot. It landed across the road, recoiled, and slid back toward him all in one swift action. Leaping high, it fastened its teeth in his collarbone. With a yell, he reached down and caught hold of its tail. He pulled it away, but it coiled around his arm and struck again, this time at his face.

Nearly fainting with pain, Robinton managed to stick his thumb into the angle of the snake's jaw and detached it from his flesh. He flung the creature to the ground and stamped and twisted with his boot until the ugly head was smashed flat. Then he slumped against the tree. The two snakebites were already swelling, and he felt ill. He decided not to move. His head was beginning to ache.

Twitch came over to sniff at him. Robinton lifted a weak arm to scratch at the beast's ears.

"You missed all the excitement, little fellow." The arm fell back, and Robinton's eyes sagged closed.

Turn to section 29.

* 175 *

He backed away from the snake, feeling behind him to determine where the branch turned. The reptile feinted at him, causing him to jump back in fright. He swiped out with his hands for the branch, but he missed it and fell. With a thump, he hit the roadway on his side. He squawked, and caught his breath. It hurt to breathe too deeply. He hoped there were no broken ribs, but he couldn't be sure. With cautious fingers, he probed at the sore places. No broken skin, but there'd be bad bruises. He'd have to see a healer as soon as possible. A rustling in the treetop made him look up again. Sidling away hastily, he scanned the branch for signs that the snake might be following to attack him. No, not yet. He listened for the rattling. Probably the creature had just gone back to sleep. Thank goodness.

Twitch trotted over to find out what he was doing. Robinton slumped under his tree again, grimacing at the pain in his back, and scratched the runner's ears. "Next time I leave the tree climbing to you."

Twitch just brayed.

Subtract 1 D6 for damage sustained in fall.

If he is now out of hit points, turn to section 29.

If not, turn to section 173.

* 176 *

Together, he and C'gan hauled his cases down to the beach and fastened them to the blue dragon's harness next to the Weyr Harper's own packages. Mettin promised to give little Twitch a good home. Robinton was grateful, having forgotten all about the little runner in the excitement. Once everything was in place, Mettin turned back toward the Hold. Robinton waved to him, shouting thanks and promises to visit.

As he prepared to follow C'gan up the massive blue shoulder, Tagath turned his head, and one gigantic eyelid drooped shut in a wink. Robinton gaped, then climbed up as he'd been directed.

"Now hold tight to me," C'gan instructed over his shoulder. "You know your Teachings, so count slowly to three when we go Between. You'll be cold, but don't worry. Tagath's done this more than once," he joked. "It's frightening the first time. And the second. And the next . . ."

With a tremendous leap that threw Robinton's head back on his shoulders, Tagath was airborne. The wind rushed into their faces, driving Robinton's hair back and

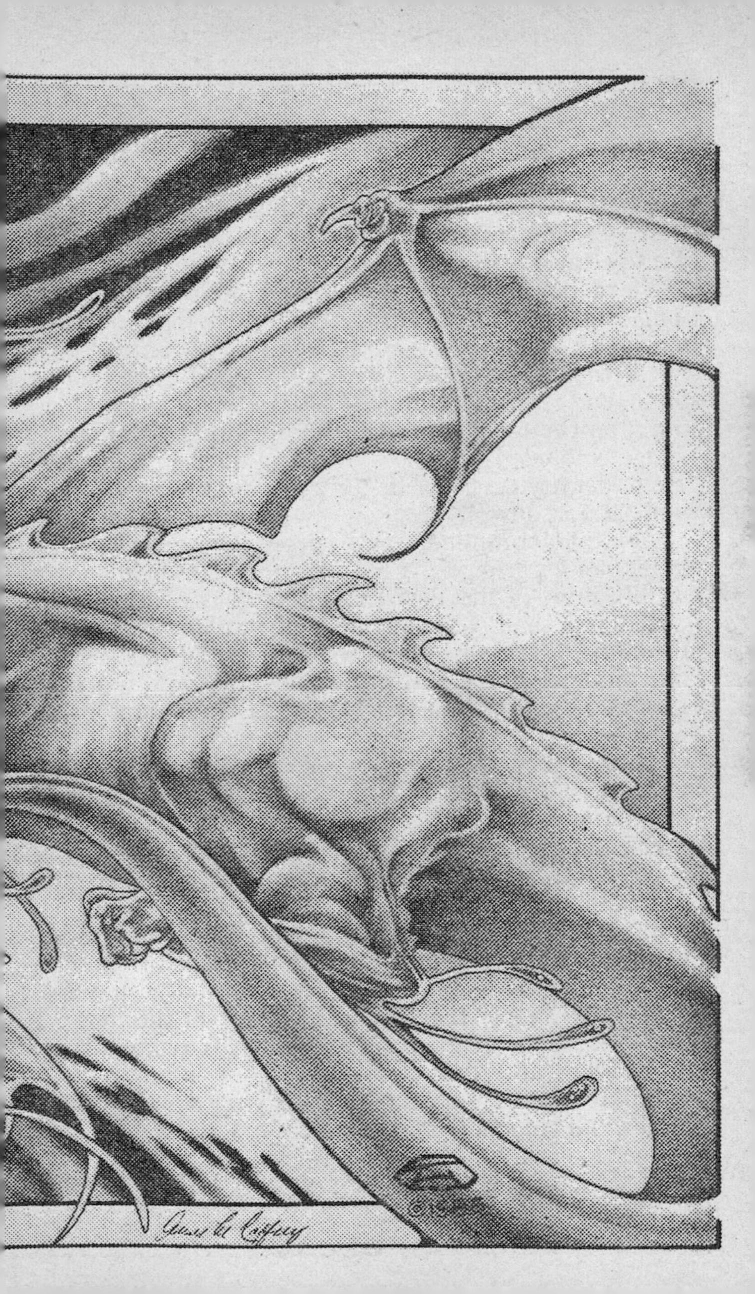

bringing stinging tears to his eyes. He tightened his knees on Tagath's neck and held firmly to the dragonrider, who appeared not to notice the strangling clutch of his passenger. When Bayhead Hold below them was the size of a toy, the world went dark.

"Black, blacker, blackest . . ." Robinton ran the traditional saga in his head interminably. He had no sensations at all, except for the bitter cold. His ears and nose ached from it, his teeth chattered, though there was no sound, and no perception that his jaw was moving at all. And after the count of three, there was light again.

Tagath roared, his voice vibrating through their legs. "He's identifying himself," C'gan shouted against the wind. "Look down!"

Robinton complied, and promptly doubled the strength of his grip on C'gan. Dragonlengths below them was the Bowl of the Weyr, a tremendous oblong crater floored with sand. The glaring sunlight made him squint at the bright scene in the bowl. At one end was a small lake, in which green and brown dragons were sporting. From up here they looked as small as did the one in his dream.

Tagath glided in to settle on the ledge of one of hundreds of openings in the inner Weyr walls. Robinton knew from his Teachings that they were weyrs of the lesser dragons. The Weyrwoman and the bronze dragons had weyrs closer to the Hatching Grounds. The two men climbed down and undid Tagath's harness, pulling all the bundles into the inner chamber. The blue dragon opened his wings and glided down to join his friends in the weyr lake. In spite of his vast size beside humans, Tagath was one of the smaller dragons in the bathing pool. The young Harper calculated their relative sizes with growing amazement.

Robinton, pulling the strap of his gitar over his head, noticed and recognized the shape of one of the packages in C'gan's arms. "Is that a harp?" he asked.

"Why, yes," the Weyrharper answered, surprised. "A fine instrument. I received it today from a trader named Keir." He opened the wrappings to display the dragon-harp Robinton had so admired.

"I know him," Robinton said, sighing. What a fine instrument that harp was.

"You do? Then . . . ?" C'gan was interrupted by the sound of humming. Not the sound of a trained chorus, to Robinton's ears, but rather a hum of purpose. "Come on!"

A shadow darkened the sky outside on the ledge, Tagath returning for them. C'gan clambered up and extended a hand down for Robinton. The Bowl was full of dragons a-wing, picking up their riders and swooping toward the Hatching Grounds.

Tagath flew in at the upper entrance and settled on a ledge with a perfect view of the eggs. Men and women hurried to take their places in the Galleries. Robinton felt taken up by all the excitement around him. So many dragons! The human hubbub echoed through the cavern, underscored by the dragons' urgent humming.

Nemorth, the gold queen dragon, hovered protectively over her clutch, pacing and hissing every time there was a new noise in the cavern. She was nearly twice the size of Tagath, only some of that size might have been an illusion because she seemed to be glowing. There was a spicy aroma about that Robinton took to be a dragon's natural scent. It was pleasant, though heady. The bronze dragons glided to perch on ledges around the inner walls, and the other dragonriders, with or without their beasts, sat near Tagath in the Galleries.

They were just in time. As soon as they were settled, two narrow lines of boys dressed in white Impression garb filed in and spread out in a semicircle around Nemorth and the rocking eggs. Humming filled the air, growing louder. C'gan and the other dragonriders leaned forward, waiting expectantly.

Section 176

Robinton, with his feel for tone and mood, was perhaps as much in tune with the humming as many of those who'd lived in the Weyr all their lives. The sound was an instinctual reaction of the dragons. He could sense the hope and urgency in their voices. It reached a sort of crescendo, and Robinton's spirit rose with it, higher and freer, until *crack!* The first egg split, and pieces broke away from the shell until the infant dragon stood unsteadily on the sands. Robinton was holding his breath in anticipation. The crowd murmured with delight. It was a bronze. The boys moved forward to greet it, their faces shining with hope.

Speculation echoed around Robinton, seated high above the hot sands. Whom would the little bronze select? Crying plaintively, it tottered from boy to boy, searching. Robinton experienced a brief surge of hope. Was it perhaps meant for him? Could he ever hope to Impress a dragon? But the baby dragon stopped before one of the boys, its jeweled eyes whirling. Impression! Ecstatic, the boy called out the dragon's name, and Robinton released his breath in a rush. Another egg rocked and burst, its tiny green occupant glistening in the glowlight, bleating for attention. The candidates moved away from the newly Impressed pair and formed a loose circle around her. Robinton drew in his breath again.

In a matter of minutes, it was over. The fourteen eggs Hatched, and the new dragonets filed out with their child weyr-mates. Cheers and congratulations were called down to them as they left, but the pairs were much too involved in one another to notice very much. More than one of the boys had tears dripping down his face for sheer joy.

Such an incredible experience. The young Harper felt almost exhausted from the tension. He'd seen a Hatching. Down on the sand, Nemorth stopped pacing and flew out of the Cavern toward the herdbeast pens.

Section 176

Robinton sighed deeply and settled against the stone.

C'gan looked up at the sound from the note he was making on the Impressions and smiled understandingly at Robinton. "It takes you that way. Of all the Hatchings it's been my privilege to attend, they've all been like this. And I've felt the same as you at each one." He got to his feet. "But come, there's a feast now, to celebrate."

Robinton followed the older Harper down to the Living Cavern. As they walked, C'gan told of his own experience, the day he'd Impressed Tagath. Robinton hung on his words as if by concentrating, he could live the experience with the other Harper. It was clear that C'gan was as moved by it now as ever. He knew what it was to share the unquestioning love of a dragon. The young Harper felt somehow left out, as if C'gan and the others moved in a world in which he could have no part. But he had no time to worry about it. In the Living Cavern, he was introduced to dragonriders whose names he knew from the Naming Song, a tune intended to train children to remember the names of the Weyrmen, but had no faces to which he could connect them. That fellow was S'lel; he rode a bronze named Tuenth; that S'mon, who flew green Delianth.

"Who are you?" a small boy demanded, poking Robinton in the knee with an imperious forefinger. He didn't look to have more than five Turns at the very most, but he had the air of a Lord Holder. A toddler clung to his hand.

Robinton hunkered down to the child's eye level, smiled at the wide-eyed brown-haired toddler holding on to the bigger boy's fingers. "My name is Robinton. I'm a Harper, a friend of Weyrharper C'gan. And whom do I have the honor to address?"

The boy threw back a proud shock of black hair. "I'm Felar. My father is Weyrleader F'lon."

The small boy tugged on the hem of his tunic. "My father is Weyrleader F'lon, too!"

"Right," the older child said. "His, too. He's Fanor."

Robinton extended his hand, palm up, to each of them. "I am very pleased to meet you," he said, gravely.

"The feast is beginning," Felar said. "Come sit with us? Please? We don't have much company."

The journeyman looked for C'gan, who joined them. "I've told the Weyrwoman you're here. Tagath already bespoke Nemorth when we arrived. The Weyr wasn't expecting you yet, but Jora said it's all right. Shall we eat?"

"May I introduce Masters Felar and Fanor?" Robinton said, formally.

C'gan eyed them humorously. "We've met. This big rascal is already of Teaching age. But," he sighed, "I have them both together. They're inseparable."

As they sat down at one of the long tables, a voice growled, "Who's this? A candidate I knew nothing about?" A tall, black-haired man stood behind them, rumpling the boys' hair. They regarded him as adoringly as the dragonets had their new weyrmates. He smiled down at them, and looked inquiringly at C'gan.

"No, Weyrleader," C'gan said, getting to his feet. "He's a journeyman Harper named Robinton, bound for Benden Hold to assist Master Evarel there. I met him in Bayhead. You will possibly remember that I mentioned him to you? He's a fine lad, a discreet one. I thought it wouldn't hurt to give him a special treat."

"All right, but it's irregular. A Hatching is not a public exhibition." F'lon nodded curtly to them and moved over to the head table. Robinton exhaled with relief.

C'gan smiled at him. "Don't worry. A Hatching can be a draining experience. He's suffering from reaction. We all are, a little. Besides, you have to sing for him later."

"I do?"

"Of course, do you think I'd pass up a chance to play counterpoint for a change?" C'gan chuckled, tapping Robinton's gitar.

Section 176

The fourteen new dragonriders were brought in as soon as their young charges were asleep. The children were still excited and filled with the wonder of Impression. Robinton leaned over to C'gan. "They're so young. Why are children used for candidates to the Egg?"

"A dragon lives many, many Turns. When its rider dies, a dragon goes Between forever. It's a tragedy when that happens. So, the younger a candidate, the longer dragons will live."

"I'll ride a bronze dragon someday," his little seat companion piped up. "And his name will be Mynyth."

"You can't know what a dragon's name'll be, silly," his brother informed him, disgusted. "They name themselves. And I'll have a bronze dragon, too, and he'll be bigger than yours."

"Will not!"

"Will too!"

C'gan touched Robinton's arm. "Come on. They're waiting for a good song. I hope you know something new."

Robinton's comic ditty about the Lord Holder was well received. He got many a sly look from the dragonriders, but managed to keep an innocent expression in his gray eyes when they asked him about his model. In honor of the Hatching, he sang the lullaby written for the child of Lord Micawl and Lady Caryda of Ruatha, to much applause.

It was followed by his favorite sea song, which he discovered C'gan knew, too. Robinton had decided that all Pern should hear all music, no matter where it came from, if he had to sing it to everyone himself.

"The fickle wind's my foe,
With tide his keen ally . . ."

To Robinton's satisfaction, they liked that one as well.

At evening's end, the Weyrleader came up to clap him

on the back. "My thanks for the entertainment, Journeyman. I'm minded that we should make contact with the outer world more often. You'll be welcome back. Not a reflection on you, C'gan. But I have enjoyed this evening."

"So have I, Weyrleader," the Weyrharper said.

"You'll see me in the Hold, Journeyman . . . Robinton, is it? Good night."

"Thank you, sir. Good night."

They returned to C'gan's weyr to pick up Robinton's possessions. Tagath stood patiently as they tied the harness back on him, and loaded it with cases. "And one more," C'gan said.

Robinton counted. "No, that's all I had with me, C'gan."

"That isn't what I meant. It was supposed to be a surprise, a welcoming gift to you, but since you've already seen it, you may as well have it." And he presented Keir's bundle to him.

The young Harper's mouth dropped open. "Oh, I can't accept that."

"Why not? It was meant for you. Thank the Egg Keir didn't know that. He'd have spoiled the surprise. Go on, take it." He thrust the dragonharp into Robinton's arms. "Well, hurry up. I'd better get you into Evarel's care before the Hold doors close for the night. You'll make quite an impression, arriving on a dragon." He chuckled at his own joke.

Robinton followed, clutching the harp and still muttering soundless protests and expressions of gratitude. Tagath rumbled his amusement as he knelt for them to mount. Robinton stowed the harp tenderly among his baggage before climbing up to his place on the neck ridge.

Now he had the last possible thing he could want to give him confidence toward his new job. He'd successfully completed a long and difficult journey. He'd met people and new ideas and, hopefully, grown somewhat in wisdom. He'd ridden a dragon and sung for the Weyr—new songs. And that was just a little of what he was going to do, starting tomorrow morning.

The cold of Between this time only exhilarated him, made him feel eager to begin. Stars were beginning to appear in the indigo sky when he felt the dragon under him circle down and around.

"There it is, Robinton," C'gan pointed down over Tagath's shoulder at the hulking cliff far beneath. "That's Benden Hold."

THE END